ORB

By

Gary Tarulli

To My Wife
Forever Young

CONTENTS

Approach...........................1

Kelly Takara......................17

Orbit.............................29

Thompson 41

Landing...........................57

Possibilities.....................73

Ixodes..........................87

Sighting.........................105

Intelligent Life................117

Spheres..........................131

What Are They?...................145

Many More........................155

Internalizing....................165

Ambassador.......................185

OceanOrb.........................201

Larry Melhaus....................213

"But We Must Try"................233

The Unthinkable..................245

Heartfelt........................261

D Major op. 61...................281

Imagining the Unimaginable.......297

Visionaries......................311

Addendum.........................325

Approach

I WAS TRYING to escape the confines of the box I found myself in—the one I had spent the last forty-one years of my life creating. Watching Earth disappear from view, a thought belatedly crossed my mind: Was I taking introspection a bit too far?

I'm writing this while on the research vessel *Desio*, outbound on an eight-hundred-trillion-kilometer journey to a planet some galactic cartographer devoid of imagination had named 231-P5. Four scientists and a medical doctor are traveling through the Void with me as we endure a unique and protracted form of solitary confinement.

You will learn more about me soon enough, but be advised: I'll be earning my keep as the mission chronicler. By trade, I am a writer. This "failing," as crewmate Dr. Melhaus once sarcastically described it, has led him and others to question my inclusion in *Desio*'s crew. My snap back: "I may lack a doctoral degree in the hard sciences, but last checked, the universe was big enough for all of us."

There's no escaping that virtual entertainment choices have turned my profession into a footnote. Reading, demanding of time and attention, is out of favor. (The quaint phrase "I can read you like a book" has come to mean "not at all.") AI-generated fiction notwithstanding, the decline in reading has resulted in a steady decline in writing. Can a *living* author subsist without a sympathetic (and paying) audience?

A few persist—those who can defend against charges of plagiarism alleged by an army of copyright lawyers who compare each new work of fiction to the millions that came before.

The lawyers would have us believe there's nothing new under the Sun. I shall avoid their complaint.

Where I'm headed, there is a different sun.

They tell me it's blue.

My assignment on board this star-class vessel is to observe, document, and create an "accurate" written record of what transpires during what the Central Space Agency (CSA) believes will be a historic scientific voyage.

Their statement prompted me to reflect on the word "accurate." It is a quality that is both subjective and elusive. How can the truth be determined when what a person observes is selectively chosen? And once chosen, is not the observation filtered through the senses before entering the brain, where it then suffers repeated collisions, loses momentum, only to be expelled at some later date in altered form?

Nevertheless, I shall do my best. And because I am the *first* filter evaluating what is to follow (you, the reader, being the second), a necessary word about this "box" I had created for myself and why I was attempting to climb out.

The reasons may be evident. Like others plying my craft, I struggle to earn a living. The expedition to 231-P5 and this narration may ultimately result in some desperately needed name recognition, a rocket boost to a flagging career. It might even induce a wellspring of creativity. I am also borderline antisocial, tending to keep to myself and, save one, I forgo meaningful relationships. I'll be challenging that personality quirk by spending the next seven months trapped in a glorified tin can, hurtling through the abyss with people who, until recently, were complete strangers.

So I begin my exposition, but not before repeating a final word of caution. I will not be providing much scientific detail about what will soon transpire. For such information, I encourage you to peruse the ship's extensive logs, compiled by my five crewmates, each preeminently qualified in their respective fields.

Good luck trying to read *their* accounts.

Although several months would be spent aboard *Desio*, I knew nothing about the person, likely long deceased, whom the ship was named for. With a minimum of research, I uncovered a full name and bio.

Ardito Desio. Born 1897, died 2001. Explorer, geographer, and geologist. Leader of more than twenty scientific expeditions; organizer of the first team to reach the summit of K2 after attempts by others had failed; author of several hundred scientific papers—in sum, an adventurer who consumed eighty of his one hundred and four years traversing Earth when strange and mysterious lands still awaited discovery. A remarkable individual who, along with his name, has been relegated to the back shelf of history by the passage of time.

Gone but not wholly forgotten. Somebody had bestowed the man's good name upon our ship. I learned that it was the commander, Bruce Thompson. His choice told me a little about him. I would soon discover a whole lot more.

As for the *Desio*, form followed function. She was a sturdy, compact, and highly automated vessel. I became intimately acquainted during intensive training sessions when, along with the other members of the crew, Thompson drilled us on the proper function of everything from recycling toilets to the gravity compensator. By teaching us himself, "he'd never hear bitching, 'would he?'" that we had not been adequately instructed.

Each member of a starship crew is typically responsible for one or two specialized assignments. Thompson insisted this was nonsense, saying we were sufficiently intelligent (simultaneously telling us not to let the remark go to our heads) to have a working knowledge of nearly all of *Desio*'s systems. His first objective was to rotate the crew through the tasks necessary to keep his ship running efficiently. Secondarily, he believed that the challenge of acquiring and utilizing multiple skills would reduce boredom. If you needed a third reason, it was because he said so. During training, I came to respect Thompson. He certainly knew his ship. There was no question about her that he could not answer. I also came to appreciate his brand of sarcasm.

Although I did not always comprehend the highly technical intricacies of propulsion, guidance, waste treatment, artificial gravity, and a host of other critical systems, I was amazed by their elegant and imaginative design, which approached an art form.

Mission engineers had concentrated on the crew's physical and psychological well-being, their efforts sometimes producing uneven results. One example is the noise-canceling sound system that had been installed to mask the persistent hum from engineering and life-support. It's too damn effective, rendering the ship as quiet as the grave, as commented on by every crew member save one: Dr. Melhaus, the ship's illustrious physicist.

For the rest of us, the eerie silence heightened a pervasive feeling that lurking just beyond that thin protective bulkhead was a kindred eternal silence—a troublesome reminder that our long voyage made us among the most isolated humans in history.

Isolation, the cause of psychological distress during prolonged space travel, had been well-studied. There are many ways to counteract these detrimental effects, but I did not anticipate the extent to which CSA tried to address the problem.

Early in the crew's training regimen, we were ordered to complete questionnaires regarding personal preferences in the arts—music, painting, sculpture, and the like. To find out if anyone was truly paying attention, I answered that Edvard Munch's *The Scream* was my favorite painting. I guess someone was paying attention, because two days later, Thompson was compelled to affirm my sanity to the mission psychologist.

Questionnaire responses were used to help outfit the ship: Monet reproductions adorning the bulkheads, Mozart symphonies wafting over the sound system, and mocha-colored paint gracing the cabin walls. All were attempts to keep the crew happy and well-adjusted.

I am starting to doubt their effectiveness.

A word about compartment layout. There were six sleeping quarters or cabins—one per crew member. Space being at a premium, each was just large enough for a bed, a workstation, and a small enclosed area for toilet and personal hygiene. Cabins were soundproof and had an entry door with a coded lock. For safety, Thompson had override capability. There was precious little privacy elsewhere on the ship.

Two of the crew, Paul Bertrand and Diana Gilmore, elected to share a cabin. Never finding a reason to marry, their relationship flourished during two decades of successful cohabitation. It was an admirable and increasingly rare example of the possible. Still, it failed to deter mission engineers from designing separate quarters for each "just in case they elected to dissolve their living arrangement." The remark did not sit well with Diana, who sarcastically chided the engineers for their inspirational vote of confidence. Early in the voyage, the ship's physician, with Thompson's permission, converted the unused cabin into a treatment room.

The common areas consisted mainly of four compartments, the largest suitable for meetings, meals, and socializing. The mission room's most notable features were a sizable composite worktable that occupied the center and an oval viewport that dominated one wall. An adjoining compartment served as the science lab. Here lay the domain of the scientists, which I had little cause to invade. It housed built-in stations for conducting experiments, an equipment storage area, and a secured enclosure for quarantining and retaining specimens. Centered above these compartments was a smaller level equally split between a command and control room with viewports and the ship's navigation/communication/nerve center.

Above all was a rotating turret equipped with a guided laser weapon. The official justification for the system was to facilitate the obliteration of space junk—a real and present threat to vessels in or leaving orbit. There were also unsubstantiated rumors of privateer ships circling Earth.

The doors to every compartment and the laser turret were installed with high-tech security locks that could be activated at Thompson's discretion.

Outbound.

Three very long, uneventful months have elapsed, and *Desio* and crew have nearly completed the journey to 231-P5. I was not alone in my cabin. Angie was quietly sleeping in my bed. She is the exception to my reluctance to form personal attachments. Her presence warrants an explanation.

Flash back several months, when I stood before the Crew Selection Committee with a petition to allow Angie to become the expedition's seventh crew member. I had come to the late realization that abandoning her on Earth would not be an acceptable option. If need be, I would relinquish my seat on the *Desio*, and a trained alternate would eagerly take my place.

And so I did my best to emphasize my companion's extraordinary attributes. There was no need for hyperbole. She was, after all, exceptionally bright, disciplined, well-trained, healthy, and personable.

Unfortunately, there were more practical concerns to contend with, which made the likelihood of Angie's inclusion highly improbable. She was excess payload weight, requiring engineers to recalculate *Desio's* oxygen and waste-processing requirements. There was also the matter of her special dietary needs. And, as one committee member stated with a fair attempt at humor, "The ship already has, in Dr. Bertrand, a French crew member."

The committee seemed intent on denying her inclusion, but agreed to defer their final decision. I remember one crewmate, Diana Gilmore, advising me not to give up hope. Two days later, they relented.

How could they not? Angie is a damn cute pooch, miniature poodle by breed, weighing seven kilograms, with a black coat, a medium shaggy kennel clip, bright, clear eyes, and a sweet disposition. With one exception, the crew was delighted, welcoming her with open arms. In no time at all, she became our little mascot.

If there was an onboard routine that Thompson rigorously enforced, it was for the crew to convene at precisely the same time every morning. Rightfully thinking of herself as an essential part of the group, Angie rose and stretched. Leaping off my bed, she followed me to the ship's central mission room. As we entered, Thompson greeted me with his usual friendly sarcasm.

"That dog follows you pretty much everywhere."

"Can you blame her?"

"Her ears are slightly asymmetrical; her tail was docked too long."

"Perhaps she wouldn't win best in show."

"Coincidentally, Kyle, neither would you."

"Angie and you have something in common," I said. "Neither of you shed."

I was trying to redirect the spotlight onto Thompson's shiny shaved head. Like house paint, the sheen could vary from matte to satin to gloss, depending on lighting and the closeness of the shave. Today, it was semigloss. Highlighting that particular feature had become my sworn duty, but Thompson shaved by choice. A smooth head was simpler: washing, combing, vanity, all neatly dispensed with. After three months, though, I was nearly out of bald jokes. Thompson's other rugged features were relatively immune to criticism.

As on most occasions, he got in the last word. "Sit! Stay!" he barked, commanding me to an empty chair. "We're about to begin." While I obeyed, Angie sniffed about the floor, searching for breakfast crumbs.

Seated at the conference table, consuming what passed for breakfast, were Commander Bruce Thompson, Ph.D., Geology and Engineering; Kelly Takara, M.D.; Diana Gilmore, Ph.D. in Marine Biology and a M.S. in Astrobiology; and Paul Bertrand, Ph.D. in Climatology.

The final member of the crew, Larry Melhaus, Ph.D., Physics, Mathematics, M.S., Chemistry, was, as usual, in his cabin, probably in the throes of solving an advanced problem in mathematics or particle physics. A moment later, he strode in and grabbed some coffee. Without uttering a word, he sat at the far end of the long table.

Thompson couldn't let it pass. "Good of you to join us."

"Yes," Melhaus said without a trace of sarcasm. During the last three months, we learned he was exponentially more proficient at solving equations than interacting with us.

"With your permission, Bruce, I'll start," Paul offered.

Thompson nodded.

"We're approaching within one million kilometers of P5, allowing partial confirmation of the meteorological data collected by the prior expedition. The planet's elliptical orbit produces winter and summer seasons of nine months' duration. Transitional seasons, within close approximation, are six months long. The last crew had the bad luck to emerge from the wormhole and stumble on the planet at an inopportune time, midwinter, thereby preempting the possibility of a thorough survey. Average surface temperatures then were hovering—poor word—at minus thirty degrees Celsius. You might say conditions have improved. Long-range scans indicate the current midsummer temperature is averaging a balmy *plus* thirty degrees. After we enter orbit, I can assess localized weather conditions. A few days after landing, I'll have a detailed picture of extended climatology."

"That was mostly a rehash of what the first mission surmised," Thompson said. "You have nothing further?"

The commander was typically blunt. We expected as much. It was his way of keeping us focused. The crew, all in their early forties, except Dr. Takara, who was thirty-five, was far too self-assured to be offended.

"I'm not finished," Paul said. "I have some preliminary readings on the ocean, which covers ninety-six percent of the planet's surface. The previous expedition encountered ice three meters thick at the equator. That ice, except at the extreme poles, has completely melted. Given the planet's elliptical orbit, the melt was anticipated but never considered a sure thing."

The news was welcomed by the crew. The abundance of available water was an exciting development, increasing the probability of the planet harboring complex life forms. Even Angie, having sensed the rapid change in mood, responded with a couple of delighted yips.

We were familiar with the reports compiled by the first expedition's scientists. Sterile technical language could not hide their disappointment when no life was found at their landing site, one of the tiny islands dotting the planet's surface.

Nevertheless, core samples extracted from ocean ice were found to contain significant numbers of frozen plankton-like organisms. It was only the third time that a life form had been discovered beyond our solar system, and the most complex yet.

"Larry, your report?" Thompson asked.

The physicist, choosing to avoid eye contact, answered while staring into the 3-D images floating above the AI Device (A.I.D.) unrolled on the table before him.

"I've extrapolated existing data concerning the quantity of frozen phytoplankton found per unit volume of ice. By estimating the organisms' theoretical ability to produce oxygen during the planet's cyclical warm season, I have calculated that they are responsible for producing and, more importantly, *maintaining* P5's breathable oxygen atmosphere. As for Dr. Bertrand pointing out that the ocean ice has melted? That eventuality was predicted by the calculations I performed of P5's solar orbit, the anticipated amount of solar energy, the atmosphere's composition, and other factors."

Melhaus's unflinching, self-assured (some would say arrogant) phrasing made me wonder: if he had not dutifully performed his calculations, would the ice have dared to melt?

"Let me know if your conclusions change," Thompson remarked.

"It is unlikely."

"Humor me. We'll soon have sufficient sampling of active phytoplankton to precisely measure their oxygen production." Thompson turned his attention to Dr. Gilmore. "And how about you, Diana? Anything to add to this discussion? Anything *new*, that is?"

"I do. When's the last time any of you had a wet dream?"

At least the question was different, I thought. Nobody volunteered an answer. Thompson, with a bemused look on his face, waited her out.

"That long?" she said. "Pity. Well, I'm having one now."

"Care to share with us?" Thompson said.

"Okay. Just this once. Ninety days getting here. One day till we enter orbit. Awaiting us is the chance to discover advanced life forms on an Earth-sized planet *covered* in water. Can you possibly imagine anything more apropos of a marine biologist's wet dream?"

"Do you always blurt out whatever pops into your head?" Thompson asked, amused.

"Why?" Diana responded, smirking. "Doesn't everybody?"

"Has this verbal ejaculation reached its climax?"

"I'm sure it has."

Thompson had to laugh. Diana's outburst and other spirited remarks she made from time to time were more diverting when you considered how out of place they were coming from a person who had a display case crammed full of prestigious awards in the fields of marine science and astrobiology. Yeah, she could sometimes be a bit of a wiseass, but she certainly gave the word a fuller meaning.

The crew needed her irreverent comments. Anything that could elevate our individual and collective moods was welcome. Months ago, psychiatrists warned us that deep space exploration was a mentally taxing business. At the time, we considered ourselves adequately prepared. We were not. The extended period traveling the *Void* had induced troubling bouts of depression and feelings of isolation—despite sharing quarters not much bigger than a small house.

As I was mulling this over, I looked across the table at Angie. Paws in the air, she was lying stretched out on her back across Kelly's lap, happily getting her belly stroked. Angie did more than any one person or thing to keep us entertained. She had become a favorite of the crew. I had the additional benefit of receiving her unconditional affection. Glancing up from her to Kelly's smiling face, I wished human interaction was as simple and easy to understand. Kelly and I occasionally shared a cabin. Our relationship, starting as friendship during mission training, had developed into something more. How much more was a question I was finding difficult to answer.

Thompson broke my reverie by asking her a question.

"And, Doctor, what is your report on the physical condition of the crew?"

Thompson wasn't just looking for generalities here. Given the closeness of quarters and how interdependent we were for survival, there was essentially no doctor-patient privilege. Kelly could invoke an exception to the rule, but she could not withhold patient information from the commander. Once medical information was in his hands, he had sole discretion as to whether the crew needed to be apprised.

"Under the confining circumstances," Kelly began, "we are in good health. Larry was complaining of mild insomnia. Since he wasn't responding to non-pharmaceutical alternatives, I dispensed a mild sleep aid, the one some of you have occasionally taken. Time-released liposome capsules with the usual warnings: Do not take if you are nursing, pregnant, might be pregnant, want to become pregnant…" Her voice trailed off.

"What if you inflect a sentence with a pregnant pause?" the Writer in me asked.

"Is it working?" Thompson asked, ignoring me.

"Too soon to tell," Melhaus answered.

"I suggest you keep taking them."

"I'll sleep on it."

Humor? Did I detect a slight smile? I was glad to see he could, on rare occasions, interact with the crew.

"We haven't heard from you, B.A.," Thompson said, centering his attention on me.

"B.A.?" I inquired, though I should have known better.

"Bachelor of Arts. The rest of us have useful science degrees."

I took up writing as a career a dozen years ago. The crew was well-aware of my educational background.

"Somebody," I clapped back, "has to rein in you mad scientists."

"And just how do you propose to do that?" Thompson inquired.

I considered for a brief moment. "Shall I entertain you with a short story?"

"You have the ultimate captive audience," Thompson replied. "Make the most of it."

"I intend to. Have you heard the tragic tale of the *Mars Climate Orbiter*?"

"Can't say I have," Thompson said.

"Good, because it's the only pertinent story I know. By way of introduction—minus some slight literary embellishments I've added to help hold your interest—this story was passed on to me by my old college communications professor."

"I love a good story," Diana said. "Any sex?"

"No. A long time ago, in a faraway land called Earth, humankind explored the nearby planets using unmanned spacecraft. One of these was called the *Mars Climate Orbiter*.

You will come to appreciate why it was a good thing it did not have a human crew.

"The objective was to journey to the Red Planet, enter orbit, then collect and transmit climate data back to a waiting Earth. The brightest scientists and engineers labored for years in designing and building the mission. On launch day, they nervously watched their intrepid little spacecraft as it ascended through the clouds and sped off on its long, expensive voyage. Imagine their excitement when it approached Mars twelve months later. As planned, there was a short engine burn, and the *Orbiter* passed behind the planet. Picture, if you will, hundreds of scientists eagerly anticipating the craft's reappearance."

I paused for effect.

"Only the signal never came."

"Saw that coming," Diana interrupted.

"The scientists were devastated. 'We must have answers!' they cried."

"What, you may want to ask, could cause such a calamity? Computer glitch? Thruster failure? Breakdown of complicated electronic components?"

"Micrometeor?" Paul suggested.

"Good guess, but no. Here is where the tale gets interesting."

"I was wondering when," Diana said.

"It was a misapplication of thruster force that sent the *Orbiter* much closer to the planet than intended—near enough to be affected by its thin atmosphere and send it crashing to the surface. It had nothing to do with computer or equipment failure. You see, the team who designed the computer-operated thrusters had programmed them to *receive* commands in the metric system, specifically in

Newtons. A second, independent team of scientists had programmed software to *send* commands to the thrusters in the old English system, pounds of force. It doesn't take a rocket scientist to know that won't work. A fourfold overapplication of thruster force was the *technical* reason for mission failure."

"Blatant incompetence," Melhaus commented, a bit irritated. "Your point being?"

"I'm getting to it. The Space Agency thoroughly investigated the two teams that handled the navigational commands. The report they issued made it crystal clear that it was the scientists' *failure to communicate* that caused the Orbiter's destruction. And that, boys and girls, is why my professor told this story."

I didn't expect a standing ovation, and I didn't get one. Then again, it didn't look like I had put anyone to sleep, either.

Thompson, who had listened with an impassive expression, chose to speak up.

"Interesting story," he said. "Brought us scientists back down to Earth."

I couldn't tell if he was being serious or sarcastic.

Sometimes, he was good at being both at the same time.

Kelly Takara

AFTER THE MORNING meeting and the informal discussions that followed, I returned to my cabin, intent on recording my thoughts. Naturally, Angie accompanied me, sporting what can best be described as her happy face. She had unilaterally decided it was playtime by whipping her head back and forth to throttle her stuffed toy duck and then ceremoniously dropping it at my feet.

There was no denying her. Sitting on the floor, my back to the bulkhead, I threw the toy out the open cabin door and into the corridor. Anticipating, she emitted a short, excited yip, ran, caught the duck in her mouth, throttled it anew, and then trotted back to dump it in front of me. Jubilant, eyes glistening, she gazed up expectantly. Long ago, I learned that this sequence could be repeated three times or three hundred times, depending on her mood. The funny thing is that neither of us tired of this game, simple as it was.

She and I were an unbreakable pair, discovering each other three years ago when I decided to take on the responsibility of caring for a puppy. And so I headed to a reputable breeder of miniature poodles that were larger and sturdier than most—precisely what I wanted since I had no intention of raising a lap dog.

One puppy frolicking in the litter caught my eye. I reached into the pen to play with her, and we connected. The breeder then subjected me to an extensive battery of questions that, in retrospect, was good preparation for the CSA's psych profile testing. With Angie vouching for my character (and with a substantial hit to my dwindling bank account), I was allowed to take her home. I never imagined what would come to pass, the restrictive environs that would masquerade as that home. Nevertheless, she had adjusted far better than the humans on board.

After nearly an hour of bolting back and forth and no indication that she was tired except a sloppy wet tongue hanging loosely from her mouth, Angie quit playing. I was about to settle at my workstation when I heard a quiet rap on the door. An obligatory bark told me I had protection.

"Would you like company?" Kelly asked from the doorway.

"What do you have in mind?" I said, pretending I didn't know.

"You're way overdue for a routine physical exam," she responded, pushing inside and closing the door behind her.

"So you're making house calls now?"

"Lie down," she ordered, shoving me backward onto the bed. "Try to relax. This won't hurt... much."

Suddenly, I was flat on my back, straddled, with a shirt being pulled over my head. "This is your *routine* exam?" I asked, caressing the small of her back.

She flattened her body against mine and pressed an ear against my chest. A tumble of silky jet-black hair cascaded onto my bare skin. "Hmm. Do I detect an elevated heart rate?" she asked. "Perhaps you are afraid of doctors. A bit of 'white coat syndrome.'"

"No. It's that I don't have medical insurance..."

Trying hard not to laugh, she clasped my hand, slipping it below the unbuttoned waist of her pants to where she was wet and warm. Her hand was now resting on top of mine, but I reversed the positions, my hoarse voice urging her on to self-examination. She locked our fingers together as her hips rose. A silvery sheen moistened on her skin. A hazy, faraway look came into her eyes, and I heard a low, throaty moan, unsure if it was hers or mine.

Afterward, we rested, slipping into the pleasurable zone between sleep and wakefulness, where the only sensation is that of floating above and away from the physical part of oneself. But the feeling soon receded, disturbing thoughts intruded, and I was compelled to open my eyes and accept where I was; that what surrounded me was the uncompromising emptiness, the stark and deadening silence of infinite space.

Struggling to fight off a feeling of isolation and loneliness, I stared at the woman next to me, lying on her side, unguardedly naked, eyes closed. Her lips, the deepest red, formed a slightly suggestive smile as if she were aware of being completely exposed and vulnerable. Did she realize how achingly beautiful I thought she was and what she meant to me? I had yet to tell her in anything but a casual, guarded way.

Her smile widened as my finger slowly traced a path on warm skin, delicately traversing the contour of her leg, pausing at the inviting curvature of her hip. Her eyes, with their alluring Asian arc, fluttered open. For the first time, I noticed her deep black irises sparkled with tiny flecks of gold.

"I felt your stare," she said, stretching luxuriously, her expression provocative. Reaching down, she twisted the bedsheet into something resembling a thick rope and seductively wrapped it between her legs and up and over one breast.

I wanted to express how much I cared for her, but couldn't find the right words. Pathetic, when you consider my chosen profession. My poor excuse: language is inadequate to communicate the depth and subtlety of human emotion. If they exist, the "right" words often evoke feelings other than those intended. The most familiar words, so carelessly bandied about, become too commonplace and lose their meaning. Words such as "soul," "god," and "love."

Best to avoid these words.

But that logic was flawed. I was merely rationalizing my shortcomings. The quarter-million words in the English language can produce a staggering number of word combinations. It was a damn good possibility that if I opened my mouth to speak, one or more of those combinations would do magnificently well right now.

Perhaps my silence was more a symptom of indiscriminately applying a lack of faith in people to one person in particular. Whatever the cause, I was letting an opportune moment slip away. Recalling that Kelly was born and raised in Japan and that Japanese was her native language,

I hedged my emotional bets, asking, "How do you say 'I need you' in Japanese?"

Hesitating, she gave me a long, strange look and answered, "*Aishiteru.*"

"*Aishiteru,*" I repeated.

"*Aishiteru mo,*" she replied, a bright smile lighting her face.

Neither of us spoke as she slid into her clothing.

Feigning jealousy, I asked, "You don't give this complete physical to the entire crew?" When she didn't respond immediately, I widened my eyes with a pretend look of shock and added, *"Do you?"*

"You idiot," was her reply.

"I'll take that for a 'no.'"

I let Angie leap back on the bed. And why not? Kelly had become her second favorite human.

Admittedly, I had a slight advantage by dispensing Angie's food supply. Small treats were a great way to keep her occupied within *Desio's* restrictive confines. She would be in a "sit-stay" position while I went about the ship, finding new and clever places (including inside the crew's cabins if their doors were left open) to hide those treats.

She never failed to find each one. My crewmates (excluding Melhaus) found this highly entertaining, welcoming her inquisitive visits.

I also taught her to sneak into Thompson's cabin, snatch a T-shirt off his bed, and scamper back to me for a waiting morsel. The profanities he hurled in our direction from down the corridor made this antic quite enjoyable. I don't think Thompson minded the temporary abduction of a shirt. Why else would he consistently leave one in the same location?

"You love Angie," Kelly said matter-of-factly, watching us interact.

"You could say that," I responded.

An odd look of bemusement came to Kelly's face. "I do, too," she said and was about to say something more, reconsidered, and then began scratching the base of Angie's tail. She knew the exact best spot. You could tell because it sent my pooch drifting hypnotically into space, snout pointed upward, abbreviated tail cocked so far to one side it almost appeared broken.

Rapture.

Kelly and I had ours. Angie was entitled to her own.

The opportunity arose to get Kelly's opinion on how the crew was faring during the long outbound voyage. I wondered if she had observed, as I had, behavioral changes that were too insignificant to bother Thompson.

She was the right person to ask. After graduating near the top of her class and completing her residency training, she fulfilled her lifelong ambition of opening a family medicine practice. Daily contact with a diverse patient population honed an innate ability to read people, not only by what they said but by what they failed to say. Me included.

I had an ulterior motive for inquiring about my crewmates. Examining my feelings of isolation (always present but voyage-accentuated), I discovered a potential cause applicable to all. My primary concern was Melhaus, but singling him out might, in some subconscious way, influence Kelly's opinion. Instead, I couched my question as a generalization.

"Overall," I asked, "do you see any subtle changes in the crew's mental health?"

Her reply was immediate.

"I assume you mean the esteemed Dr. Melhaus?" Seeing my surprise, she laughed, then added, "I thought so."

"Meaning what? You believe there's a problem?"

"No, not necessarily. But it makes sense to consider him first, remembering the morning's meeting when you became aware of the sleep medication I prescribed. It's not unusual for sleep patterns to be disrupted during extended periods of space travel."

"Did he come to you for help?"

"No. The insomnia came up during a routine examination. He was reluctant to start medication. That is why I made that little joking comment about it. You inadvertently helped with your remark. I took it as a positive that he could respond to Thompson with humor."

"He was testy at the end of the meeting."

"True, but I think whatever you see in his behavior is Larry being Larry. He closely fits the classic stereotype of the genius who concentrates on his work to the detriment of social skills. To the detriment of almost all else, for that matter."

"So you don't see anything troubling in his behavior?"

"Not presently. With the crucial part of the expedition at hand, we'll all be subjected to greater pressure. I *will* tell you that Thompson gave me a specific order to report any signs of abnormal behavior in the crew. Without delay, he said. He included himself."

"That's interesting."

"Mildly. Why the sudden interest in Larry—if it is sudden? Does delving into our personalities help with your writing? After all, he is a bit of a character."

"The mood of the crew is of interest. Our vulnerability— and Larry seems most on edge—has the potential to jeopardize the mission's success and our safety. Admittedly, there has been nothing exciting to write about."

"Our little romps in bed haven't been exciting?"

"Uh-huh," I answered sheepishly, knowing I would be greeted with the next logical question.

"Well…?" she repeated, with a wry, accusatory smile.

I didn't need it spelled out. Kelly had the right to know if details of our intimate physical relationship were being incorporated into my work for everyone to read.

"There are passages about us," I admitted. How could there not be? It's my assignment, my purpose for being on board. I'll use some discretion, of course, but unless our relationship has no bearing on what transpires during the expedition, personal details will likely remain in my work."

I had answered truthfully, hoping it wouldn't be an issue between us.

She thought for a long moment and said, "I respect your professional judgment. And *nothing* we do together, in or out of bed, could ever embarrass me."

She half-smiled and turned to leave without allowing me time to respond, which was fortunate since I was a little choked up by her faith in me. I stopped her at the door and kissed her.

No further words were exchanged. They didn't need to be.

I returned to my workstation to write, wondering if something was affecting my relationship with Kelly that I was not fully conscious of, an outside influence that, together with my emotional baggage, would explain why I might be holding back my feelings for her.

An answer suggests itself in how this artificial environment, a self-inflicted prison with no chance of escape, has come to define the crews' lives. Sure, we have any number of AI-generated distractions at our fingertips. For a short while, they seemed to be enough. No longer. How unimaginably far we are from the sight of the open sky, the touch of a warm breeze on skin, the sound of a summer songbird. Isolated from nature and everybody and everything that makes us feel human. Even the harshest of Earth's prisons does not deny *all* these simple pleasures. For the crew of *Desio*, they are trillions of kilometers away.

So distant that we have begun to doubt, in our darker moments, that they exist at all.

Could this deprivation artificially foster a relationship between two people? Would not the all too human response be to hold onto somebody, almost anybody, to fill the emotional void? Are Kelly and I deluding ourselves (if we believed) that we could continue our relationship back on Earth? If that is the unlikely future, is it not presently unfair to place expectations on one another?

Despite all my strained logic to the contrary, the greater part of me says the risk is well worth taking. That Kelly was the best woman to have ever come into my life. The rest of me says shut up and be thankful for the temporary solace we gave each other.

But what of Paul, Diana, Thompson, and Melhaus? How are they coping?

Diana Gilmore and Paul Bertrand are a matched pair, a partnership begun several years ago on Earth's firm footing. They seem to be doing well on board, especially Diana. Short, red hair, fiery and profane, her demonstrative enthusiasm for the mission is infectious. In some ways, she acts more like fourteen than forty-one. I once saw Thompson use this to his advantage during a heated argument. When her complaint deteriorated from reason to accusation, he abruptly changed tack, calmly stating that if she didn't behave, she'd be sent to her cabin without supper. Nothing is as satisfying as witnessing a raging argument doused by a good laugh.

On the other hand, Paul is more reserved, possibly because Diana has enough excited energy for both of them. As she sets fires, he sits back with a bemused look and takes it all in. If she is effervescent champagne, Paul might be labeled vin ordinaire, an analogy he'd likely take umbrage at, being of French nationality. He is very much devoted to Diana. As the mission planners discovered, they are, in fact, inseparable. During this outbound portion of the voyage, they have taken great comfort from each other's company.

And what of Thompson? Although it may appear he has nobody to care for, that isn't entirely true. He has his ship and the crew. We are his primary responsibility, and he takes it seriously—despite the sarcasm he doles out routinely. We're five mature (except, maybe, Diana) "children" to watch over, each with our peculiar personality quirks and problems. You could say that to him, we're one big, adopted, and sometimes dysfunctional family.

Melhaus is a strange case. What comfort he derives from the company of others is difficult to say—our incomplete knowledge of him has been obtained indirectly and somewhat indiscreetly through CSA psychologists. He can be hard to read because he reveals so little of his inner self, content to keep his emotions hidden.

He is brilliant. While attending Imperial College in London (at age fifteen), he scored 178 on a standardized IQ test. His mental skills developed so rapidly and at such an early age that his social skills suffered. Because personal relationships are something he can never be proficient at, he has withdrawn from most unnecessary contact, thereby avoiding a potential blow to his ego by trying to relate and

26

failing. He isn't very accepting of failure. He isn't used to it in the arenas of academia and science.

During the outbound voyage, he has been prodded, coerced, and cajoled to participate in our little group, sometimes by Thompson's sarcasm, other times by Diana's enthusiasm. Even Angie gets into the act by dropping a stuffed duck at Melhaus's feet and looking up at him with her expectant, silly look. Who can say if Melhaus appreciates any of the many small efforts made on his behalf? He keeps to himself.

As I ponder these observations and attempt to make them more coherent, I feel Angie's soft pink tongue licking my hand. Out of nowhere, I think there is something vaguely sensual about the act. Now *there's* a thought, innocuous though it is, best kept to myself! Remarkable, is it not, that like Melhaus, we all hide things from each other, even from ourselves? Perhaps the quality and extent of this mental editing are good signposts of how well an individual fits into society.

As we near P5, I wonder if an alien civilization, if they can understand us at all, would be startled, even afraid, of how extraordinarily selective and inhibited human thought processes can be.

ORB

Orbit

THE NEXT MORNING, I entered the mission room and was immediately confronted by an astonishingly beautiful sight. P5, which had been a fuzzy, golf ball-sized glow yesterday, now loomed below us, almost filling *Desio's* main observation window.

In crystalline clarity, and without the benefit of optically enhanced augmentation, was the shimmering surface of a silver-blue, planet-sized droplet of water suspended in the ultimate blackness of space. This fantastic image, surreal in size and scope, had my mind fighting a battle between the irrational fear of being inescapably drawn toward the planet and the overwhelming urge not to look away.

As I gaped, Diana and Paul entered the room. At the same time, I heard Thompson say something purposefully irreverent, something like, "An entire planet of ocean, and I left my fishing poles and tackle at home."

I don't know if it was Thompson's remark or the expression of amazement etched on Diana's face, but Kelly, already a fixture at the viewing port when I arrived, laughed and said, "Give me a moment, Bruce, I'll get her sedative ready."

With Paul standing close by her side, Diana appeared transfixed by the image in the viewport; you could tell she was having trouble working through and expressing her emotions. Her response was late, but it was still typical Diana.

"Yesterday I was excited, but today, Kelly... you need scientific notation to quantify the orgasm I'm having."

We all commented, but Paul, forgetting that the onboard language was English, expressed himself most eloquently when he spontaneously blurted out, *"Elle est presque aussi belle que vous, mon amour!"*

Caught unawares, Diana looked affectionately up at her mate and squeezed his arm. She seemed more than a little pleased.

"Care to translate?" I asked.

She was more than happy to oblige. "It is almost as beautiful as you, my love."

"Ah, you have a way with words, Paul," I said. "Maybe you should be the person chronicling this voyage." Before Thompson expounded on *that* observation, which I could see he was eager to do, I faced him and added, "Just saving you the trouble of pointing that out."

"Much appreciated," he replied.

I was relieved and pleased to hear my crewmates' first joyful reactions at seeing the planet, especially in light of how previous glimpses out of this same port only exacerbated the feeling of isolation I have already described. The crew was experiencing a renewal of purpose. Even Angie, softly whining at the viewport, seemed enthralled. I issued a "quiet" command, though I understood how spending three months holed up on a small ship was, to her, a lifetime. She was telling me she wanted a place to run, sniff, and play, and that the big glowing ball offered the best opportunity.

The ball grew more prominent as *Desio* accelerated into a semi-synchronous orbit above the planet. Our velocity, double the planet's rotational speed, allowed us to experience one full planet day (twenty-six Earth hours) in less than half that time. We would soon see the world below become enveloped in darkness as it rotated away from the system's massive blue sun.

Gazing "down" at the planet allowed the eye and mind to become better at resolving and assimilating smaller and smaller details, which we took great pleasure in pointing out to each other.

The most prominent feature was the imposing ocean, a slightly iridescent blue-gray with minor disturbances the scientists attributed to currents upwelling colder water, changeable winds across the water's surface, or the relative distribution of phytoplankton. The number and intensity of bright light flashes, called sun glints, radiating into space, suggested that the ocean was extraordinarily calm. Coupled with uniform coloration, it gave the planet a polished, shiny look.

The ice-capped poles were identical in size, perfectly circular, and crisscrossed by an intricate webbing of cracks and fissures. Along their jagged fringes were countless icebergs created by the calving of giant slabs of fractured ice. These ice islands appeared to be dividing and diminishing as they entered the warmer waters now encompassing most of the planet.

Tiny puff balls of cirrocumulus clouds dotted the colder regions bordering the ice shelves. Closer to the equator, bands of cirrus clouds, behaving like white whiffs of smoke, stretched into twisted shapes. Elsewhere, they merged into denser patches that reminded me of tufts pulled from a cone of cotton candy. The atmosphere had dynamic weather systems, though compared to Earth, they were markedly less common and more benign. Rarely did clouds congregate into threatening disturbances, and rarer still did flashes of lightning brighten clouds from within.

Great land masses were noticeably absent, replaced by tiny islands strewn like so many brown, tan, yellow, and gold-colored pebbles across the planet's one vast sea. I heard Paul describe how the absence of continental masses radically affected the formation of planetary weather and how, ultimately, the meteorological data we obtained here could reveal much about Earth's climate.

While we enjoyed and commented on the visual treats, the ship's daunting array of scientific instruments tirelessly collected and stored massive amounts of data. A fraction of that information would be evaluated onboard. The more significant portion would be analyzed by teams of scientists in the months following our return home.

As I previously remarked, I was interested in the crew's behavior, and none more so than Dr. Melhaus's. When he finally entered the mission room, he displayed no emotion, and I wondered if he had taken the time to appreciate the planet's beauty. Before I could ask, he exclaimed to no one in particular: "We have a lot of work to accomplish in a relatively short time. Don't you think we should get started?"

Kelly and I exchanged glances, but Thompson answered, saying, "I appreciate your work ethic, Doctor. We'll get to it soon enough. There is one item of business we can discuss as a group. You're aware that we have permission to rename the planet. I want to hear suggestions."

"I see no reason," Melhaus quickly responded, "to change the logically assigned star map coordinates."

"You know, Doctor…" Thompson paused, quickly reconsidered, and then deliberately let himself be interrupted by Diana.

"We can name it *anything*?" she asked.

"Just about," Thompson responded, then, reflecting on the little trap she had set for him, looked at me and added, "Uh oh."

"So, we could name the planet 'Larry' if we wanted?" Diana asked.

"As far as I am aware, there are no other planets named Larry," Thompson replied, willing to play along.

With good intentions, Diana hoped to elicit a positive reaction. None was forthcoming, for the physicist had deliberately parked himself in one corner of the room to stare at a screen cluttered with Greek, Latin, and other mathematical symbols that few people would recognize, let alone decipher. This was *his* language, and he was fluent in it.

"Well, then, does anybody have a better name?" Diana asked. She was a little put off by her colleague's behavior, but didn't want to say anything that would dampen our collective spirits.

"May I make a suggestion?" volunteered Kelly, throwing a glance my way. "Kyle is creative with words. I'm positive he can come up with something."

"I like the idea," Thompson responded. "Kyle?"

"Sure. But I'll need to give it careful consideration. You can't rush into naming an entire planet, you understand. The biggest thing I ever put a name on was a compilation of short stories."

"And how did that turn out?" asked Thompson.

"Nobody reads. Even short stories are too long."

Thompson let the opening pass. He'd find a more suitable time to explore my questionable career moves. Plenty of work was at hand, and he was responsible for giving us direction.

"Listen up," he said. "Use the next few hours to evaluate those sensor readings that are helpful for getting our butts safely on the planet. We'll meet again at 1200 hours for a working lunch. The plan is to touch down on P5 in the early morning, and I do mean early. I'll need a projection of the weather at potential landing sites from you, Paul. I'll provide the potential locations once I finish preliminary mapping. Diana, I appreciate that your real work begins on the surface. For now, review the biochemical data we're accumulating on the atmosphere. I'd prefer not to have any nasty surprises. The first expedition confirmed the air is breathable, but that was in winter. Larry, listen up. You and I need to perform a final readiness check on *Ixodes*. Kyle, you'll assist Paul; Kelly, you assist Diana."

Ixodes was the name Diana gave to the squat, ovoid-shaped submersible probe that clung like a tick to the ventral side of *Desio*. It had been out of sight for the last three months but not out of mind, having been repeatedly inspected and upgraded via remote comms. Capable of operating at a depth of ten thousand meters, it would be detached and sent plunging into the ocean to gather and transmit data on currents, temperature, and water chemistry. The sub's engineering team boasted that if a life-form inhabited that first ten thousand meters (a technical and scientific compromise, since the ocean approached an incredible depth of twenty thousand meters in locations), it would be detected. If the organism were small enough, it would be sucked into a collection chamber and eventually brought to the surface for analysis.

Mission planners had made the convenient and all—too—expedient assumption that the organism would be oblivious to being forcibly captured and removed from its natural environment. Unaware or not, it would almost certainly expire in the process.

When 1200 came around, the crew assembled in the mission room. I sensed that the day's initial excitement was being tempered by nervous tension, and with good reason. Expectations for the mission's success, and therefore the crews' need to fully execute their assignments, had been set exceptionally high, perhaps unreasonably.

In the months before our departure, the mission was the object of intense debate by a critical public that had divided itself into two distinct and very vocal groups: those who were intrigued by exploring the wonders of a new planet, and those who believed the king's ransom needed to explore that planet was better used reducing misery on planet Earth.

Although the weight placed on the scientists' shoulders by a demanding public was high, it was exceeded by the pressure each put on themselves. I knew this to be true from sharing with them every recycled molecule of air and water for the last three months, and because it is a truism that accomplished individuals are self-motivated and driven. The mission was the high point in their professional careers, a rare and unique opportunity not to be squandered. Accordingly, a silent but constant voice reminded them they were expected to conduct pioneering work in their respective fields. The scientific community summarizes this relentless need to produce with one concise and merciless phrase: "Publish or perish."

And so it logically follows that very much indeed was expected of, and by, Dr. Larry Melhaus, one of the world's preeminent physicists and chemists. He did not have a double standard. What he demanded of himself, he expected from others.

I was not wholly immune to the same career pressures, either societal or self-imposed, for I, too, had a function to perform on the *Desio*. And, having to earn a living as a writer, I was certainly no stranger to the fear of not being published. To that end, and because my forte was not expounding on the hard science (though I did try to keep up), I occasionally attempted to elicit personal details from the crew. They understood this, and the conversations that ensued from my prodding provided an enjoyable diversion.

But not always.

With the planet looming as a backdrop and our meeting almost concluded, Kelly absently said, "I miss Earth." And all talking stopped. "Sorry, all," she quickly added, as if the topic were forbidden. "But seeing this world, the ocean, the clouds, has me longing for home."

"You only said exactly what I was feeling," replied Diana.

"Isn't this what we all feel?" I added. "So why fight against it? Why not, at least for the moment, go with it?"

"Perhaps," responded Melhaus, impatience adding an intolerant edge to his voice, "because some of us have better things to do?"

I decided not to press on, and the conversation would have ended right then and there, but Thompson chimed in.

"Kyle's looking to see which of us has some sort of emotional catharsis."

"That would be good material," I said, "so don't hold back." I then decided to persist. "Come on, any of you, what's the hardest thing you had to leave behind on Earth? What do you miss most, excluding family, friends, and lovers? That's too easy."

"I miss going to the theater!" Diana blurted out. "The excitement of a Broadway show, taking in a play on London's West End!" She had no sooner finished when her eyes lit up, and her mouth started moving again. "Wait! Wait! Can I change my answer?"

"No," said Thompson.

"Then can I have two things? Please?"

"No," Thompson repeated, continuing his teasing. "You heard Kyle. One thing. Anyway, what else could you possibly miss? Your dollhouse?"

Stretching herself across the table, Diana gave a quick, hard punch to Thompson's thickly muscled shoulder. Based on his smirk and her silence, this seemed to satisfy them both.

"For me, give me my rose garden," Kelly said, the reminiscence causing her to smile. "So many new genetic varieties. Digging in the warm soil. The warmth of the sun on my face." She looked warily at Thompson. "Is that three things?"

"We'll accept it."

"And for you, Paul?" I asked.

The climatologist considered momentarily and said, through a frown, "It may sound a little corny or sentimental."

"Probably," said Thompson, "But try us."

"Paris," he said, starting to laugh. "Yes, in the springtime, if you must have it out. The charged atmosphere. The cafes.

At night, the glittering lights of *Champs-Élysées*. Have you been there, Kyle? No! *Mais pourquoi?* You live in New York? But it is only an hour away! Diana and I must show you!"

I willingly agreed to be their guest. Looking across the table, I noticed Thompson staring into space.

"What do you miss?" I asked. "Visits to the dentist?"

Coming back from wherever he was, he said one word: "Maryann."

"Some day, I'd like to hear about her," said Diana with satisfaction, "but *you* know the rules. Absolutely no family, friends, and lovers."

"Maryann," Thompson responded, "came to mean more to me than the woman—in a moment of insanity—I named her after. She's my fishing boat."

"You tricked me," Diana said, annoyed but smiling.

"At seven meters, she's a bit small…"

"I'd rather hear about the woman," Diana interrupted.

"That's never going to happen."

"Ever hook into a striped bass?" I asked.

"Sure," said Thompson. "Caught a twenty-two-kilo-grammer off Block Island, New York."

"I speared a smaller striper, skin diving. With the spear and trailing line still hooked in, it took me for quite a ride. Anyway, it's my turn. What I miss most is scuba diving. If I had to pick a particular memory? Being immersed in a school of spotted eagle rays as they arced and glided above me in the warm waters of the Seychelles."

And so it went as we happily, almost greedily, took our turns, each of us sharing a memory, making a small connection, temporarily setting aside the pressure of the mission.

All but Dr. Melhaus, who, through the awkward anticipatory silence that followed, remained quiet. To ease him past his reluctance, I tried to make light of it, saying, "Pardon the obvious pun, Larry, but you can't get off the hook that easily."

Looking up distractedly, almost as if he had heard none of the previous conversation, he said: "Do you realize 231-P5 is round?"

It was an obvious statement, uttered at precisely the wrong moment, delivered with a flat and emotionless voice — and it gave me a momentary start. A quick flash of concern crossed Kelly's face. I couldn't tell what Thompson was thinking; perhaps he was annoyed, but he seemed to understand where Melhaus was going with this. In any event, he said nothing and let things unfold.

"And Earth is not. Not round, that is," the physicist continued, raising his gaze from his A.I.D. to acknowledge us. "I'll explain. The Earth is an oblate spheroid due to the effects of its moon, variations in internal mass, and geological factors. These influences, no moon, for example, are inapplicable to 231-P5. Using data Dr. Thompson provided, I have calculated that P5 is at least as round as can be detected by *Desio*'s instruments; that is to say, the planet is within one kilometer of being perfectly round. Highly unusual."

In all likelihood, Thompson, with his doctorate in geology, anticipated Melhaus's findings. He deliberately chose not to make an issue of precedence but instead said, "Larry, the crew has been spending some necessary time here sharing personal feelings. Would you care to add something of your own?"

"Yeah, *Larry*," said Diana, trying to goad him into responding.

"Nothing pertinent comes to mind," the physicist replied, apparently having some vague sense of what we had been discussing.

The conversation was going downhill, so I hoped to stay out of it.

"Nothing," Thompson repeated matter-of-factly. He paused, looked at Angie, then looked at me and asked, "What does Angie miss?"

I was a bit surprised by the question; the answer, however, was easy. "Angie misses mousing. She's an eight-kilogram ball of fury when she finds a mouse."

"There you are, Larry," said Thompson. "Something to think about. Even the damn dog misses something."

Judging by his expression, Melhaus was formulating a confrontational reply. Anticipating as much, Thompson gave him a long, hard stare, then issued a command that could not be mistaken.

"Now, let's all get back to work."

Thompson

LATER THAT SAME afternoon, Thompson requested that I join him in his cabin. Entering, I observed he was busy at his workstation, accessing personnel files.

"Have a seat," he said, pointing to the room's other chair. "I'll get right to the point. You took several psychology courses with the communications degree and have writing credentials, correct?"

"That's right, I majored in communications and minored in psychology. I didn't actively pursue either one as a postgrad. I elected to make a living as a writer."

"Understood, but do you believe for a minute that your psych minor went unnoticed when the Selection Committee worked through the complicated process of choosing a crew for this ship?"

41

"At the time, I didn't give it much thought."

"Recently, I have. I'll answer the question for you. Not a chance in hell. In my twenty years of experience with the CSA, I have reluctantly accepted that very little gets by them. On board the *Desio*, I consider it my duty to see that *nothing* gets by me. I vaguely remember you saying that being picked for this mission was as much luck as anything else."

"I said that?"

"Yeah, you did. I didn't believe it then; I believe it less now. I suspect your credentials were *exactly* what the Committee was searching for. The reason I came to this conclusion may best be served by asking you a question or two."

"You have my undivided attention."

"Do you know the number of CSA ships, other than ours, that have artwork decorating their bulkheads?"

"I couldn't say."

"I can. There are none."

"Pity."

"Do you know how many interstellar ships are designed with separate sleeping quarters for each crew member?"

"Don't know. Will these all be rhetorical questions?"

"With you, might as well be, but I'm going to ask them anyway. The answer is none. Or how many ships have Vivaldi, Schubert, and Mozart wafting over their intercom systems?"

"Same answer?"

"Right," Thompson said, scowling but not expecting much in the way of an informed response. He then gestured over his shoulder. My gaze followed.

"You see that hunting bow I had mounted over my workstation?"

I nodded. "If there's a story behind it, which seems pretty damned likely, I want to hear it."

"Just shut up and listen. That bow is on a list of personal items mission engineers gave a derisive name: 'Nonessential Mass.' You might guess some other items on their list: Kelly's violin, Diana's houseplants, and Paul's antique barometer collection. The only person with no items on the list is Melhaus. You can also call your dog 'nonessential mass,' though I doubt she'd come when called. Have you ever known of a crew being allowed to encumber a ship this way? Do you realize how prohibitively expensive extra mass is?"

I admitted I hadn't and didn't. I still wasn't exactly sure what Thompson was getting at, but despite receiving no answers to his questions, he seemed to be gaining momentum.

"As expected, you're batting a thousand. A month before our departure, I thought having a little friendly chat with the commander of the previous expedition to P5 would be useful. By the third drink, he informed me that elevated levels of stress had led to a serious morale problem during his voyage. By the fifth drink, he let on that a violent argument erupted between two crew members. He grumbled about having been ordered to keep what happened under wraps. The Agency told him they had more than enough difficulty funding deep-space missions. Said they didn't need a private matter turned into a public distraction."

"Interesting," I said.

"Yes, isn't it?" Thompson said, leaning back in his chair. "I'll say this: a fight during a mission is unheard of."

"I think I'm catching on," I said. "But the CSA, in addition to taking the remedial steps you pointed out, repeatedly informed us that we'd be exposed to stressful situations. They warned us—in fact, trained us to identify the obvious causes."

An expression of doubt passed over Thompson's face. "Of course, they warned us, but I suspect the Agency was also reacting to something they could not understand. And I'll tell you what else I think. I think they believed your psych minor would be an additional benefit to this mission. Especially when coupled with your communications training and your ability as a writer to make observations about human behavior. You appear to be proactive in trying to lift the crew's spirits. As you did earlier today."

"Am I so transparent?"

"Not transparent. Self-effacing perhaps."

"Careful—there may be a compliment somewhere in there."

"If there is, it's the closest you'll ever get to one. So I ask you, besides the usual reasons, what do you think is contributing to the heightened stress levels?"

I had considered this question without knowing of the prior crew's problems. Still, I hesitated to volunteer an opinion, for when an idea receives a voice, it gains a life it might not deserve. Based on what I knew about Thompson, if my idea did not deserve to live, he would be the first and best person to kill it.

"I only have a theory, based almost exclusively on my behavior and casual study of the crew during the last three months. I can factor in what you just told me. It's this: Deep—space missions carry us too far from Earth for too long."

"You have my attention," said Thompson. "Go on."

"Has there ever been a study of the psychological effects of being outside Earth's solar system for a protracted period? Of being so absolutely separated from all verbal and visual communication forms? Or of the behavioral changes brought about by being utterly devoid of contact with Earth?"

"Not that I've been privy to. There have only been five interstellar voyages, including ours."

"I believe that, on a subconscious level, we are having difficulty coping with the stark realization that the Earth and our life-giving sun were reduced to insignificant, disappearing specks. What is left for us when the Earth is removed as our refuge and sanctuary?"

For the briefest moments, I saw a sadness register on Thompson's face. It was soon replaced by one of skepticism as he contemplated my concerns. He wasn't a man to rush to judgment. And he rarely equivocated. But he did so now. "Must say, I'm torn between thinking that's a pile of crap, or a clever insight. Let's say it's the latter. How do we address it?"

"Stress is harder to deal with when the cause is unidentified," I answered.

"Understood. Go ahead and advance your theory with the rest of the crew. It should make for some amusing dinner conversation. Notwithstanding your theory, however, the more obvious causes of stress remain to be dealt with."

"Yes," I responded, "and we have seen everyone onboard affected and coping differently. And not coping." "Which brings us to our principal concern, Thompson said, which is Dr. Melhaus."

"You've been speaking to Kelly?"

"She approached me earlier. She wasn't comfortable with Melhaus's antisocial behavior today. I concurred, but let's face it, he's always set himself apart. Arguably, more now. Kelly believes he is putting too much pressure on himself, but has yet to see warning signs of a meltdown. There are additional drugs that may provide stress relief, but she's sure Melhaus

45

would refuse to take anything he believed would impair his cognitive abilities."

"Let me guess, he's not very receptive to discussing this topic, is he?"

"No. I already tried. He was in here before you. For the present, we'll do what we're doing, which is letting him work his butt off. Keep an eye on him. Anything that represents a change, better or worse, I'll probably see it, but keep me informed. As for the rest of the crew, they seem to be doing OK. Paul and Diana seem to be rock solid."

"Seems so."

"And you and Kelly? On duty and off, that is."

"Fine," I responded, choosing not to elaborate. I was not surprised that the Commander was aware of the relationship. There was no reason to hide our affection for each other, but we didn't think it appropriate to flaunt it either.

"Good," said Thompson, apparently satisfied with my answer.

"Now you'll tell me about that bow?" I asked.

"What makes you believe there's something to tell?"

"You're being evasive."

Thompson gave me a long, scrutinizing look. "You're a persistent pain in the ass."

I agreed.

"I have many pressing things to attend to before tomorrow's set-down. You'll have to be satisfied with the abridged version."

Thompson made his weathered hands into tight fists. He then slowly unclenched them, staring pensively at palms and fingers, almost as if his hands were triggering a memory or were an integral part of the experience he was about to divulge.

"You've heard," he began matter-of-factly, "of the vast wildlife preserve in South Africa named Kruger National Park. It was established around 1900, I don't recall exactly, but could anyone living then have imagined how the planet would look three hundred years hence? How we could foul our nest so badly that the park would become one of the world's last sanctuaries for large mammals? In any event, I was afforded the rare opportunity to serve two years there as a wildlife warden. Little salary, mind you, but I was permitted to hunt game when doing so benefited the ecosystem. Sanctioned culling, for example, or removal of a diseased animal. Mostly, I did a lot of walking and tracking, searching for snares—they're a cruel business, I can tell you—and apprehending the poachers that set them. The state government set a very high penalty for violators, and poachers were heavily armed. For that reason, and the hunting, I carried a rifle. Nothing high-tech, mind you.

"I was out searching for snares when I stumbled upon three San poachers butchering a Cape Buffalo. You need only to comprehend two things: the few remaining San tribesmen were skilled trackers and hunters, often using nothing more than a primitive bow and poison-tipped arrows to kill game; an average Cape Buffalo weighs eight hundred kilograms, stands one and a half meters tall at the shoulder, double that in length, has formidable horns, a thick hide, and a mean, some say vindictive, disposition. In short, you have to admire the San's nerve.

"I was about sixty meters from the three of them, and, lucky for me, two were busy dressing the buffalo carcass, knives in hand. The third San drew a poisoned arrow from his quiver and let loose a shot at me. I distinctly remember the whistling sound of the fletching as it sailed past my ear. That got my attention. In the next instant, I had him squarely in my rifle sight, but he underestimated me or didn't believe I'd fire. I'll never know, but he notched another arrow and was shot dead for it. The other two San quickly disappeared into the bush.

"You're looking at the native bow and remaining arrows with the poison removed for safety. Out of respect for the natives' skill, I learned to use that bow. In the process, there was one thing I was forced to consider. A Cape buffalo may take days to die from poisoned arrows, so it is conceivable the animal had been hunted onto the park from adjoining lands where hunting was permitted. The San likely believed they were justified in doing what they knew: hunting bush meat, maybe getting money for the horns. They may have had families to keep alive, who knows, but I'd be lying if I told you what happened doesn't still trouble me. I mounted the bow as a reminder of a disappearing way of life, a reminder that there can be a heavy price to protect what you believe in, though the San paid a dearer price by far."

I thanked Thompson for telling me the story. I then asked him if he remembered how we felt months ago when we watched as the Earth and then the Sun shrink to pinpoints of light and vanish; how our emptiness might tell us something about what the San and other cultures felt as they watched their world disappear. He seemed to have anticipated the question, for he immediately and emphatically replied that he believed so, yes.

My question and his story put Thompson in a somber mood. I made an educated guess that he wouldn't entertain any more inquiries. What helped tip me off was being told to *let* the cabin door hit me in the ass on the way out.

Typical Thompson, on the outside coarse as forty-grit sandpaper, ignoring what others consider verbal niceties. He had a tireless appetite for dishing out sarcasm and encouraging riposte. It was then (and only then) that he deliberately waived his due as mission commander. Arguments were of great entertainment value to him when not waged in anger.

On the inside, he was quite a bit smoother. Though he tried to mask it, his concern for each crew member was absolute. His cabin door might hit you in the ass on the way out, but that same door was always wide open if you needed to make your way in.

I thought I saw other contrasts in Thompson. Self-taught in native culture, a hunter, fisherman, and geologist, he seemed preoccupied with chipping away at the past. As mission commander, treading where few—or none—have gone before, he was on the cutting edge of the future. Of these two colliding worlds, I wondered where he was more at home. If there was a common denominator, it would be in the pure adventure he sought and found in excavating the unknown.

He certainly was intelligent enough to confront all the many challenges he set for himself. He was near the top in his chosen field, but unlike Melhaus (and most other scientists, as well), he didn't care about peer recognition. His physical appearance also flew in the face of the stereotypical bespectacled, lanky scientist. He was not overly tall but heavily muscled in the chest, legs, and forearms—likely due to his many pursuits.

Given his physical and mental attributes, if I were in a tight spot, Thompson would be on my A-list to be there with me.

At dinner, I shared the theory I had broached with Thompson. Not only was I seeking the crew's opinion, but I was hoping that verbalizing the idea would provide a beneficial effect.

"Help me with something I'm working on," I began. "Call it the Sanctuary Theory, if you will." I then explained my thinking on the matter. "Maybe something in your respective disciplines, or perhaps a personal experience, would be relevant. Or you can diplomatically tell me that the theory isn't worth a damn."

I was grateful when Thompson, wanting to give the conversation some impetus, chimed in first.

"I had the advantage of hearing Kyle's idea earlier," he said. "Two thoughts came to mind. The Sun's magnetic field extends throughout the solar system, and its effect on brain waves is well known. Could the absence of these fields have a detrimental effect? My research came up empty. Anyone?"

No one had heard of a study concerning the matter.

Diana was eager to chime in. "I know of experiments done on subjects living in caves. They showed signs of depression. During solar eclipses, animals exhibit behavioral changes that resemble symptoms of stress. I can add a personal note. The day we lost sight of Earth, I wept. I thought it was hormones, but the feeling has been hard to shake."

"There are studies related to my expertise," Paul added, "human behavior is also affected by barometric pressure, temperature, wind, precipitation, too many consecutive days of identical weather, variation in the length of the day, and changes in season. That would suggest that the absence of *all* weather strongly influences behavior. It is not a new phenomenon, however. Extrasolar missions were preceded by three centuries of intrasolar spaceflights."

"New or not," Kelly volunteered, "we cannot underestimate the psychological effect of losing every vestige of contact with family and friends. Whatever the cause, stress levels on board are likely to increase. I shouldn't have to chase after you if you are experiencing problems. For now, I want to see everyone, without exception, for a full exam. And I have a question for you, Larry."

I watched as Melhaus visibly tensed up, then relaxed after realizing the question posed to him was not of a personal nature.

"For the next eight days," Kelly continued, "our exposure to *Desio*'s artificial sunlight will be lessened, supplanted by the sunlight available on P5. How does that sunlight compare to Earth's?"

"Favorably," Melhaus responded, "P5's sun radiates a light that is more beneficial to human health. Blue, green, and yellow wavelengths of four hundred seventy to five hundred seventy nanometers predominate. The average intensity of surface sunlight as the planet reaches its perihelion is a relatively bright three hundred ten watts per square meter."

"Thank you for that information," Kelly said.

Avoiding what he believed to be useless discourse, the physicist failed to acknowledge the gratitude. Instead, he addressed me.

"Regarding the idea prompting this conversation, Mr. Lorenzo, your proposition should be identified as conjecture—not theory. A theory is formulated after careful observation and measurement. You've done no measurements and only scant observation."

"You're correct, Larry," I replied, careful to keep any trace of irritation regarding his blunt manner out of my voice. "I should have been more careful with my choice of words."

"That said," he continued, "a well-designed study would entail submitting human subjects to conditions that duplicate extrasolar spaceflight with subsequent administration of psychological tests on these same subjects. Barring that near impossibility, a logical starting point is an examination of those individuals who *have* left the solar system to determine if they experienced behavioral problems. A very rudimentary question follows. Excluding this crew, what data is available for individuals on extrasolar missions?"

I hesitated a moment. "Not much," I cautiously answered, unsure if what the commander told me about the previous expedition was suitable for general consumption.

"Earlier today," Thompson interjected, "I informed Kyle that the last mission commander alerted me to the inordinately high levels of stress, cause unknown, seen within himself and his crew. That disclosure coincides with the Agency's unusual efforts to address stress on our mission."

"And you were going to notify the rest of the crew of this *when?*" Melhaus said in an accusatory tone.

"When I judged the need to know arose," Thompson responded in an even voice. "Are you questioning that?"

"And what prompted the release of information at this juncture?" Melhaus continued. His anger was building, but for the moment, he was avoiding an overt challenge to Thompson's authority.

"The answer can be found in your recent deportment."

"I see," said Melhaus, not at all satisfied. "An answer couched in a riddle."

"No, Larry, you're too intelligent to say that was a riddle. Intelligent enough to understand that if I have a problem with you, you will be the first to know—plain and simple."

The ship's eerie silence descended, which only Thompson ventured to disturb. "I'm not sure you got what you wanted here, Kyle, but unless you or anybody else has something to add, I suggest we go about the pressing business at hand."

I thanked everyone for their input, but struggled to keep an expression of dismay from my face. As the crew dispersed to go about their work, I caught a brief look of sympathetic understanding from Kelly.

Despite my best intentions, broaching my theory with the crew did not have the positive effect I had hoped for. On the contrary, the ensuing conversation ended with everyone feeling ill at ease. Worse, I may have inadvertently helped widen the divide developing between Thompson and Melhaus.

Several hours had elapsed, and *Desio*, now in a lower orbit, was accompanying the planet as it entered the night.

What was awaiting us down there? Would the unknown conveniently fit within the realm of human experience or rise to challenge, perhaps exceed, the limits of our imagination? One tantalizing mystery had already presented itself.

Unaccustomed to seeing a world without a web of artificial light marring its surface, the crew had crowded at the main viewport to watch as the planet spun from the blue sun into night. Unexpectedly, countless tiny flecks of colored light appeared on the surface! They emerged slowly at first, like early evening fireflies, then with greater prominence and frequency as we progressed further into the realm of darkness.

A baffled Diana said there was no evidence to indicate the phenomenon was caused by the plankton-like organisms prolific in the planet's ocean. Paul suggested that the colors might be an unknown type of atmospheric disturbance. At the same time, he wondered why there were no lights above the steadily shrinking icecaps.

Telescopically, each speck resolved as perfect circles of varying sizes, ostensibly residing on, or very close to, the ocean surface—at least as observed from our top-down view. None was greater than twenty meters across.

Thompson and Melhaus, reviewing every scrap of sensor data, could offer no plausible explanation. A similar phenomenon had never been seen, and our present altitude rendered it impossible to explain. This gave the four scientists secret satisfaction; they wanted nothing more than a great mystery to solve.

The crew had turned in for the evening, and I found myself alone in the darkened mission room, inexplicably drawn to the unspoiled world. The inscrutable mystery of the glowing lights, the distant and untouched beauty, and the surrounding panoply of stars were captivating wonders to behold. Together, they conspired to affect in me a singular thought—not of science and solutions, but of fancy, of literature. An ancient compilation of fables, *One Thousand and One Arabian Nights*, came to mind.

The fable is centered on the storytelling ability of Scheherazade, who marries a Persian king known to wed—and execute the following morning—a succession of virgins to exact vengeance for the actions of his unfaithful first wife. To save herself from the same fate, Scheherazade tells the king a fantastical story, only to leave it unfinished, or claiming that a more imaginative story will follow. By doing so, night after night, for a thousand and one nights, she postpones her death until she is spared.

No untimely thought, this. The evocation of a collective work of Middle Eastern folklore needs no apology. Not in an age where science rules and the precious few storytellers remaining are bereft of an audience.

As I stood at the viewport, self-absorbed in thought, Kelly quietly entered the room. Approaching from behind, she wrapped her arms around my waist and pressed tightly against my back. We gazed at the mysterious lights below with her chin resting on my shoulder. Softly, she whispered in my ear.

"Thinking of a name?"

"Beautiful, isn't she?" I said. "It's hard to believe she was encased in ice a few months ago. There must be a name befitting such a world, but it will never be as sweet sounding to me as yours."

"Hmm. You'll have *me* melt."

"Stay with me tonight." I implored.

"I'd like nothing better. You seem lonely."

"I often am."

"Sorry. Why?"

"Sometimes, I guess, my inner thoughts isolate me."

My response was cryptic and didn't explain anything. Nevertheless, Kelly accepted it gracefully, even giving me an easy way out if I chose to take it.

"Maybe," she said, "someday you'll share those thoughts with me."

I said nothing more, letting her wish disappear into the emptiness of space.

As we walked to my cabin, I silently criticized myself for missing another opportunity.

Not for what I said but for what I somehow couldn't say.

Landing

EARLY THE FOLLOWING morning (for the first time in a hundred days, the word took on real meaning, for we eagerly awaited sunrise), *Desio*, in the capable hands of Commander Thompson, sliced a path through the planet's atmosphere.

Transported within one hundred meters of P5's surface, we became the first humans privileged to behold the moving, living ocean in liquid form. Our elevated perspective revealed a strangely placid expanse of widely interspersed, low-rolling swells unmarred by wavelets, sea foam, or disturbances of any kind. An endless, unbroken line of glare cast upon the water by the planet's slowly rising blue sun highlighted and bisected this elemental scene.

Mesmerized by the ocean's overwhelming serenity, my mind wandered into uncommon imaginings and fanciful abstractions: the water—shiny-smooth, metallic-colored, fluid-moving—as though it were a boundless, polished sheet of cobalt blue steel undulating through the will of a fundamental and unknowable authority!

Perhaps I was alone in my daydreaming, but there was an undeniable calming feel to this tableau, a quality possessed and imparted by the muted blues and grays, the simplicity of shape and line, the grandness of scale, and a sense of timelessness. Yes, there was something beyond comprehension here, something intangible at play. We were not original to this picture and were humbled to silence.

And in that silence, unfeeling instruments performed the vital process of sampling the atmosphere, ruling out the presence of chemicals or pathogens that could have threatened our shared hope to experience what had for so long been denied: to touch solid ground, to breathe fresh, unrecycled air; to see a sun gloriously rise and set. In short, if only in part, a return to life's natural, cyclical order.

We traveled onward as the sun—twice the size of Earth's—continued its slow rise, growing dominant, emerging from the ocean to appear as an atmosphere-distorted disc hovering on the horizon. With the planet dutifully spinning into a new day, the last vestiges of dawn receded, and the disc started brightening, rounding, repeating what had been accomplished nine hundred billion times before.

In awe, we venerated the start of the new day.

Thompson, taking pleasure in ignoring *Desio*'s automated piloting, decreased forward velocity to bring us within a ship's width of the water's surface. The feeling of motion that had been lacking for the past several months was exhilarating, even though we were moving at a minuscule fraction of our former velocity.

The crew agreed to select a landing site that satisfied three criteria: a suitably flat area of geological significance and natural beauty. The first landmass encountered, a collection of sharp rock slabs rising dramatically from the ocean, was smaller than five square kilometers. It was deemed unacceptable. A neighboring island, twice the size of the first and with an area to land, seemed adequate but was insufficiently enticing for Thompson, despite our protestations, to land.

Desio's control panel displayed yet another isolated island out of view beyond the horizon. This became our new destination. It was only minutes away, but we had become increasingly impatient to land. Because Thompson had passed on the first suitable location, two crewmates felt obliged to make him the object of some teasing.

"I was wondering," Kelly asked Diana, "if you agree with a basic and universal premise that some men are too stubborn to ask for navigational assistance."

"I'm not so sure I can agree with the premise. I'm having trouble with the word 'some.'"

Paul and I exchanged glances and leaned back to enjoy.

"I get that," Kelly responded. "I should have said many or a staggeringly high percentage."

"And I," interrupted Thompson, "am thinking of words such as stifle, muzzle, and gag."

"Oh, I'm sorry," said Kelly, "you don't think we were referring to you, do you?"

"What could give me that crazy idea?" Thompson responded. "But if either of you would like to assume the flight controls…"

"Oh, no!" Diana said in shock, "We would never think of such a thing, would we, Kelly?"

"Never."

"Personally," Paul said, "I'd give the commander a break. A delay of thirty kilometers out of seven hundred trillion isn't too shabby."

And so the little comic scene played out, the actors knowing full well that Melhaus, who had not participated, was the only other crew member rated to pilot the ship. Moreover, Thompson would never relinquish control. Moments later, he pointed out a landmass lifting itself from the horizon.

"I see it!" shouted Diana.

As we obtained our first close-up view, Thompson, an excited edge to his usually calm voice, asked, "Have any of you been to Moscow?"

"No," Diana said, confused. "And I'm not likely to get there any time soon."

"That's what you think," Thompson replied, reducing forward speed. "Make preparations. Looks like we'll be landing there in two minutes."

To starboard, lofting into the sky were crudely sculpted replicas of the spires, towers, and twisted turrets of St. Basil's and Kazan's Cathedrals—the iconic buildings bordering Red Square. Seemingly resistant to time and the elements, there were a hundred or more stone pillars ranging in height from fifty to two hundred meters. All were dressed in striking yellows, browns, and gold tones, with darker veins of each color spiraling throughout.

Red Square required more imagination, for it was not as level as its Russian counterpart and dwarfed it in size. An expansive plateau of flat rock spanned the distance from the base of the spires (which formed an imposing backdrop) to the water, where fissures and cracks created steps and accessible shallow pools. Far beyond, the ocean's clarity permitted an unobstructed view as the slabs descended steeply into the abyss, finally disappearing from view.

"Incredible," said Kelly.

Even Melhaus, who had characteristically shown little emotion, shifted in his seat to get a better look.

"I can't see how weathering could produce such unusual formations," Paul said, referring to the spires. "Do you believe you can develop a geological explanation, Commander?"

Thompson left the question unanswered. Viewing the casual remark as a challenge, he confirmed the island as the preferred landing site, but not before moving *Desio* away from the island to locate deeper water. One task required tending to first, arguably the most crucial of the entire mission. With a series of commands, *Ixodes* was magnetically detached and sent plunging headlong into the ocean. Submerging, it became fully operational, as planned and without mishap.

Moments later, in June 2233, after six months of training on Earth and three months of travel, at a place we were now calling the Square, the crew of *Desio* gently touched down on the ocean planet.

"We have arrived," said Thompson. He activated the external hatchway with those simple words, allowing six metal steps to unfold—our gateway to another world.

"Captain, sir," said Diana, inflating her deference to Thompson by assigning him a military rank he did not have. "May I have your permission to be the first to leave the ship?"

The request was unusual, a departure from the long-standing tradition that being first on the planet was the privilege of the expedition leader. Thompson, who had little use for formality, could not deny her. "We'll be right behind you," he said, though the look on his face said more. We all knew Diana well enough to expect an ulterior motive hiding behind her request. We weren't disappointed.

Setting foot on the surface of P5, with the rest of us close behind and the onboard camera recording for posterity, Diana exclaimed in a clear, steady voice, "That's one small step for a woman, one giant leap for womankind."

Thompson, unperturbed, raised an eyebrow at her and said, "Working on the male-female theme today?"

Diana gave him an unabashed look. "What can I say? We double—Xs waited two hundred fifty plus years to rectify that B.S."

The prior expedition had comprised five males. Diana was the first female on P5 and the first female on a planet outside our solar system. There was no reason to be anything but amused at what she said.

Melhaus, however, wasn't entertained.

"What I...," he began, then corrected himself, "...what *we* are about to accomplish here doesn't deserve to be trivialized by you, or anyone else, in some ill-conceived attempt to right some perceived wrong."

The remark did not go over well. Paul and Kelly seemed intent on wading into the pending fray. Diana abruptly preempted them.

"Why, Larry," she shot back, "I see your ego, like your reputation, *exceeds* you."

"I have no time to waste participating in a juvenile insulting match," Melhaus countered, his voice tight with restrained anger.

That was more than enough for Thompson.

ORB

"*And I*," he said, emphasizing each word while staring hard at Diana and harder at Melhaus, "expect my crew to bind and gag their personal demons, or I'll do it for them."

Yet another awkward silence ensued. The episodes were getting to be routine. Fortunately, what transpired next provided a welcome distraction.

I had forgotten about Angie, who certainly hadn't forgotten there was a world to explore. She had managed—no easy trick—to extricate herself from her custom-made flight harness. Poised at the top edge of the landing stairs, she sniffed her expert evaluation of the planet's atmosphere, liking what was detected. In the next instant, she bounded down and out of *Desio* and, with fantastic speed and agility, began to run back and forth across the expanse of the Square, all the while barking excitedly.

"Let it be known," I said for Diana's benefit, "that's one small step for a dog, one giant leap for canines." I was happy to elicit a laugh, but it was Angie's unbridled happiness that was contagious.

"Looks like Angie is the second bitch to set foot on this planet," Thompson added, earning him a swift, hard punch in the shoulder from Diana.

"I don't think I have ever seen her so animated," said Kelly, "but don't you feel it, too, Kyle?"

Taking a few strides, I wondered why we had not noticed sooner. "Of course! I had forgotten! Angie, like us, weighs ten percent less here!"

"Diana insisted I should shed a few kilograms," Paul added. "Now I have. Mission accomplished."

Work began in earnest. Thompson, who had wisely allowed us time to acclimate to new surroundings, now held a scanning spectrometer to examine a walnut-sized rock. Paul

63

carefully erected a laser Doppler anemometer. Diana began calibrating an ion-buffered off-gas analyzer. These—and many other scientific instruments I was helping unload from *Desio*—had descriptive labels that gave me an erudite air of familiarity with devices. A familiarity that I did not have.

Thompson picked up on my ignorance when he requested, and I failed to retrieve, an unlabeled protonic nano-introscope.

"I wasn't sure if you wanted the red or green one," I said.

"I don't have a preference. You choose."

"OK," I admitted, "you're acquainted with every damn piece of equipment on the ship, and I am not. But can you tell me how many stanzas are in a Shakespearean sonnet?"

"Stanzas?" Thompson replied as if confused. "Oh *yeah*, I remember—the three Italian counts. Enrico, Giuseppe, and Philippo. Brothers, I believe. Weren't they the three gentlemen of Verona?"

"I won't dignify that with a reply."

"Can you dignify fourteen?"

"How in hell did you know that?"

"An undergraduate elective. If I recall correctly, my only choices were Shakespeare's plays and sonnets or an entire course on James Joyce's *Ulysses*."

"You made the right decision."

"I think so. I've continued to read Shakespeare."

After hours of hard physical work unloading and setting up equipment, Thompson took me aside and said, "Grab Kelly and your mutt and visit the other side of the island. Stay alert. We don't want to provoke the indigenous population." As Kelly, Angie, and I were partway across the Square, he shouted after us, "Needless to say, don't ingest the water."

He correctly anticipated we'd go for a swim. The crew had gone three months without a real shower or bath. Even if the water was cold, it was going to be irresistible.

"Pity we don't have bathing suits," I remarked to Kelly.

"Pity," she repeated, deliberately bumping into me as we walked across the Square, knocking me off my stride like a delighted child. Side by side, we made small talk as we idly walked along.

"Did you bring the sunscreen?" she asked.

"Forgot the sunscreen. You bring the towels?"

"Forgot the towels."

The temperature was rising to that of a midsummer's day on Earth, the ascending sun, now a faded shade of blue, pleasantly warming the exposed areas of our skin. The dull heat rising from the stone did not bother Angie's paws; she scampered ahead of us, occasionally looking back to ensure we followed, impatient when we lagged. She reached the base of the spires well ahead of us, having skillfully navigated the intervening boulders and crevices. I was happy she handled the terrain well after initially worrying about her safety, seeing how she ran full speed out of *Desio*.

"Can you believe we are here?" Kelly said, stopping to grab my hand as she tilted her head to gaze up at the spires looming over us.

I took her other hand and wrapped her arms around my waist, hugging her tightly. She was a few inches shorter than I, and her jet—black hair, warmed by the sun, was in my face. I saw highlights in the strands that could not possibly be there— reds, purples, and oranges. I heard my heart pumping blood through my veins.

Turning out of my grasp, she clasped me by the hand and pulled me along. "Let's see if we can find a secret path through these sleeping giants."

There was little chance of getting lost on such a small island, but we tried. Winding our way among the spires, backtracking several times, we eventually arrived at a small, secluded cove. By this time, we were feeling the heat. Kelly had the foresight to bring two liters of cold water. We drank half, and then some was steadily poured into my tightly cupped hands as Angie eagerly lapped.

I spotted a stone slab at the water's edge, suitably flat and broad for us all to lie on comfortably. One end was elevated above the water, where we could sit high and dry, legs dangling over a ledge, our bare feet immersed in the shallow pool below.

"It's delightful!" said Kelly, laughing with surprise. "Nearly as warm as the Caribbean."

"You're right. I expected colder." I reached down and waved my hand beneath the surface. "Did you see that?!" I asked. "A flash of color when I swirled the water."

"Yes! Very faint, but I see more than one."

"The hues intermingle but don't seem to blend—if that makes sense."

"Every test so far has proven the water safe," she said. Then, with surprising urgency, "Let's jump in!"

I needed no encouragement, but Kelly provided more, reaching across and tugging my shirt out of my pants. I raised my arms, and she pulled the thin fabric over my head. With both hands, I swept her long hair off her shoulders and onto her back, then unbuttoned her blouse. For the first time, I noticed that her moist skin took on a sultry, satiny sheen in the ambient light. We removed the rest of our clothing and slipped into the water. With a few careful steps, we were in water up to our waists, facing each other but not touching. Looking into her eyes, I said, "Ready? One. Two. Three!" and we let the water completely envelop us.

She rose out of the ocean with me, splashing into the bright sun, rivulets of water streaming down her skin and hair, hair blacker, if ever possible, and shinier, clinging to her back, shoulders, and breasts. I urgently reached for her, pressing against her so forcefully that we lost our breath and started panting. I didn't want us to separate, but she deliberately pushed me away, a sad, vulnerable look of bewildered desire welling in her eyes, a gasped, choked-off sob coming to her throat. I was terribly unsure if passion or emotion was about to make her cry; she deliberately prevented me from knowing by clinging to me, kissing me so violently our teeth clashed.

From nowhere, a moment with *half* this intensity involuntarily flashed into my consciousness. I was twenty years old, young and carefree, burning up most of the summer body-surfing on the beaches of the United States' East Coast. It was a sweltering day, and a storm out to sea generated waves big enough to chase everybody out of the water. I jogged to the far end of the beach to find a secluded sandy cove where the sun, glowing orange in the summer haze, had begun lowering its bulky self onto the incoming waves.

I remembered the waves cycling in, plumes of salty spray sweeping backward off their towering crests. I remembered the wave's exhilarating energy, primordial and powerful, carrying me to shore.

Half as intense. I understood why. Kelly had not been with me then.

"Kyle."

Funny-strange, then and now, water as the common element.

"Kyle."

There are times, too rare, when one loses all sense of self in ecstasy.

"Kyle," I heard Kelly say, lips pressed hot and moist against my ear. "You disappeared. For a moment."

"Did I hurt you?" I managed to say, breathing hard. "I never want to hurt you."

"No."

"Let's lie on the rock together. To dry."

Unwrapping from each other, we climbed out of the water. Lying on our backs, resting, we stared up at the sky.

"Do you think Diana will be mad?" Kelly finally said with a small laugh.

"How so?"

"She likes being first. She and Paul won't be the first."

I laughed. "You'll tell her?"

"No. But she'll know."

I turned onto my stomach to look out at the ocean. "The sun feels good."

"Yes."

"I'm feeling guilty. Have we been gone too long?"

"We'll make up for it when we get back."

I was resting my chin on folded arms, looking at the razor-sharp line where the ocean met the sky. It was then that I viewed a tiny disturbance in or on that line—a mere blip, way out. I cupped one hand over my eyes to block the sun's glare, squinting to improve my vision, but to no avail. By the time Kelly looked, the disturbance, real or imagined, was gone.

"What do you think was there?" she asked, intrigued.

I stood up, continuing to gaze out. "Probably nothing."

"Could it be the *Ixodes*?" Kelly asked.

"Maybe. But she wouldn't be spending much time on the surface."

Dressing to leave, we continued to look oceanward.

Nothing.

We held hands, and Angie stayed close as we headed back through the spires. How should I tell Thompson what I saw—or didn't see?

Halfway back, Kelly, also deep in thought, said in a little voice, "I have a small confession to make."

"Yes," I said as we casually walked on. "Go ahead."

Her voice began to waver, saying, "Remember when you asked me how to say 'I need you' in Japanese?"

"Of course."

"I could have answered differently... a lot differently."

"Really? How so?"

"The special word I said, *aishiteru*, isn't often used. Sometimes never. It's a cultural thing not to. It doesn't mean 'I need you.' It means 'I love you.'"

"You made a mistake translating?"

Kelly stopped walking. We were holding hands, so I stopped with her. She faced me.

"No," was her simple answer.

"So why...?" I was refusing to catch on.

That look of sadness returned to her eyes, only this time, the look and feeling weren't intermingled with passion.

"Will you make me spell it out?" she said.

"No...," I began, yet no words came out, partly because I was stunned speechless by my monumental stupidity. I tried to start again. "Should I..."

"Well, then I will," she said, releasing my hand and backing away a step, striving to keep her voice in control, believing, and she was right, that anything I said or did now was going to be too late, or much worse, a fabrication.

"I made you say it. I was very wrong to make you say you love me. I was afraid. Afraid it was the only time I would ever hear you say it."

"I'm sorry." I managed to blunder, taking a step toward her, but she retreated, fighting back the tears coming to her eyes.

"I know you are," she said, her voice quivering with emotion. "Can we go?" She picked up Angie and hugged her, receiving far more comfort and affection from her than from me.

Resolutely, she walked ahead, leaving me with the last person I wanted to be alone with: myself. I was sorry, more than I could express, for hurting her. Where were the words to make everything right? "*A mistake translating?*" I actually said that to her, didn't I, damned dishonest fool that I am, incapable of admitting that I had deliberately pushed her away!

Before we were in sight of the Square, I ran to catch up with her.

"Wait!" I shouted.

She slowed, then went on.

"Please. Wait."

She stopped but determinedly looked straight ahead.

"I'm sorry," I began, groping for words. "You deserve more. If you can, stick with me a little longer. Maybe this is not all you deserve to hear, maybe not all I want to hear from myself, but it's a start. I need you. I want you. No one else has ever come close. Doesn't *that* mean something?"

She turned to face me.

"Do you think I'd give up on you so easily?" she said. "Do you think I can?"

70

"I don't know..."

"There's no other way for me. You'll have to do a much better job of turning me away."

She stooped to put Angie down, looked up at me, and said with a sad little frown, "Besides, if I lose you, I lose Angie too."

With this hurt, we returned to the ship. I would need to think seriously about what Kelly had said and what she was coming to mean to me.

For now, however, my duty was to update Thompson.

ORB

Possibilities

KELLY AND I had been gone for less than two hours, but much had been accomplished at the landing site. Equipment that needed to be placed in service had been removed from the ship and, when necessary, assembled. The four scientists had established their workstations and were preoccupied with conducting experiments, reviewing instrument readings, or collecting samples.

Kelly sought out Diana while I located Thompson, who was closely examining an assortment of rocks he had collected. He looked up distractedly as I approached, simply saying, "And?"

My response wouldn't be straightforward.

"No natives to displace. There's a path meandering through the spires, terminating at a small cove on the island's far side. The geology, to an untrained eye, is the same. The only discernible difference is that the spires gradually decrease in size." I wavered and then said, "Perhaps there's more."

"For general consumption?" Thompson asked, looking at me closely.

"Can't see why not."

He called to the crew, not wanting to waste time hearing my report twice. I now had an audience. "Go ahead," he said.

"There's a small cove about four kilometers away, due north of here. I was resting on a rock overlooking the ocean when I saw, or imagined, a slight disturbance on the far horizon. Barely visible and undefined."

"Imagined or saw?" Melhaus prodded. "Which is it?"

"I said it that way because I can't be sure."

"Which direction were you facing, or more specifically, looking?" Thompson asked.

"The island was behind me, completely blocking the view south. Spires on my right were blocking the view east. I was looking north to northwest."

"Larry?" Thompson asked, expecting an answer to an unspecified question.

"No," Melhaus responded, "*Ixodes* is operating due south of here."

"Could you tell," Paul asked, "if what you observed was in the water, on the water, or just above?"

"No," I answered, and then, on reflection, added, "Probably not elevated above, or it would have been easier to focus on."

"The sky is cloudless today," Paul said to Thompson. "But we can't completely rule out that possibility."

"Did *you* notice anything, Kelly?" Diana asked.

"No, but by the time Kyle had pointed where to look, he said there was nothing to see."

"I'd like to be more certain," I added.

"What's your vision rated?" Thompson asked.

"Twenty/ten."

"As far as you can tell, was this disturbance at the horizon line?"

"Yes."

"The line is approximately five kilometers away, but gauging the distance to an object is impossible without knowing its size. Larry? Paul?"

"No, can't be done," Paul agreed.

"If I had the object's height, the calculation would be simple," Melhaus replied. "We can, however, substitute an extreme. If the object were fifty meters tall, the sighting distance would be approximately twenty-five kilometers."

"OK, let's use that as an extreme assumption," Thompson responded. "So somewhere between five and twenty-five kilometers. Diana, is there any reason not to send *Ixodes* to the general area?"

"Can't give you one," she responded. "The submersible has collected, and I'm in the initial stages of examining live plankton samples. Unfortunately, more complex lifeforms remain undetected. Because of that, I'm stressing."

Thompson studied her carefully, weighing, I think, the extent to which she was joking. After considering it a moment, he then turned his attention back to Melhaus.

"Send *Ixodes*. Program her on a mapping course. Keep all of her other operational commands as is."

Melhaus went off to make it happen, content with the decision.

"Is that cove worth a special visit?" Thompson asked, looking at Kelly. She blushed slightly, so I answered for both of us.

"You could say that." As I was speaking, Kelly excused herself and headed for *Desio*.

Thompson looked after her, then devoted his attention to Paul and Diana. "If you two take a break to go there, which seems a good idea, just let somebody know first."

"A little later?" Paul asked Diana.

"Definitely," she responded, nudging him. "But for now, there's a batch of weird phytoplankton under the scope."

The meeting was over, and I was about to head for my cabin when Thompson stopped me.

"And you and Kelly? Together and separately, that is?"

Thompson phrased the question precisely as he had a day ago. Had he picked up a subtle alteration in our body language?

"Fine," I responded.

The commander deserved a more truthful answer. He was only looking out for the welfare of his crew.

Kelly and I performed routine maintenance and upkeep for the next few hours. When directed, we assisted the other four crew members. I should say three. Dr. Melhaus never requested assistance.

The time I spent alone with Kelly was brief and work-related. An uneasy politeness replaced the casual intimacy of past conversations. Although we tried to minimize the damage, a dull hurt lingered. The best I could manage was to ask if she'd like to take Angie for a while. The gesture was eagerly accepted.

Later in the day, Paul and Diana, looking wet and relaxed, returned from a visit to the other side of the island. Shortly after, I overheard Thompson urging Melhaus to take a short break at the cove, advising that he could still control Ixodes' functions by bringing his A.I.D. along. From the tone of the conversation, I gathered the physicist wasn't interested. Thompson didn't press him.

Deep into the afternoon, a pleasant breeze came up, followed by a few widely dispersed cumulus clouds marching in from the north—from the location I had seen… nothing. I wasn't entirely convinced, but the crew was, especially when *Ixodes* came up empty after hours of searching.

A decent-sized swath of ocean had been explored without indicating life other than the phytoplankton. It was still early in the mission, but the disappointing findings visibly subdued the crew. With our expectations moderating, Melhaus asked Thompson for permission to reprogram Ixodes for operation in water depths that exceeded its engineered maximum. Thompson said he'd consider the request—but not so early in the mission. Melhaus did not argue the point.

As evening approached, a decision was made to remove the table and chairs from the mission room and set them up on the Square. From then on, we enjoyed our communal meals outside in the warm, fresh air with the ocean as a stunning backdrop. A science-based discussion ensued as we ate dinner in the fading ambient lighting.

"I just don't understand it," Diana said, exasperated. "Or maybe I don't want to. All the grab samples that *Ixodes* analyzed, coupled with the volume of water samples taken from shore, and not a single indicator of life other than the plankton. Nothing more complex, nothing less complex. Only the damn plankton. How in hell is that possible? It's almost as if they were somehow deposited here. From what you're telling me, there's a good chance nothing else will be found."

I was not privy to the ongoing discussions among the mission scientists. "Fill me in," I asked. "What's driving this conclusion?"

Diana began to reply, then thought better of it, and said, "Paul? Why don't you tell him your piece of the puzzle? I could stand to hear it again myself."

"Unlike Earth, the climate appears to be extraordinarily stable. One likely cause is the absence of geographical features such as deserts, large land masses, or mountain ranges known to generate or influence weather systems. Let me amend that. There is one dominant feature, and you're looking at it—an enormous heat sink of an ocean, with its capacity to moderate temperature swings. The Northern and Southern hemispheres have the same weather because the planet has no axial tilt. This means there are no microclimates to act as suitable incubators for life.

Oh, yeah, I left out something. It's a good lead-in for you, Bruce. P5, unlike Earth, never had a period of volcanic activity to alter the atmosphere. There is no indication the planet ever had a protracted ice age."

"No sign of an ice age *or* an extended period of global warming," Thompson submitted. "OK, Kyle, here's my part in this," Thompson said. "For you, in liberal arts form. Two years ago, I examined rock samples returned by the previous expedition. We determined P5's age as 2.5 billion Earth years, which is to say, one billion P5 years. Despite the planet's relative youth, it is geologically stable. My current thinking attributes this to the absence of tectonic plates and a moon. I have measured no meaningful seismic activity. There are no volcanoes, earthquakes, or tides—good reasons for little sand and no soil.

"I am admittedly mixing fact and conjecture. Many things remain a mystery to me." Following Thompson's stare, watching the look of concentration on his face, there was no mistaking that he meant the spires forming the backdrop of our landing site. "Much is left to be accomplished here. I'm sure Dr. Melhaus will attest to that. You're up next, Larry."

I was wondering what the esteemed physicist would add to the discussion. He had been attentive but didn't appear to be exuding his usual excess of self-confidence. I looked across the table at Kelly, who followed the conversation with interest.

"Within the boundaries of this discussion," Melhaus began, "I can provide only rudimentary input. Decide for yourselves if it coincides with what you're starting to believe. First, on the approach to P5, I determined that the solar system is nearly devoid of asteroids, suggesting they never existed in appreciable quantity or were swept clean by the sun's gravity. The scarcity of asteroids equates to few, if any, meteors impacting the planet. Those making it to the surface would have their energy absorbed by the ocean. In sum, unlike on Earth, meteors can be eliminated as a potential source of climate change.

"As for an analysis of the chemical composition of the ocean, well, uh, the salinity is one percent versus three percent found on Earth. Not much else can be offered without further analysis."

Curious, I thought, that Melhaus was unsure or holding back something. Was he keeping scientific terminology at a minimum in deference to me? If so, he was overcompensating.

"Larry, maybe you noticed this," Kelly said, eyeing him closely. "There are colors, barely noticeable when the ocean water is agitated."

"If you press me on it, there are unusual forms of inorganic molecular compounds—some of which are metalloids—forming a unique heterogeneous mixture. I have never seen anything like it. Suffice it to say I am pursuing the matter with vigor."

We took our cue from Thompson and decided, for the present, not to pursue the subject. The conversation naturally flowed back to Diana.

"Kyle, my colleagues have explained the central tenet for the formation of life: Change. Despite this, the phytoplankton are evolved enough—ha, I shouldn't use *that* word—*complex* enough to have had precursors, rudimentary organisms occupying the same environment. But where the hell are they? I mean, did the phytoplankton suddenly materialize out of thin air? If they existed, did they wholly and suddenly die off? I see no evidence of it. Compounding the mystery is that the organism has no gene sequences. Not as we've come to understand them. So, what's left to explain their existence? That the little critter is now, and has always, occupied an entire planet all by its lonesome? I'm not looking forward to postulating *that* theory when we return home."

Diana appeared crestfallen, which was completely understandable. Her hopes of exploring an ocean rich in biodiversity had been crushed. Paul's words, "Don't despair," were small comfort.

"Oh, it's not so bad," she responded. "It's exactly *because* the little critter is so different that it can represent a lifetime of study." Her attempt to portray a better mood was unconvincing. I decided to try a different tack.

"I have a solution to your problem, Diana."

She looked at me skeptically. "And what would that be?"

"The phytoplankton, I've heard you say, produces a prodigious amount of oxygen, correct?"

"Yes."

"It produces all the oxygen, both in the air and water, on the planet?"

"You've been paying attention."

"Well, I think the little critter was brought here by a highly advanced alien race and deliberately seeded in the ocean. And for what purpose? It's obvious. To generate sufficient oxygen to create a hospitable and habitable world."

It had been a long time since anyone elicited a spontaneous laugh from Dr. Melhaus, but I did so now—quite a deprecating laugh.

"That's Kyle," Thompson said, "for better or for worse, always giving us something to think about."

"I aim to please," I said, giving him a wry grin. "Is the idea too far-fetched, Diana?"

"Let me put it this way," she answered, "there isn't a single shred of evidence to support your contention."

"You realize, Diana," Thompson interjected, "Kyle here has a serious problem."

"And what exactly is that?"

"I've mentioned it before. He's desperate for something bizarre or sensational to write about. That something has yet to materialize, so he's trying hard to invent shit. Or should I say, Kyle, you're trying to get us to do it for you?"

"Just trying to help out," I said.

With darkness nearly upon us, Kelly and I cleared the remains of dinner from the outside table, allowing the crew (minus Paul, who was measuring the diffusion of light through the atmosphere) to put their equipment to bed. The day had been emotionally, intellectually, and physically demanding, and we intended to claim our just reward. The landing site was well situated on an open expanse, facilitating a panoramic view westward over the ocean toward the setting sun.

The sun would not disappoint. Huge, fiery blue, it appeared poised to boil the waiting ocean.

There came a stillness, a suspension of time, as the world awaited the orb's final submission. It did so reluctantly, relinquishing heat and blazing color in a glorious surrender, then casting two divergent beams of light skyward while a watery blanket spread over its disappearing head.

Alive with radiant shades of blue, the sky turned progressively darker—sapphire blue to Persian indigo to midnight blue—until blue was lost to black and day was lost to night. A moonless night resplendent with countless silver, red, and blue pinpoints of light shimmering in astonishing clarity all the way to the horizon.

A pleasant light breeze had stilled in the early evening, and the ocean was eerily quiescent. We were about to retire when Thompson (adept at spotting objects on open water, a skill honed from time spent as a boat pilot) sighted something moving far out to sea.

"At first glance, I thought it was a star," he said, trying to point out the location, "but the planet's rotation cannot explain the object's velocity and direction. The binoculars aren't helping. I'm losing it now! It's gone. Anybody else see it?"

We couldn't confirm what he saw.

"I can send *Ixodes* to that quadrant," Melhaus volunteered.

"Not a good idea to move her about at night when we'll all be sleeping," Thompson responded.

"I can monitor the submersible for a few hours and still get sufficient sleep."

Thompson considered a moment. "OK," he said, "but no more than two hours, then give it and yourself a rest. We can't afford to jeopardize her this early in the mission."

"Understood," Melhaus answered.

"Perhaps it was an electric discharge into the atmosphere," suggested Paul, his eyes following Melhaus rushing into *Desio* with an AID in hand. "But, no, I can't prove that."

"Or perhaps Kyle and I are starting to see objects that aren't there," Thompson added.

"There's always that too," Paul said. "If we take a page from Kyle's psychology handbook, you both want something to be there that isn't. No offense to either of you."

"Can't fault you for thinking it," I said. "The Commander is less subject to imagining things than I am. A bit more grounded."

"A *bit*?" said Diana, mocking me, and then in the next breath, mocking herself. "If wishful thinking applied here, I'd be seeing creatures resembling plesiosaurs humping in the water."

"Is that the best you can do?" I asked.

"Red ones? With gossamer wings?"

"A bit better."

"With that dream," said Diana, "I'll turn in. I'm exhausted."

"We're a tired bunch, no doubt," said Kelly. "I'm ordering seven hours' rest."

As the crew headed into *Desio*, I held back, wishing to enjoy the warm night air and allow the solitude, a million stars, and the serene ocean to encourage introspection. I couldn't escape how badly I reacted to Kelly's expression of emotion.

Angie was with me now, having gravitated back from Kelly. We found a suitable boulder to sit on roughly a hundred meters from the ship. It was hard to imagine that if I were somehow sitting in this exact spot several months from now, I'd be staring out at a flat sheet of ice. Of all the times I've seen large bodies of water, never have they appeared like this—so perfectly flat that stars reflected off the surface.

Fascinating substance, water. Ubiquitous. Unifying. We equate it with life. Did I see something out there today? I could almost swear I *felt* something present, but the feeling, as intangible as the sighting, was more complicated to explain. I kept it to myself.

I advised Thompson that isolation might result in adjustment problems for the crew, with no two people reacting the same way. As for me? One part of me abhors the isolation. Another embraces it. A handy explanation of why I chose to become a Writer. It's a lonely profession—observation, essential; interaction, optional.

More troubling, however, is I sometimes feel alone when with people. Even with Kelly.

What is the actual value of my introspection? How well do we know ourselves? How well *can* we? Can a person change?

"I have a better understanding of you, pooch," I said, nestling her little head in my hands, "than I do of myself."

I lost track of time and started drifting when Angie, shifting in my lap, alerted me to Kelly's approach.

"You weren't in your room," she said. "You should come in and get some sleep. Doctor's orders."

"I'm glad you came to get me."

"Are you? I didn't want to disturb you. I thought you might want to be alone out here."

Reaching into the darkness, I took her two hands in mine and urged her to sit beside me. Angie was between us, where she wanted to be. For the moment, where I needed her to be. For several minutes, and without saying a word, we gazed at the ocean and stars.

"Will you help me to understand something?" I asked.

"Anything."

"Is it right to feel lonely even when you're with someone you care about?"

"Here's one answer," she said after a time. "It applies to me, so possibly you, too. Loneliness is an unwinnable battle that never ends. You have the right to expect the person you care about to fight the battle with you. You did that earlier today for me. Knowing I was hurt and lonely, you gave me the best thing you could under the circumstances. You gave me Angie. If you let me in, I'll find a way to do the same for you."

Determined this time not to drain the life out of the moment, I squeezed her hand to let her know that I'd consider what she said.

With her clasping my hand, we entered the ship.

Kelly to her cabin, Angie and I to mine.

And that was OK.

Ixodes

I WAS STANDING alone on a tiny island of crystal ice, not knowing when, why, or how I got there. A misstep in any direction would send me tumbling into the ocean below. The air was warm, but the only ice melting was under the soles of my feet. I looked straight ahead, finding only an endless expanse of perfectly still water. Suddenly, at the periphery of my vision, there was movement. I turned my head to both sides, but whatever was there stayed behind me, out of sight. I tried turning my body to see, but my feet, planted firmly in a growing puddle of water, would not move.

I was lying flat on my back in a spacecraft on a planet of ocean, a wormhole separating me from Earth. As it was, I had more than the usual difficulty establishing whether I was awake or asleep, distinguishing reality from dream. My only clue was that reality tends to linger.

I jotted the dream's fading imprint on an old-fashioned writing pad. The one kept handy by my pillow in the hope, a writer's version of the tooth fairy, that a creative idea would be found scribbled there in the morning.

One thing was sure. I needed to haul myself out of bed to be punctual for Thompson's usual morning meeting. Angie stared at me expectantly, stretching out on the bed like a miniature sphinx.

"What do you dream about, my faithful dog?" I asked.

Cupping my hand, I petted along the top of her head, starting at her snout, rubbing over her eyes and across both ears. Her puffy tail rapidly vibrated as she happily faced a world of prospects. Time to eat, time to drink, time to explore, and time to pee—thereby scenting and proudly proclaiming as hers the entire planet. Like the humans on this trip, she was (thanks to specially designed nano-substitutions) microorganism-free. We would have to find other ways to contaminate the worlds we visited.

Opening my cabin door, expecting a peaceful early morning, I heard two loud voices. Exiting the ship, I observed Diana, as angry as I've ever seen her, shouting at Melhaus. At the same time, Paul and Thompson, responding to the commotion, were rapidly approaching from across the expanse of the Square. A split second behind me, still adjusting her clothing, was Kelly.

The first sentence that I could make out was from Diana. She was right in Melhaus's face.

"How could you let this happen?!"

"Evidently, Diana, you've closed your mind to possible explanations!"

"Have I? You're the bloody math genius. What are the probabilities? Give me a plausible one!"

"Are you trying to tell me a malfunction on *Ixodes* is impossible?!

"Are you *listening* ?! Diana shouted. "Whatever happened, it was due to *your* fucking negligence! *You* left her unmonitored! Let's call this what it is! It's what you'd call 'blatant incompetence'!"

I was starting to understand. There had been a mishap involving Melhaus and the submersible. I thought back to my story regarding the demise of the Mars Orbiter and how he expressed contempt for the mission's engineers and scientists. His own words were now being used against him, causing his face to flush red and leaving him groping for words.

Diana, momentarily taken aback by the marked effect of her insult, halted her assault and retreated a step. Neither antagonist intended for this interlude to last.

Thompson, on the other hand, did.

"You two again?!"

"Well, he—" Diana started, but was immediately cut off.

"No, not another word from either of you," Thompson declared, "unless it's to answer a question from me. Is that clear?! If not, I will lock *both* of you in the spare cabin."

The combatants shifted their attention from each other to the commander, for there was no doubt he meant what he said. He always did.

"Larry, your version," Thompson demanded. "What's going on here?"

"There is no signal from the submersible."

Thompson's jaw tightened, and a look of concern flashed across his face. "Including the emergency transponder?"

"Yes."

"Any precursor to this? Any record of a system malfunction before signal loss?"

"No. And I cannot explain why, or what, may have caused a complete failure."

"Have you determined her last position?"

Melhaus hesitated. His eyes shifted back and forth.

"Well?" Thompson asked again.

"Coordinates were 361.2 and 423.1."

"Is that where we agreed to send her?"

"Yes."

"What time was the signal lost?"

Again, the hesitation.

"Don't make me pull it out of you."

"Zero one hundred hours."

Not good, I thought. It was several hours after Melhaus should have placed Ixodes in quiet mode, clearly violating Thompson's directive and further angering Diana. She was poised to make a bad mistake by speaking, but Paul quickly intervened by placing an imposing two meters of himself squarely in front of her.

"That's a good three hours past the time the sub was to have ceased operation for the evening," Thompson said. "Why didn't you bring her back sooner?"

"I programmed *Ixodes* for a specific quadrant of operation, then placed her on auto navigation. I fell asleep sometime before she went missing at zero one hundred hours."

"How much before?"

"I can't say exactly."

"We'll come back to that," Thompson said, unsatisfied with the response. His expression told me he decided that Melhaus's choice of words was suspect. He turned his attention to Diana.

"*Ixodes* has gone missing. Now I understand why you're upset. Fair enough. So, before you bust a gut, what's your problem with Larry? Keep it civil."

"He doesn't know what time he fell asleep?!" Diana said, expressing disbelief. "He never sleeps. And even if he did, it would have been *hours* beyond when you ordered him to place Ixodes in quiet mode! That's not what he did, is it!?"

Kelly positioned herself next to Melhaus. She was taking a cue from Paul, ready to intercede if he unwisely spoke out of turn.

"So let's cut to the heart of the matter," Thompson said, addressing Diana. "You've concluded that Larry countermanded my directive, resulting in the loss of the submersible?"

"Yes," Diana said, sounding placated, believing the commander was sympathetic to her accusation. What he said next disabused her of the notion.

"You then decided to make a bad situation worse by not bringing the matter to my attention and then insulting Larry?"

The statement surprised Diana, and it would make her either combative or contrite. If I had Thompson's measure, he deliberately intended to force the choice. He was a good judge of character, having correctly anticipated her response.

"I'll shut up," she said, looking glum, her anger turning to resignation. "For now."

"Wise choice," Kelly said, trying to break the tension.

"Larry," Thompson said, refocusing his attention. "Will the log indicate that you programmed *Ixodes* to enter quiet mode when I specified?

"No."

"Then I'm forced to conclude you deliberately disobeyed

my explicit instructions. Do you wish to explain or argue the point?"

"There's no point."

"The loss of Ixodes is a serious matter," Thompson said, looking troubled, "that must be noted in the expedition log."

On the face of it, the commander's action did not appear to be excessively punitive. We all knew otherwise. When the public and, more importantly, the scientific community were made aware of his error in judgment, he would have to endure the humiliation of explaining himself to those he considered intellectual inferiors. The illustrious Dr. Melhaus would have a glaring stain on an otherwise spotless reputation. Weighing these consequences, his shoulders drooped, and a dark expression seeped into his face.

"I'm pushing back the morning meeting an hour," Thompson said, addressing us all. "Dr. Melhaus. Ten minutes. My cabin. You and I shall reexamine Ixodes' operational records."

I grabbed Diana by the arm, indicating that we should speak privately. Thompson gave me a quick nod to indicate that was precisely what he wanted me to do. At the same time, I noticed Paul initiating a conversation with Melhaus. Good, I thought. If you can't calm him down, nobody can. Paul and Kelly were the only crew members with whom Dr. Melhaus had not engaged in a verbal altercation.

"The arrogance of the man," Diana told me when I had her alone.

"You have a right to be very upset," I said.

"Two days ago, I was so excited about the potential here," Diana lamented. "Now…," Her voice trailed off as she tried to face diminishing expectations.

"I can't imagine how you feel, but you've done your best."

"I wish *I* believed that," she said.

"If you don't believe me, ask any member of the crew. OK, maybe you shouldn't ask Larry right now."

"Thompson was right," said with a small smile. "I didn't handle the situation very well."

"Could have been a tad better. But listen, considering what you were reacting to, it's hard for anyone to fault your language. Especially me, given *my* recent history in the verbal arena."

"Kelly did tell me she was disappointed with herself. That she made you unhappy."

"What?!" I said, wondering if I heard correctly. "Is that what she told you?!"

"Yes," Diana answered. "Isn't it true?"

"At best, it's a charitable explanation of how I was a complete ass. In the space of thirty seconds, I unloaded a lifetime of insensitivity on her. *That's* how it was."

"You being an ass is more believable."

"Thanks. It qualifies me to offer you this advice: if you think you overstepped with Larry, the sooner you try to apologize, the better."

"He's a difficult person to apologize to."

"I did say *try*. You can claim the moral high ground if he doesn't accept graciously."

Diana reflected and then said, "Let me ask you. Do you think Melhaus is on thin ice?"

"Just enough to support him, but the ice does seem to be cracking."

"Puts Thompson in a challenging position," she said.

"Not too many viable options considering where we are, what we're supposed to accomplish here, and how we rely on each other."

"No doubt," Diana said, then went unusually quiet as she contemplated possible scenarios. Not wanting to press her on the matter, I waited. "OK, I'll apologize," she reluctantly said. "If, for no other reason, keeping the peace makes Thompson's job easier."

"Can't hurt," I said. "I'll let you in on a little secret. On at least one occasion, and there'll probably be several more, I've resisted the urge to tell the esteemed Dr. Melhaus to go drown himself in the nearest ocean."

"Very funny."

We climbed the steps into *Desio*, heading for our respective cabins. As I was about to enter mine, Diana stopped me.

"Oh, Kyle, by the way, I know a little secret, too." She flashed me an evil little grin. "About you and Kelly. Yesterday. At the cove."

"Oh, you do, do you?" I said, feigning ignorance.

"Of course." And to prove to me she did know, she childishly hugged herself and puckered her lips to mimic two people kissing.

"Well, since you know all my little secrets, I'll have to come up with another." I closed my cabin door on her while she stood there smirking.

Flopping on the bed, I put my hands behind my head and stared at the metal alloy ceiling.

I felt good about the conversation with Diana. I had intended to help her out of her melancholy mood, and perhaps I did. Her willingness to apologize to Melhaus was a bonus. Deliberately referencing my relationship with Kelly certainly helped, but in retrospect, I wondered if I walked away from the conversation getting more than I gave.

My thoughts were interrupted by Angie barking in the distance. At what? There didn't appear to be anything on this planet to bark at. With the submersible gone, if a creature lurked in that bottomless ocean, it would have seven days to come slithering up to us and extend a dripping tentacle.

I exited *Desio* and walked to where Angie was romping at the shoreline. Bending down to pet her, I looked toward where she had been barking, discovering only an endless expanse of ocean. "What are you up to, my inquisitive little friend?" She stared back at me, eyes glistening, tail vibrating. No answer. "You're no longer talking, eh? Perhaps that is for the best. Talking to people can get you in trouble."

I left her at the shoreline while I joined Paul, seated at the table immediately adjacent to *Desio*. "And?" I asked him as I sat down.

"Cloudy, with a chance of light showers," he said, correctly inferring that I was inquiring about Melhaus. "And your conversation?"

"You have a smart mate."

"Please don't let her hear you say that."

"Never," I said, returning his smile.

Diana slipped into the chair across from us. "You two talking about me?" she asked.

"Never," Paul and I answered in unison and much too quickly.

"Liars," Diana said, reaching over the table to punch each of us hard in the shoulder.

Kelly and Melhaus exited *Desio* together. Kelly sat beside me, a long leg casually brushing against me under the table. I was going to have trouble concentrating. Melhaus, looking stern, assumed his usual place at the table's far end.

Thompson, already seated, deliberately made eye contact with each of us before speaking.

"Did any of you expect this to be easy?"

Nobody was foolish enough to answer him in the affirmative.

"I didn't think so. But we seem intent on making it harder. Let's retrace a bit and consider the problem of *Ixodes*.

Larry and I agree on one thing. The AI log indicates she was fully operational until her signal ceased at a depth of thirteen thousand meters. The signal from the emergency transponder terminated shortly after, suggesting to me that the onboard guidance system malfunctioned and sent her to the bottom.

Manual override may have mitigated the problem, but that is conjecture. For all practical purposes, we must consider the submersible irretrievably lost.

"Diana, I realize that's a major blow to your efforts and the mission. But let's look at it from a different perspective. We arrived here safely. *Ixodes* was detached and made operational, and data on thermoclines, currents, water chemistry, and the prevalence of phytoplankton were gathered. Bear in mind your own words, too, that there are good reasons to believe that no other life forms are present. That would be no less true if we had one sub or one hundred exploring this planet's ocean."

So far, I thought, Thompson was taking just the right balance.

"You are aware," Thompson went on, "that for safety concerns, CSA issued orders not to task *Desio* with unnecessary take-offs and landings. I will consider what happened to *Ixodes* as an extenuating circumstance that warrants overriding that directive. I'll take it under advisement if anyone wishes to move to another location."

"That would suit me just fine," Diana said. "But in fairness, I'll defer to the others. Dismantling our equipment and setting it up again is a disruption."

We needed no reminder of the "safety concern" Thompson referred to. Timely rescue was an impossibility. Our limited food supply meant any malfunction that prevented *Desio* from leaving the planet would be tantamount to a slow death sentence. The grim possibility had been planned for. Kelly was responsible for distributing six merciful L-capsules (and a smaller one for Angie) to be swallowed at each person's discretion.

"One more thing," Thompson said. "Our short time here limits what we can accomplish. If Earth's ocean has yet to be completely explored, what does that say about an ocean with twice the volume of water? The secrets this planet holds will not be uncovered in one week or one year, and perhaps not in several lifetimes. Now, is there anything anybody wants to add before we get down to specifics concerning our work?"

"There is one thing I'd like to say," Diana began. "To Dr. Melhaus."

Diana deserved credit for what she was about to do. Apologizing is never easy when you're convinced it's unwarranted. As for Melhaus, he raised an eyebrow and appeared leery (who could blame him) about what might be said.

"There are times," Diana continued, "when I open my mouth, people are surprised at what comes out. Sometimes, so am I. And sometimes, Larry, I regret the unfortunate words I use. You have my apology."

Melhaus had listened impassively. "Acknowledged," he said. We had come to expect nothing more and often got less.

"Fine...," Thompson began, hoping to move on. Melhaus had other ideas.

"—but the apology just as well could have come from Mr. Lorenzo."

"I'd accommodate you," I said in response, "but I'm not sure what you are referring to."

"It was *your* comment that impugned the work of us scientists."

I was at a loss, but to keep the peace, I offered the day's second apology. "That certainly wasn't my intention," I said, hoping it would suffice to end the discussion.

"That's difficult to believe," Melhaus persisted. "'To rein in you mad scientists' were your exact words."

"Said in jest, Larry." The "mad scientist" remark was simply a reaction to a comment made by Thompson about my B.A. degree. Wherever this discussion led, I did not consider it a good idea to bring the commander into the mix.

"Yet I find it hard to believe," Melhaus responded, pressing his argument. "You've made other offhand insults."

"Let me tell you plainly, Larry, I don't have a high or low opinion of scientists as a class. That would imply I distinguish their innate character as different from everyone else's."

Melhaus was unmoved. I found an ally in Paul.

"Why not take Kyle's words at face value?" he said, seeking rapprochement. "Anything else said was friendly banter that we all took part in at one time or another."

"Exactly," Kelly added, "It's not as if Kyle hasn't received teasing about his lack of science credentials."

Melhaus said nothing. Words of explanation would not move him. I conceded the argument, swallowed my pride, and used up the remnants of my patience.

"Larry, I'll say it again: I'm sorry if anything I said offended you. That was the diametric opposite of my intention."

Again, nothing. I would have settled for an "acknowledged."

Having grown impatient with Melhaus's intractability, Thompson appeared on the verge of interceding. I, however, thought it best to move on. With deliberate emphasis, I quickly pushed back my chair and stood.

"With your permission, commander, if the meeting is about over, I'd like to investigate what Angie is up to."

Thompson looked at me steadily. I gave him a slight nod to let him know I was using the renewed barking coming from the water's edge as an excuse to stave off the worsening tensions.

"Other than discussing a few specifics concerning the tests we are conducting," he said, "we're just about finished here." He returned to the meeting while I headed to the shoreline.

As I approached, Angie stopped barking and trotted up to me. "You were a smart pooch to stay away from us," I said. Looking around, I again found nothing that would have consumed her interest. And while I failed to understand her, she had no such problem when I shouted, "Come! Let's run to the cove!"

As Paul had predicted, the daily temperature swings were moderate, and the day had begun pleasantly warm. I was looking forward to a swim in the refreshing water. Perhaps whatever I saw would reappear.

My recollection of the path through the spires was good. I stripped off my shirt to prevent it from being soaked in sweat, then ran the entire way at a fast sprint. At the cove, I immediately immersed Angie in the ocean to cool her down. She had run beside and ahead of me, and now we both needed to hydrate. The crew was confident that the water was potable, but I noted with interest that Angie deliberately avoided drinking from the clear pools lining the shore. Instead, she eagerly lapped water from the portable filter I remembered to bring along. While she contentedly splayed on a rock slab to dry, I shed my shorts and sneakers and jumped in the ocean. In a few strokes, I was a good distance out. Floating on my back, I stared up at the steel-blue sky. I felt buoyant. Was that due to the lower gravity or the unique water chemistry?

I abandoned the thought for one less complicated. Cool, refreshing, invigorating water. In Arabic, *al-ikseer*. The elixir of life. The substance from whence all life springs. Proven true everywhere life has been found.

An indeterminate amount of time passed. Angie stared at me from the shore and emitted a barely audible whine. I hauled myself out of the water in one swift motion by gripping onto the edge of a stone slab. Lying on my stomach, I stared out into the distance.

Nothing. What did I expect to conjure?

I heard a voice coming from the edge of the spires: Thompson. Approaching, he put away the hand-held device he had used for making field observations.

"Couldn't resist," he said, looking out over the ocean to the horizon. "I've heard the water's fine."

As he stripped naked and entered the water, I noticed a ten-centimeter scar on his buttocks. Asking him about it could be tricky, I thought with amusement. Some people might avoid doing so.

But not me. After several minutes of swimming, he climbed out and, winded from the exertion, lay on his stomach beside me.

"Damn, that felt good," he said.

"I'm going to open a day spa here," I said. "Charge admission."

"No, not you. Never. Nor me, for that matter. We're not cut out for dealing with people."

"You got that right. There's a theory that I have been developing—you'll notice I'm using the word *theory*—that, statistically, one out of five people is an asshole."

"I'll need a definition of 'asshole.'"

"Right now, it's anyone who irritates me."

"And it's no coincidence that, other than you, there are five in the crew?"

"It is the theory's very foundation."

"Personally, taking a statistically larger sample, the number is one in ten."

"That's a generous view."

"I like to think of the beaker as half-full. So how long have you been working on this so-called 'theory'?"

"All my life. This expedition was an experiment in socialization for me."

"And, on balance, how's it going?"

"All the results aren't in yet."

"The way I see it, you're way ahead."

"Care to explain?"

"I'll spell it out for you, dummy. K-E-L-L-Y. You're concerned about one in five. How about one in a million?"

"Diana put you up to this?"

"What?" Thompson said, leaving no doubt that what he said was based solely on his keen perceptions.

"OK. I got some things to work out."

Thompson chose not to ask for further explanation. He had encapsulated everything he wanted to say in a couple of sentences. I had done the same in one.

"How did you get that scar on your butt?" I asked.

"I was wondering why you were staring at my ass. Ever hear of a razorback?"

"Sure. A wild boar. Pretty mean."

"My ass is the last part of me that went up a tree."

"Shit," I said, laughing.

"I got the last laugh."

"How so?"

"I'm up the tree with my ass bleeding, not feeling particularly good about it, the boar snorting below, waiting for me to come down. If that wasn't enough to ruin your day, I received a sting or two from a hornet's nest in the branch above me. An idea came to me. I wasn't sure it was a good one, but I didn't let that stop me. I took out my pocket knife and, as carefully as I could, cut loose the branch holding the nest. I then whipped the branch down onto the back of the boar. Hard to tell which became more agitated, the nest or the boar, but hornets can sting multiple times. They gave the boar the worst of it until it charged off, grunting, squealing, and as angry as anything I've ever seen. Except, possibly, Diana."

"That's called making fertilizer out of the shit handed to you."

"Speaking of being handed shit," Thompson said, "don't think the way you handled the load Melhaus just handed out went unappreciated by me or the rest of the crew."

"You've got one helluva balancing act dealing with him, that's for sure. I don't envy you."

"Whatever the cause, I'd prefer not to lose him. The problem is, he knows that. Considers himself indispensable. I may have to convince him otherwise."

"It's tough getting past that intellectual arrogance of his. I wonder how much of what we're seeing is his glaring lack of social skills. Other times, well, I almost think he's against us."

"None of us are simple."

"Sometimes, Bruce, I wish we were."

"Now that would be boring, wouldn't it?"

"Point taken," the writer in me said.

We dressed and headed back to the Square.

Sighting

DURING THE OVERNIGHT, a brief shower came out of nowhere to leave a wet, color-intensifying sheen on the rock formations ringing The Square. It was before the morning meeting, and Paul, Angie, and I sat on a large oblong boulder, enjoying the striking view of spires and an ample slice of ocean.

The blue sun, now a sun's width above the horizon, had already begun its work for the day. Around us, the wet rock was absorbing heat, sending columns of steam tumbling and twisting high into the air, where they were dissipated by a gentle breeze. Within minutes, only the rainwater collected in the deepest depressions remained to be evaporated back into the atmosphere.

I had discovered that Paul was a man of few words. Unlike Melhaus, whose silence was a sign of distancing, it was more of an economizing of thought for Paul. He chose his

105

words carefully, and I paid close attention to what he had to say when he spoke.

"There's an elegant simplicity behind all we see," he said, eyes glancing skyward at the cascading steam. "Rainfall rises as vapors; water vapors condense to droplets; droplets collide, collect, and fall as rain. Simple. Beautiful."

"Why then," I asked, hoping to elicit more, "is simplicity sometimes so difficult to discover?"

"Like $E=MC^2$?"

"Good example."

"Some would say from looking too hard."

"Isn't that heresy for a scientist?" I asked.

"No. It's a matter of approach. It's not about viewing the subject of inquiry as unraveling something complex but recognizing the simple truths comprising the whole. Often, that is where the profoundest insights come from."

"The graceful arc of the horizon," I said, looking over the ocean. "The ability to discern simplicity is a valuable attribute for a writer, too."

Paul considered for a moment. "Diana, I believe, might see simplicity in the varied shapes of Diatoms or the elegant whipping motion of flagella."

"And for Thompson," I said, making a game of it, "the crystalline structure of quartz."

We spied Kelly and Diana, heading toward us from across The Square, walking hand in hand like schoolgirls on a summer's day.

"And Kelly?" Paul contemplated, watching her approach. "She visualizes the notes of a violin concerto?"

"And I see a woman's neck that is enticing with its graceful curve. Beautiful, no?"

Paul responded with a laugh, and I found myself laughing with him.

"Kelly, Diana? Beautiful? Beyond compare," he said. "But is understanding them simple? *Il n'est pas!* You have, or rather they have, completely undermined my assertion."

We were perched on the boulder's edge, Angie between us, our legs dangling over the side. When Kelly arrived, she positioned herself between my knees. Diana assumed the same position with Paul. He and I exchanged telling glances, both sensing they were plotting something.

"Thompson canceled this morning's meeting," Diana said. "We're here to tell you—and no, you don't have a choice—that the four of us are going to the cove later for a group picnic."

Judging by the "I'm pleased with myself" smirk on her face, the picnic was Diana's idea, her way of getting Kelly and me back to the cove. Kelly flashed me a broad smile. Leaning into me, she placed her lips to my ear and whispered, "Clever, isn't she?"

In a blatant attempt to give us privacy, Diana yanked Paul from the boulder he sat on. They were steps away when Angie, emitting a short bark, leaped off the boulder and bolted down to the ocean's edge, where she faced the water and whined. Yesterday, she exhibited a similar behavior. I had not taken sufficient notice. I jumped off the boulder and ran to the shoreline, determined to discover what my clever little pooch was up to.

"This isn't the only time she's done this," I said as the others came beside me. "She knows something. The other day, I doubted myself. The other evening, Thompson doubted himself. But I'm *not* going to doubt her. Angie is never wrong. *Something* is out there." I bent down and scooped her in my arms while the five of us intently scanned the horizon.

"If we can't see anything out there," I said, "she won't be able to either. She could be smelling something. More likely hearing something. Did you see her head turn slightly and her ears flicker?"

"I did," Kelly confirmed. "She can hear twice what we can from three times farther away. But what would she be hearing? Could it be a distant thunderstorm?"

"Not according to my instrument readings," Paul responded. "There are no storms within five hundred kilometers."

"There are species, including canines, sensitive to earthquakes," Diana volunteered. "Only Thompson said there are no earthquakes."

"So then… what?" I asked.

"I'll get the commander," Paul said and ran off.

Paul, with Thompson and Melhaus in tow, returned with a pair of binoculars.

"What's your mutt up to now?" Thompson inquired.

"Not sure yet."

Trying to be patient, we stood by as Paul used the field glasses, methodically sweeping back and forth across the ocean. On one pass, he froze. Fumbling with and adjusting the focus, he shouted, "shit!" and accidentally dropped the delicate instrument onto the unforgiving rock at his feet.

Thompson reached for the binoculars, one lens showing a hairline crack, a fraction quicker than Paul.

"Paul?!" Diana practically pleaded. "What did you see?!"

All Paul could manage was a shrug and a shake of his head.

"Damn!" Thompson said, attempting to adjust the focus. "He doesn't know, and neither do I."

"Whatever it is, here it comes!" shouted Kelly. "I can see... *them*!"

"Yes," said Melhaus, who had lingered in the background until then. "There." He pointed. "Eight. No ten. *Twelve* I can discern."

"Try these," Thompson said, quickly passing the binoculars. "But the unaided eye seems to serve almost as well."

We were rooted to the spot, staring in disbelief. Floating, bubble-like, on the tranquil water were several blue-gray domes. The objects (I was at a loss on how to name them) were a kilometer from shore and slowly approaching. Judging their exact size without a point of reference was problematic, but I guesstimated their varying heights as proportional to those of a man, woman, and child. But were we viewing the upper half of spheres with the bottom half hidden below the water line? A million other questions flooded my mind as I wrestled with the phenomenal import of what we were witnessing.

"Somebody, please tell me," Diana implored, "what the hell *are* those things?!"

"Whatever they are, they're not coming closer," I said, watching as the objects' slow forward motion suddenly ceased.

I had difficulty holding onto Angie, who wiggled impatiently in my arms. Lowering her to the ground, she immediately entered the water up to her chest, emitted a short, happy yip, and vibrated her tail so rapidly that it disappeared into a blur. Her low whining had stopped in recognition that we humans had the good sense to finally see what she was trying to communicate.

"We need to make the most of this opportunity," Melhaus said, his face now partially obscured behind binoculars. "We need to use *Desio*—"

"Hold on," Thompson interrupted. "What are we looking at here? I'll accept guesses. Paul, can wind or ocean currents explain the objects' movement?"

"Doubtful. The sudden cessation of forward progression contradicts it. The prevailing wind does not agree with their direction of motion. There are virtually no ocean currents."

"So if I say these objects are somehow moving on their own?"

"None of us would call you crazy."

Hearing this, Diana looked ready to jump out of her skin.

"And the objects originate from where?" Thompson asked.

"*Sous-marine* ?" Paul shrugged. "You asked for guesses."

"Kyle," Thompson said, marshaling my attention. "Angie anticipated the arrival of the objects. How?"

"We think by picking up high-pitched frequencies humans can't hear."

"And do you believe this happened during yesterday's meeting when you responded to her barking?"

"I'd have to say yes. And on at least one other occasion."

"What frequencies can Angie hear that we can't?"

"I'll defer that question to Kelly. She's the expert."

"From twenty thousand hertz to approximately forty-five thousand hertz," Kelly replied.

"Larry?" Thompson said, looking for his input. Receiving no response, he tried again. "Dr. Melhaus!" The physicist reluctantly lowered the damaged binoculars glued to his eyes. "Can you determine," Thompson asked, "the objects' size and shape?"

"No. Not with accuracy. Not without utilizing *Desio*."

"Do you believe we're seeing the objects in their entirety?"

"Unlikely, given what we can see. They are almost certainly spheroid, with one-half below water."

"Why do you think so?"

"In nature, the sphere is a common shape. And one of the strongest."

"I agree," said Thompson. "Diana, what do you make of all this?"

"I don't know, I don't know," she responded, frustrated. "If only we had *Ixo*…"

She caught herself, barely, but not in time to prevent Melhaus from visibly cringing. Thompson attempted to smooth over the moment by quickly posing another question.

"What do you make of the objects' hue, a close match to the ocean, although shades darker?"

Diana could only answer with yet another question. "And what of their surfaces being shiny and extremely smooth, at least as seen from this distance? I'm trying to pull it all together. The undifferentiated look of it, with no apparent orifices or sensory equipment, begs the question: is this an inanimate object or a living entity?"

"Perhaps," Kelly volunteered, "it is a means of conveyance for an entity."

"Kyle," Thompson said. "Your opinion?"

"They may be none of the proposed possibilities, but I bet we are looking at a life form. Up till now, they have stayed beyond our capability to see them. Except two days ago, I did, at the cove, just barely, when Kelly and I split away from our main group. Now they approach us, I'd say cautiously, keeping at a distance. In those actions, I see the possibility of intention."

"Why avoid us?" asked Paul.

"Wary of *our* intentions," I said.

"All wild conjecture," Melhaus asserted. "For definitive answers, we must immediately take *Desio* in for a closer look, taking advantage of the altitude and ship's instrumentation to better assess these things."

"If what Kyle says is accurate," Kelly proffered, "a flyover may be the one thing we shouldn't do. I would expect they would respond by moving away."

"That seems to make sense," Diana said, addressing Thompson.

"So that's how it's going to be," Melhaus interjected, visibly irritated. "Taking advice from a layperson."

"You can't possibly see 'how it's going to be,'" Thompson asserted. "Not without hearing from me first. Here's what we are going to do. Larry, you, Diana, and I will board *Desio* and take her to an altitude of one hundred meters, then slowly pilot closer and see what happens. If we keep a reasonable distance, the possibility of them moving away won't materialize."

The decision was sound, and there was no disagreement voiced. Three of us would remain behind and watch from the shore. Thompson, Melhaus, and Diana were moving toward the ship when I was constrained to stop them.

"Wait!" I yelled. "They're moving again!"

"No!" Diana shouted, returning to where Kelly, Paul, and I stood. "They're heading away from us!"

Melhaus, binoculars still in hand, also turned when I yelled, but had stubbornly anchored himself in place as if to insist that proceeding to *Desio* was the only sensible course of action. In one quick motion, Thompson strode past him, took the binoculars from his hand, and said, "We stay." As he spoke, the objects were speedily heading out to sea until, quicker than they appeared, they vanished from our view like a mirage in a desert.

"This is torture," gasped Diana, then, in an instant of madness, waved her hand oceanward and cried out, "Whatever you are, you come right back here, damn you!"

"Calm yourself," Thompson admonished. "They'll be back."

"And how do you arrive at that conclusion?" Diana asked.

"If they're sentient beings, they'll be curious about the bizarre entity yelling from shore."

"There was a moment," I said, "just as I lost track of them when they slipped below the water. Anybody see that?"

"I can't confirm," Thompson responded. "I didn't have time to get a fix on them."

"Nor can I," said Kelly. "But from now on, I won't doubt what anybody thinks they see."

"My perception was slightly different," Paul said. "I saw the objects blending into the similar color of the ocean."

"And now what?" asked Diana. "Go through the rest of the day as if nothing's happened?"

"I have an idea," Melhaus said. He had decided to rejoin us. "Reconfiguring the onboard spectroscopy equipment would allow me to determine the objects' chemical and molecular composition. If and when they reappear."

"Excellent suggestion," said Thompson. "How long?"

"Five hours."

"Go to it," Thompson ordered.

113

As Melhaus headed toward *Desio*, Angie trotted out of the ocean, shook herself a few times—and found five people intently staring at her. She appeared delighted with herself.

"You're a good dog, aren't you?" I said, joining her at ground level.

"Your little mutt is finally earning her keep," Thompson said as he watched her nuzzle me affectionately. "Don't let her stray too far from you or Kelly. Just in case she barks another warning."

With Melhaus working inside *Desio*, Thompson took the opportunity to address the rest of his crew. I correctly assumed he would broach the delicate subject of Melhaus's behavior.

"We are not immune to the same pressures affecting our troubled colleague, but we seem to be coping better for some reason. I canceled this morning's meeting to break the routine. We will continue working sunup to sundown with one notable exception: forays to the cove. They seem to be, shall we say, restorative? Perhaps I shouldn't delve too deeply into why—"

"You shouldn't," affirmed Diana with a telling grin.

"—so continue to go," Thompson concluded. "The time spent there is well spent, in my opinion."

"And Larry refuses?" Paul inquired.

"Yes."

"Anything else we can do?"

"You've been doing it, each of you in your way," Thompson said. "But if his problems come to a head, let the consequences fall on me."

"About Larry—" I began, then broke off when, simultaneously, Kelly started to speak.

"No, go ahead," she insisted.

I faced Thompson. "I thought his remark, 'that's how it's going to be,' worrisome. Is he paranoid? Does he think we are conspiring against him?"

"What?!" Diana said, exasperated. "Nothing could be further from the truth."

"Only we are conspiring," Paul maintained. "To help him. Look at this from his perspective. When you strip away the ability to distinguish motive, all you see is five people acting concertedly."

"An interesting point," said Thompson, frowning. "Kelly, you agree with Kyle and Paul?"

"Yes. A developing paranoia is a possibility."

"Is slipping him sedatives out of the question?" asked Diana.

There was no telling if she was being serious, but Kelly took it so. "I don't have a full pharmacopeia onboard," she said, "and the benefits of the drugs I have are uneven. Getting him to take sleep medication was a challenge. The point is moot. He won't take anything else voluntarily. Period." She aimed her following remark at Thompson. "And slipping medication in his food is illegal and unethical. I won't do it."

"Nor have I asked you to," replied Thompson, visibly annoyed.

"I'm sorry, Bruce, I shouldn't have implied that you would. Maybe I'm starting to become a bit paranoid myself."

"The line separating paranoia and prudence can be subjective," I said, "but you both seem to be on the right side."

"Let's see how long that lasts," commented Diana, "As for you, Kyle, you weren't fantasizing about what you saw at the cove the other day. Amazing."

"I'm the picture of mental health. Just ask the Crew Selection Committee."

"You mean the same committee that recruited Melhaus?" asked Thompson.

Intelligent Life

THE REMAINDER OF the morning and early afternoon dragged on forever.

The sun crawled into the sky. Nudged by a languid wind, puffy clouds' inverted reflections slowly crossed the ocean's shiny surface.

Casting an emotional shadow on all we did was that we had a tantalizing glimpse of the unknown. Yet, we could only wonder if a historic discovery must remain beyond our grasp. We waited, hoping for the objects' return.

Was Melhaus affected even more, knowing that the loss of Ixodes compromised our ability to understand the mysterious objects? On this subject, the crew kept silent. No good could come of belaboring the obvious.

The lights of my cabin flickered, possibly due to Melhaus recalibrating *Desio's* sensor array. Tired-looking, obsessed with working every waking moment (which we knew to be most of the day), he had become even more withdrawn.

The loss of *Ixodes* was beginning to weigh on him. I again expressed my concern to Thompson, for I believed (and Kelly concurred) that the physicist was showing the initial symptoms of latent paranoid personality disorder. But how reliable was our "diagnosis" when neither of us had the skill set of a trained psychiatrist? Psychotropics used to address the condition were an unimaginable distance away, and multiple attempts by the crew to communicate with the man were rebuffed.

A percentage of individuals diagnosed with paranoid personality disorder, when left untreated, commit acts dangerous to themselves or others. This uncomfortable thought silently crept into our psyches because our remoteness from Earth placed us in additional jeopardy. In response, we resorted to keeping what we believed to be a discreet (but wary) eye on our "patient."

Could more be done before Melhaus resorts to some overtly hostile act? Thompson reluctantly adopted a wait-and-see approach.

Kelly and I continued to assist the scientists in any way we could, including doing the menial (and, frankly, tedious) chores necessary to support the ship and crew. After a stint of this drudgery, stretching into the early afternoon, I headed to my cabin to do *my* job.

By early evening, nagging hunger reminded me that the prospect of a picnic dinner awaited me outside. Angie stayed with Kelly, who assisted Diana with an experiment near the water's edge. I wasn't given much choice in this arrangement because the crew (read: Diana) felt that keeping Angie inside with me would eliminate any chance of her detecting another visit from the objects.

Gathering up a few essentials—washcloth, recorder, water purifier, and communicator—I exited my cabin. Passing through the mission room, still musing over what I had written, I absentmindedly bumped into Melhaus as he stepped down from the command and control room. An atypical grin was contorting the otherwise plain features of his face. When he saw me, the smug look of contentment changed to surprise, followed by annoyance.

"Changes to the spectroscopy array taking you longer than expected?" I asked. "Difficult work, huh?"

"Why do you ask?" he said, irritated.

Because I'm a glutton for punishment. Because I have an alter-ego that enjoys talking to arrogant assholes. Because somewhere in the infinite multiverse, I'm basking in the glow of one civilized answer...

"No particular reason," I said aloud. "Just making conversation."

"Is that all?"

"I'll let you get back to work."

I was happy to feel the welcoming warmth of the sun. Squinting in the bright light, I made out Kelly, Paul, and Diana standing beside a table, choosing items to bring on the picnic. Angie scampered up to greet me, displaying affection with a rapid tail wagging.

"We were coming to abduct you," said Kelly, beaming. "Diana was worried you'd use some lame 'I have to write' excuse to desert us.

"Not to worry," I said, turning to Diana. "But is Thompson OK with this little venture?"

"More than OK," Diana responded. "He hoped we might see the objects on the other side of the island."

"And what objects might that be?" I asked. I kept my face blank while looking questioningly at Paul.

"Haven't the foggiest," he said. Convincingly, too.

"You bastards!" Diana yelled at us. I liked teasing her, but there would be a penalty to pay. I proffered my shoulder, and she punched it hard. I pretended it hurt more than it did to make her feel better.

"Our expedition to the cove is getting a late start," I said. "I suggest we jog there."

"Jogging is for wimps," Diana responded, laughing—and took off at a run into the spires. We sprinted after her, but by the time we arrived at the cove, she was already nude from the waist up, joyously splashing in the water. Unfazed, Paul stripped down to underwear and jumped in.

"Two questions answered," I remarked to Kelly.

"Those being?"

"How constrained we'd be by social conventions of modesty."

"The other?" she asked warily.

I put a lascivious grin on my face. "What Diana's breasts look like."

"Oh?" Kelly said, stripping down to shorts. "Then you won't mind Paul having *his* question answered."

I quickly followed. And that's how, like kids on a sugar rush, we entered the water. I expected Paul to be the most reserved of the four of us. He was smart enough to anticipate that the awkward moment would arise, so maybe he was prepared.

Or, maybe people are not obligated to behave as I predict.

"Incredibly refreshing," Diana said. "I feel euphoric."

"Don't ask me," I responded, sensing the rush. "On Earth, I get that feeling *whenever* I'm in the water."

I swam over to Kelly and whispered in her ear. She smiled and nodded.

"Hey, you two," I said. "We're swimming to the other side of the peninsula. Be back in a few."

Diana beamed as she looked from me to Kelly and back to me. Having arranged the picnic, she had good reason to be gratified with herself. "Don't do anything we won't be doing," she said, pressing her body against Paul.

Kelly and I went off together, providing both couples time to be intimate.

The details of the time Kelly and I spent alone at the cove are not integral to this narrative; our evolving emotional entanglement has overshadowed our physical relationship. With growing interest, I am observing outside influences affecting my view of that relationship, such as Thompson's opinion of Kelly and Diana's machinations. Perhaps, strangely, the planet is bringing us closer together in its all-encompassing water. How significant (if at all) any of this is to the mission is presently unclear.

We rejoined Paul and Diana, and the four of us discovered a large flat area where we could eat dinner and enjoy each other's company. As we conversed, the sun began to set, and I couldn't help but notice that Diana was distracted, repeatedly stealing furtive glances oceanward.

"Angie'll let us know," I said, hoping to ease her anxiety about the objects returning.

"Sorry."

"No, it's understandable."

"Nothing works," said Paul. "She's been beside herself all day."

In the declining light, I watched as Diana's expression turned somber.

"Have any of you thought about the hell they'll put us through?" she asked.

"In what sense?" Kelly responded.

"There are twenty billion people on Earth," Diana explained, "and almost to the last man, woman, and child, they want this mission, want *us*, to discover intelligent life, or at least life that's a few orders of magnitude more complex than *phytoplankton*. OK, so we come back empty-handed; maybe they can accept that. But to come this far, to see those extraordinary objects and offer no explanation for their existence!? The entire world won't let us live down the disappointment. We'd have been better off finding absolutely nothing…"

The last words stuck in Diana's throat as she fought back her feelings. She leaned into Paul for comfort. On the other side of her, Kelly, commiserating, patted her arm.

"Oh, I know," Diana said, dabbing her eyes, "that last part about finding nothing isn't true."

But much of what she had said *was* true, and the depressing effect on her aroused my sympathy. I was ill-positioned to hug her, so she would have to settle for second best: logic.

Or my unique version of it, anyway.

"Maybe this won't make you feel any better," I began, "and I apologize if it makes you feel any worse, but twenty billion people, myself among them, don't have a damn clue what 'intelligent life' means. It's a ludicrous concept; if the arbitrary criterion 'self-awareness' is applied, it's even more ludicrous! Ha-ha… ah ha, ah *ha ha ha*!"

I intentionally ended my speech by affecting the laugh and demeanor of a madman. I was going into full attack mode, and it was working. I had Diana's attention, and Kelly's and Paul's, too, for that matter.

"Is this tirade," Diana said, "coming from the antisocial Kyle, the writer Kyle, or the just plain bat-shit crazy Kyle?"

"They're all in there somewhere," Kelly volunteered.

"Wisdom can be misconstrued as madness," Paul said. "Let's hear him out and see if we can discern the difference."

"Perhaps you shall judge me mad," I responded, "for my madness rests on this: our ability to evaluate intelligence is highly suspect. The very definition of the word is fatally flawed."

"What makes you believe so?" asked Diana, a bemused look replacing the somber expression on her face.

"Because we humans have hubristically created the definition for intelligence to fit ourselves. How convenient! Should we not obtain at least one impartial point of view? Is it not true, Kelly, that a patient would be wise to seek a second opinion?"

"*And* not to self-diagnose," Kelly added.

"Precisely! And a writer is a biased critic of his own work. If you say otherwise, I shall pronounce myself a genius, the world's preeminent author. Who's to disagree?"

"Thompson certainly would," Diana pronounced, feeling better.

"And exactly where," asked Paul, "do you expect unbiased opinions of our intelligence to come from?"

"Ah, that's the rub," I responded. "They may never come. Would we recognize and accept them if they did—humility not our strong suit as a species? Shall I venture a guess at what that second opinion would be when our world and its life groans with overpopulation, wars, and pollution—all caused by the most intelligent species, kings reigning over all? Ha! We are self-anointed, unduly coronated!"

"Weren't you trying to cheer Diana up?" Kelly asked.

"Oh, sorry…"

"Oh, no, please continue," Diana entreated. "I like not knowing what a person is going to say. Reminds me of myself."

"Very well, since you've yet to call me mad, I shall venture on. We contrived self-awareness as a 'litmus test' of intelligence and then used it to place ourselves above all life on Earth. It's become 'us' or 'them' and then use that to justify mistreating every other living thing on 'our' planet.

"But we've identified more than a dozen species that have at least some measure of self-consciousness," Diana said.

"And how long did it take us humans to reach this conclusion? And what good did it do the species we've bestowed the honor? Or is it an honor? Let's pose the question to another species, perhaps not as self-aware, but well-disposed to volunteer a second opinion."

I reached for Angie, placed her on my lap, and petted her. Her tail vibrated, her eyes sparkled, she licked my hand and gazed at me happily. As she exuded contentment, I spoke to her, sarcasm dripping into my voice.

"My poor little pooch, if only you could be as blissfully self-aware as we humans. If only you knew what you were missing—"

Angie rolled onto her back, expecting and getting her soft underbelly stroked.

"What's that you're saying, my little dog? You don't understand why examining our belly button and then realizing it *really* is our belly button is such a big deal? You say you couldn't possibly be more joyous than at this moment? That you couldn't give me one milligram more of affection?

"See?" I said. "We have our answer. Still doubtful? OK, then." I urged Angie off my lap. "Good girl. Go to Kelly! Show her exactly what you mean."

Angie, nuzzling her way onto Kelly's lap, received a tight, appreciative hug.

"She is pretty convincing," Kelly said.

"She does a lot of my talking. Sometimes, I consider self-awareness an affliction I *wouldn't* wish on a dog. Oh, I don't mean the casual 'look in the mirror and realize the reflection is me' kind, but deeper introspection, the gut-wrenching kind, where you stare at—and through—the reflection of your *self* in the mirror until you experience a tidal wave of shock, amazement, fear, and wonder that you exist. You exist, standing there naked in your clothing, part of, yet apart from everything that *is* and offered no solace, no hope of ever understanding why. And as the tide rolls out and only the memory of this experience remains, not the feeling itself, a lifetime of questions are strewn like pebbles on the shore: Does life have any meaning? Why do I feel so alone? Why do I deliberately—"

Noticing a strident voice, I stopped and connected that voice to me. Three people were intently staring at me. Hugging Diana would have been a whole lot easier.

"What do I see in your faces? I'm crazy?"

"No, you're not crazy, Kyle," Kelly told me in a low voice.

"Don't be too quick to judge," asserted Diana. "You're batshit, but not much more than any of us."

"Diana, the point I was trying to make is the world hopes we find intelligent life, but do they know what they are hoping for? What happens if we stumble on a life-form that sees no boundary between where you stop and I start? That, believing all things are intimately connected, has no concept of a *self*, yet may be more *aware* than we'll ever be?"

"Wouldn't *they* be less lonely, Kyle?" Kelly asked softly.

The words stopped me cold in my tracks; they were deliberately intended to evoke a deeper personal reflection on my part, almost challenging me to do so. My voice wavered as I grappled with an appropriate response.

"I...I don't know. Do we always understand the depth and breadth of our emotions, let alone guess those of a different life form? Birds see more colors. Angie hears sounds we cannot. Similarly, another life-form may exhibit emotions with greater or lesser intensity than humans; or different ones entirely—a realm beyond our capacity to fathom."

The twisted little smile on Kelly's face, the one I hated to see, the one I'd placed there before, revealed the inadequacy of my words. Paul also grasped my failure to personalize my response.

"You may be justified," he said, looking at me steadily, "in feeling existential loneliness more intensely than others, just as you have a right to continue searching for—and I believe you will find—a more fulfilling answer to Kelly's question. I'll add this: as often happens in science, you should not be surprised that the attempt to find an answer to one question facilitates the answer to another."

"I'm sorry," Diana said, "but shouldn't we be heading back?"

We had failed to notice the time slip away. One by one, the highest tips of the spires, shining like beacons in the fast-fading remnants of sunlight, were being extinguished by the setting sun.

"Am I correct in assuming," Kelly confirmed with each of us, "none of us had the presence of mind to bring a flashlight?"

"Afraid so," I said. "We might get hopelessly lost in the darkness of the spire maze, but what is even worse is the ridicule we will receive from Thompson for losing our way."

We needed to make our way back slowly, intent on not losing our direction in the enveloping darkness. The dusky quality of waning light, the spires' imposing and twisting shapes rising to wall us in, the muffled sound of our soles carefully seeking a path on the unforgiving stones—all these, as if portents, urged us to lower our voices to a reverent whisper.

I deliberately hung back from the group until I was alone in the quietude of a cavernous, deserted Gothic cathedral. Looking up, I stared at the first pinpoints of stars. Cold, impassive company they were, randomly blinking a meaningless message to no one.

A faint plea came to me out of the darkness.

Kelly, saving me from myself.

"Kyle? Where are you?"

"Just here," I called to her.

"Again."

"I'll come to you."

In the gloom, I made out the reflective orange of Angie's eyes. I followed the glow to Kelly.

"We want you with us," she said, clutching my hand.

"I want you."

Cupping my hand, I caressed Kelly's face in the darkness, feeling a wetness there. I wiped the wetness away with one finger, then kissed her cheek, tasting the slight saltiness.

Searchingly, I moved each kiss closer to her waiting mouth. Not long ago, near this same spot, I had been a greater fool.

She pushed me away, saying, "Come to me later?"

There was no need to ask.

Rejoining Paul and Diana, it occurred to me that I should let Angie lead the way. We were closing in on The Square when Paul's communicator chimed: Thompson.

"Are you close? There's something interesting here for you to see."

"Ten minutes away," Paul answered. "Maybe more; we have no lights."

"Figures. I'll set a lantern for you at the edge of the spires so Diana doesn't go headfirst into a ravine." Before she could respond, Thompson deliberately broke the connection.

Leaving a light on for us had been a wise move on Thompson's part. Despite the crevices veining its surface, Diana bolted across The Square, forcing us to keep pace.

"Tell me everything," she demanded of Thompson.

"Just after dark, they appeared," Thompson offered. "Other than what you see, there's not much else to tell."

We took positions on a huge stone block. Above us, a silver-speckled sky. In front of us was an endless expanse of dark ocean.

Resting on that ocean, twelve mysterious colored lights.

"Tell me," Diana challenged, "that these aren't the same objects we observed earlier today."

There was commonality in the two sightings: in number, distance from shore, and Angie's reaction. Only this time, she was vocalizing with a few abbreviated barks. A signal of recognition, no more.

The objects were emitting a pleasant soft glow, with shades of blue similar to those of the planet's setting sun predominating. Twelve in number, they appeared to be randomly and abruptly altering their speed and bearing. All but two presented themselves as full spheres. Using binoculars, we determined that most had lifted nearly their entire mass out of the water!

Comparisons between day and night observations did not definitively answer the question: were these objects or sentient beings?

"Think of it this way," Thompson said for Diana's benefit. "Starting with what Kyle saw, the visitations, if that's what they are, are becoming more regular, closer, and of longer duration."

"There is," Diana said, "something encouraging to be said for that."

"Maybe they're trying to get accustomed to us," Kelly said. "Imagine how unusual we must appear."

"Larry, I assume you weren't able…" Paul's voice trailed off. He reflected, then began again more carefully. "The modified spectroscopy array has yet to obtain a reading on the objects?"

"No." He had grown even more uncommunicative, if possible, giving terse explanations only when queried.

"Explain yourself," Thompson insisted.

"The objects' size and distance hamper focusing. You people have to realize I can't work miracles."

"Can we assist with targeting the array?" asked Paul.

"No. Absolutely not, and I'd advise you not to meddle with the system."

I performed my usual chores for the remainder of the evening while the scientists, with one eye always toward the ocean, collected and evaluated information garnered from the various experiments they had underway.

Melhaus worked on a clever idea Thompson had proposed. Patching together electronic components, he constructed a device that flashed sequentially timed light pulses in the objects' direction. They remained oblivious to the effort.

Late in the evening, as the rest of us were preparing to call it a day, Thompson exited *Desio* with a large bundle containing his bedroll and some miscellaneous possessions.

"Hope you have the weather right *this* evening," I heard him say to Paul. With the weather being pleasant, the commander preferred sleeping under the stars. He promised Diana she'd be the first to learn if the objects did anything noteworthy.

Spheres

I WAS STANDING on an island of ice in the middle of a boundless ocean. In the absence of a setting sun, darkness had replaced light. Raising my head, expecting to see a panoply of stars, I was confounded by utter blackness. Staring outward to where the horizon had been, I found a formless void. Looking down to where my feet should be, I made a frightening discovery. My vision could not penetrate the darkness! With no point of reference, *was* I looking down? Were my feet, devoid of sensation from the numbing ice, actually there? A surge of fear swept over me as I contemplated my dreadful situation. In an act born of desperation, I began frantically waving my formless hands in front of my face, revealing an inescapable truth. All my senses had abandoned me! Nothing existed but eternal darkness! Oblivion! I started to scream...

An endless, soundless, *confirmatory* scream.

Darkness became daylight. I was no longer alone. Beside me was the tangible presence of something or someone I desired to see and touch, but was prevented from doing so.

What?

I felt a nudge, and I heard a voice.

"Kyle! The objects! They've moved closer! Thompson is yelling for us!"

I understood now. The objects had returned. I was sleeping, or attempting to, in Kelly's cabin. In her excitement, she was prodding me. I began to hear Thompson's voice in the distance, calling to us from somewhere outside.

"Can't be dreaming," I said, still groggy. "I won't allow Thompson to enter my dreams." I quickly dressed.

We were about to exit *Desio* via the narrow portal when Diana appeared out of nowhere. Issuing a quick, "brains *and* beauty first," she pushed us aside and scampered through.

The reason behind Thompson's early-morning wake-up call was readily apparent. The twelve distant objects, likely the same ones sighted the prior evening, had moved to within one hundred meters of shore. In doing so, they proved to be more substantial than previously surmised (unless they grew overnight), with the largest being an impressive three meters in diameter—nearly three times the smallest. I use the term diameter most specifically here, for all were floating, or more accurately hovering, with just one tiny section of their spherical mass contacting the undisturbed ocean surface.

They were also no longer glowing, having resumed their blue-gray color from the previous day. Their polished surface had a lustrous opalescence, like a cultured pearl, but more translucent, which had us wondering if we could see into the object's center. All remained nearly motionless, almost as if they were studying us as much as we were them. Motionless, that is, until Angie barked a brief greeting, causing several to shift several meters closer toward shore. In what manner this was accomplished was impossible to determine, for nothing was emitted, nor did they rotate, spin, or extend an appendage of any kind to facilitate propulsion.

We spent several seconds in silence, thinking anything we did or said might result in the objects' hasty retreat. At the periphery of our group, I noticed an agitated Melhaus constantly pointing, adjusting, and repointing a laser micrometer at the spheres. What I could recall of the device was that it was exquisitely efficient at measuring an object's exact size and shape.

"Incomprehensible," he said, talking more to himself than to us. "The internal test verifies the instrument is functioning properly."

"What's the problem?" Diana asked, shaken from her silence. "Something about the instrument or the spheres?" "Spheres…," Melhaus responded, mumbling to himself, refusing to look up from the measuring device he squeezed tightly in his trembling hand.

"Larry…," Diana began again, her patience wearing thin.

Thompson gently placed his hand over the body of the instrument the physicist was using, compelling him to look up and notice us for the first time.

"Oh. Yes, they *are* spheres," Melhaus muttered, believing he had provided an answer.

"Explain yourself," Thompson insisted. "You can spare us the part about a sphere being round."

"You're not comprehending," Melhaus said, looking at and through us. "Shape is the very crux of the matter. In front of us are objects so perfectly round they exceed the capabilities of this instrument to measure. Orders of magnitude rounder than anything found in nature, surpassing even laboratory-engineered spheres of monoisotopic silicon crystal. Shall I change the perspective to make this more understandable? If one of those objects were expanded to become the size of this planet, all diameter measurements would be within one meter, and the enlarged surface would still be smooth as polished glass."

A long, low whistle of appreciation came from Paul.

"Tell me, how's that possible?" asked Kelly. "They're living organisms. Aren't they?"

"If they are, and *I* still believe they are," Diana asserted, "we may have to come up with a different definition of living."

I recalled a recent description of the planet's shape. "Larry, didn't you say P5 was extraordinarily round?"

"Are you trying to make a connection?" he challenged.

"Is there one?"

"No."

"Kyle's floating trial balloons again," Thompson stated, "and I'm glad of it. The worst possible mistake would be to assume a square peg won't fit in a round hole."

I glanced at Thompson. He shrugged. "Thought you'd appreciate that." Then, in the same breath, "Larry, the minute you obtain results from the spectroscopy array, let me know. I'll hold off till then."

"What are you planning?" Diana asked. "Just in case I have to be somewhere else."

"How would you and Kyle like to go for a swim?"

Two hours elapsed before Melhaus came back with his initial findings.

"What do you have for us?" Thompson asked.

"I can't wait to hear," added Diana. "Eternity flew by."

We had gathered at the outside table. Melhaus, as always, was sitting at the far end, studying chemical compounds on his A.I.D.. Scrutinizing his face, I had no idea what to expect.

"I will have to disappoint," he said impassively. "At least to determine if the spheres are living organisms."

"The modified array functioned properly?" inquired Thompson.

"Within its limitations. I have compiled a partial list of elements and compounds."

"I don't see the data on my A.I.D.," Diana observed.

"Here," he replied. "Sending. For you to peruse at leisure."

Diana glanced over the information. "You sent me the correct file?" she asked, obviously puzzled.

"You think I'm incapable of send—"

"No," Diana interrupted, "maybe I accessed the wrong one." She hesitated. "No, I have the correct file. Help me out here. I'm cross-referencing your work on the chemical composition of the ocean. The two reports look virtually identical."

"Yes," Melhaus volunteered, "there is a striking similarity. Marginally higher concentrations of certain metalloids and oxygen in the spheres, marginally lower concentrations of other compounds."

"In either case," Thompson reflected, "there are several compounds I've never seen before. Any closer to understanding them?"

"Are you any closer to understanding the geological forces forming the spires?" Melhaus shot back, realizing full well that the problem continued to vex Thompson.

A light danced in Thompson's eyes. "Point taken," he said, refusing to take the bait.

"I'm working on what created the spires," I volunteered, attempting to lighten the moment.

"Still no planet name?" Thompson countered.

"I hope to have one by this evening."

"Maybe you need some incentive," Thompson said. "We've delayed long enough. You and Diana get ready. The three of us are going for a swim."

The purpose of the swim, an up-close and personal look at the spheres, was unmistakable. The particulars—well, that had me wondering. Diana appeared nervous. She was probably experiencing the same rush of adrenaline as I.

"Here's the plan," Thompson said, addressing Diana and me, but submitted for everyone's consumption. "The three of us will swim out, *slowly*, in a loose 'V' formation. I'll take the lead. I intend to approach the closest sphere and conduct a visual examination. There's a good chance it will retreat, and the experiment will end almost as soon as we get our feet wet."

"And if it does retreat?" Diana, concerned, asked.

"We'll have more information than we do now. With any luck, the sphere will remain passive and stationary, at which point I intend to touch its surface. The experiment slowly continues if I get no reaction, or it is benign."

"If it is hostile?" I had to ask.

"Getting cold feet? You can bow out."

"Not on your life."

"Hopefully not," Thompson said. "I'll be in the lead. If there is trouble, take your cues from me."

"And Kyle and me?" Diana inquired. "What do we do?"

"When I say it's safe, swim up to a sphere. Let imagination guide your actions. Try not to do anything overt.

Perhaps a small application of pressure will be needed to see if it will respond. Maybe we'll learn how they move. It'll be tough to accomplish more while treading water."

"A low-tech approach?" Paul commented.

"Purposefully."

"You're passing up a chance to get more information," Melhaus asserted. "Why not take the portable densitometer and a diamond knife to take a sample? The knife is waterproof; the meter can easily be made so."

"Sorry, Larry," Thompson responded. "We are dealing with too many unknowns."

"Exactly my point," Melhaus responded, "Far too many—"

"Listen," Thompson said, cutting him off. "The greater risk is proceeding too fast and having the spheres vanish as quickly as they appeared. Everything indicates they come and go at will, whatever 'they' are."

"You're wrong in this," Melhaus said, "and I'd like the ship's log to reflect my recommendation as being ignored."

"No, not ignored," Thompson said. "The log will reflect your recommendation as being duly considered and deemed inappropriate for current circumstances. Now let's move on. What I'd like you and Kelly to do is observe what transpires from an elevated shoreline position. Use the height advantage to alert us of problems we cannot see."

"Why not send one person out there?" asked Kelly.

"There are twelve spheres. I'd rather not be considered tentative if we are perceived at all. If something goes wrong, one person can assist another. This brings me to the next point, Diana. You, too, Kyle. If I say we end the experiment, we end it."

"How can I assist?" Paul asked.

"You'll be operating the holo camera."

A holographic camera had been placed near the shore to obtain a visual record of the spheres. They had conveniently stayed in approximately the same position, acting like tethered balloons bobbing in a light breeze. The camera would need repositioning and refocusing depending on the reaction to our approach.

Thompson's plan was unorthodox, but his reasoning was sound. The spheres weren't coming closer, and if they disappeared over the horizon, as happened yesterday, we'd have squandered a valuable opportunity.

We were about to get wet when he addressed Melhaus, Paul, and Kelly to clarify another point. "If circumstances prevent my input, don't place yourselves in undue jeopardy. I expect you to evaluate the situation and agree among yourselves on how to respond." He had chosen his words carefully because Melhaus was next in line of command—not reassuring given his erratic behavior as of late. The physicist's blank expression showed no objection to what was said.

We prepared to enter the water, the commander in the lead, Diana, and I to follow immediately. I squatted down to pet Angie, who sensed something exciting was about to happen. Kelly stood over us, unable to disguise a look of concern.

"Keep track of Angie while I go for a swim?" I asked.

"Of course. You'll be careful?"

I showed her a confident smile. "Look at it this way," I said, gesturing to the featureless spheres. "They can't bite."

We had waded only up to our knees when the spheres' subtle and seemingly random motion suddenly ceased, then resumed precisely as before.

"Incredible," Diana said. "They somehow sensed us entering the water."

"Want to stop?" Thompson teased.

"Not on your life…," Diana caught herself. "Sorry."

Thompson laughed. "Let's swim out. Follow me closely."

The three of us were accomplished swimmers, Thompson and I from our hobbies in and on the water, Diana from her "hands-on" approach to marine biology. The odds of this being overlooked were slim to none.

The twelve spheres were dispersed in an area half the size of a football field. Thompson swam to within a few strokes of the nearest, a rather large one, and started treading water. Keeping himself afloat took effort, but that wasn't a reason for his hesitation. No, it was because he was now gazing up at an object too massive to fit through a double doorway, yet it was effortlessly resting on a patch of water smaller than a lily pad. I was further away, but my heart, already racing from the swim, added a few extra beats.

"Everybody fine?" Thompson inquired. He seemed to be enjoying himself.

"No issue here," Diana replied.

"One oversized beach ball," I said in between breaths.

Nearly motionless, the sphere seemed perfectly content to stay exactly where it was. There were no marks, seams, or openings of any type marring its pristine surface, and yet I began to sense that this entity (if I dare call it such) was closely scrutinizing me in some inexplicable way.

"This one is too big to mess with," Thompson decided. A short distance away floated one of a more manageable size. Thompson pointed. "Let's head for baby brother."

The smaller, less intimidating sphere was just shy of Paul's height. Thompson swam to within arm's reach, then glanced back to assure himself that we were trailing an appropriate distance behind.

"Here goes," Thompson said, doing an admirable job of maintaining outward composure. An off note in his voice gave him away. He had every reason to be excited. He was about to be the first person in history to reach out beyond the confines of Earth and touch something that conceivably, and in who knows what manner, might *decide* to touch back.

To contact the center of the sphere's curved surface, he needed to maneuver into very close proximity and simultaneously reach up with his arm. As he strove to do so, Kelly, gesturing wildly and pointing, suddenly started shouting, "Look there!"

Startled, I looked past Thompson to see the largest of the twelve spheres barrelling toward him like a colossal curling stone sliding across a patch of slick ice.

We froze. Angie started barking. Kelly and Paul started shouting, "Bruce, look out!"

Thompson, his view partially blocked but now mindful of the danger, paused his attempt to touch the smaller sphere.

"Don't anyone move!" he shouted, even as the large sphere came upon him with great speed, a violent collision unavoidable. Then, impossibly, as if in utter contempt of Newton's first law of motion, it came abruptly to a complete and utter stop, barely an arm's length from Thompson's head!

As time and our hearts began again, so did his hand—to reach out and softly touch the surface of the smaller sphere!

Diana gasped, and I held my breath, expecting the worst.

"Beautiful," I heard Thompson say.

The small sphere and its larger guardian had remained stationary, tolerating, it seemed, our presence. The commander was equally unfazed, a look of amusement, damn him, plastered on his face as he calmly asked if we were all right. Upon receiving two tentative and labored affirmatives, he shouted, "All's well!" toward shore.

He continued the experiment, commenting while he moved a hand gently over the object's gray-blue surface. "Incredibly smooth. Frictionless. A slight, very slight, stimulating sensation on contact. Chemical, electrical? Almost like the faint vibration of a tuning fork. Diana, come feel." She scissor-kicked over to him, leaving me alone to ponder the larger sphere.

If one chose to subscribe motivation, the sphere's rush at Thompson was calculated to be intimidating. But conventional thinking was a trap. Judging that isolated action based on its *effect* without knowing the intent or even if the sphere had one was a mistake. I was also a slave to the natural human tendency to assign greater threat to objects of greater size (hell, the damn thing could overfill my cabin) even though, to it, the concept of physical size might be completely meaningless.

Suppositions, yes, but I was confident of one thing. If the sphere had accelerated in my direction, I would have hastily dived beneath the water's surface. Poor comfort, for it was my turn to take a risk. Using a sidestroke, I swam over to make my acquaintance.

What a marvel it was, balancing on one tiny point of ocean contact, gently swaying and bobbing like a boat in a slight swell! Only there were no swells—just the ripples caused by my effort to stay afloat. Closer, peering down through the surface, I could see rays of sunlight being refracted and diffused, the hues created imparting a pearlescent color before being attenuated several centimeters within. Beyond that limited distance, there was no ability to discern. Was there an entity inside? I thought not.

I had to be practically underneath to reach up and touch the curve of the glossy surface. Thompson was correct. On contact, there was a slight tingle and, with it, something he did not voice, something less definable—a feeling of elation to be here, to be alive, to experience this moment in time. Did this feeling originate from within or without? If there was a difference, I could not tell.

I backed away a meter or so. What the hell, I said to myself, somebody should do the obvious. Then, out loud: "Care to tell me what you are?" As expected, there was no reaction except a chuckle from Thompson.

On impulse, I decided to try another experiment, expecting nothing to come of it. My mass appeared to be a small fraction of the sphere's, and my untenable position in the water made applying force exceedingly tricky. The sphere, however, was unaware of these restrictions (again, they were mine), for when I gave it a gentle push, it instantly and rapidly slid back across the ocean, retracing its trajectory to where it had come! Had I chased it away, as imposing as it was!?

"What was that about?" Thompson asked through labored breathing. We had been treading water for some time, often using one hand.

"A scientific experiment... testing the laws of physics. I exerted a force. There was an *unequal* and opposite reaction."

"You're joking?"

"No. See for yourself."

"Why not? We need to return to shore." Thompson turned his attention to Diana. "Anything more?" he asked.

"No." She had been closely examining the smaller sphere and appeared reluctant to remove her hands from its surface.

"Well then, stop fondling the thing and give it a shove."

Raising both arms, Diana prepared to push, but at that moment, all twelve spheres, by some yet unknown method, began rapidly moving away. Shouts from shore told us more. From out to sea, our local group was being joined by many others.

We swam in, Kelly and Paul welcoming us with towels in hand. I received a hug from Kelly. Angie acted as if I had been gone forever.

"Just look at them all!" Diana remarked while drying off. "There must be seventy, maybe more, out there!"

"Seventy-two, to be precise," Paul submitted. "Makes you wonder how many inhabit this planet."

"Commander," Kelly began, "what went through your mind when that sphere came rushing at you? I would have set a new hundred-meter freestyle record."

"Experience gave me an advantage. Many years ago, a bull elephant charged me."

"What did you do?"

"Same thing you saw me do in the water, not move a muscle, although every fiber of your being tells you to do so."

"You had no idea what would happen, did you? You still insisted on touching that smaller sphere." Diana leaned in and gave the commander a quick hit to the shoulder. "You gave me a damn heart attack."

"I prefer not giving in to a bluff. *If* that's what it was." Thompson turned to Paul. "You caught everything on the holo cam?"

"To be examined and reexamined a million times."

"Give us ten minutes to dry off and dress. We'll review everything."

ORB

What Are They?

I STEPPED OUT of *Desio* to witness a lively conversation in progress. Diana, still pumped from her ocean swim, was in a back-and-forth with Thompson, who, for his part, was relishing the exchange.

"And what," Diana demanded, "shall we call a group of spheres? A pod? No! No! Better yet! A raft! The spheres float on the water surface like a raft of ducks!"

"Come now, Diana," Thompson said. "We have yet to identify the spheres as living organisms."

"Oh, yes, they are," Diana asserted. "Who's the biologist here?"

"Why you, of course," said Thompson, as if relenting. A smirk said otherwise. "Then I suggest we use the name given to a group of buffalo? An obstinacy. Which also happens to be an apt description of your personality."

"Two can play that game," Diana warned.

"Well, then," Thompson challenged. "Take your best shot."

"This should be amusing," Kelly remarked as she took a place near Paul at the table. "The biologist vs. ex-game warden."

"Perhaps," said Diana, "the spheres should have the same name given to a grouping of Bullfinches. A bellowing. Like what you're doing right now."

"I'd stick with Starlings," Thompson replied. For your edification, that's called a chattering. What you're *always* doing."

"That's more pleasant than a cackle. Hyenas."

"Rhinos. A stubbornness."

"Doves. Piteousness."

"You're stretching," Diana said. "That's not a word."

"Let's ask the writer," Thompson said. "Kyle?"

"Sorry, Diana," I replied. "It's a word."

"So is implausibility," Diana responded. "Gnus."

"Goldfish—troubling."

"I rather think of myself as a charm... of goldfinches."

"Can somebody please put a stop to this?" Kelly pleaded.

"Agreed," I said, "Listening to this is murder. Of crows, of course."

"You're a big help," Kelly said, laughing.

The exchange had the potential to last forever. Only I had forgotten that Melhaus was present. "Are you people finished?" he asked. "So we can get down to the work at hand?"

"You know your problem?" Diana chided. "Somewhere out in the vacuum of space, you lost your sense of humor." Then, under her breath, "Tortoises."

"Larry's right," Thompson interjected, heading off another argument. "I know it pains you, Diana, but we'll have to call it a draw. Listen up. Thanks to Paul, the visual record of what transpired in the water was uploaded to you A.I.D.s. Hold off commenting till you see it to the end."

Watching what took place made it even more incredible. Thompson broke a long silence. "Shall we view it again?"

"Why not?" Paul commented. "Maybe we'll believe it the second time."

We gave our impressions after completing the second playback.

Then came the questions.

How do spheres move? How do they suddenly cease moving? Why was I capable of sending a sphere skimming across the water? How do they levitate themselves? What causes the slight tingling when touched? Is it related to the subtle sensation of well-being we get when immersed in the ocean? What's responsible for the spheres' perfect roundness and smoothness?

Every question gave birth to three more.

A consensus was reached (Diana abstaining) that the spheres' physical attributes were those associated with an object.

But what about the spheres' reaction to Angie's barking and Thompson's entry into the ocean? Or their rapid approach when another was about to be touched? Did they not form into a group? Didn't one group join another?

A second consensus (Melhaus abstaining) was reached: sufficient evidence suggests that the spheres exhibited behavior associated with a living organism.

Thompson sat at the head of the table, pondering two seemingly irreconcilable conclusions. He stared into space. We stared at him. Despite the crew's unparalleled learning in scientific disciplines, they were stumped.

"What the hell are they?" Thompson said, equally intrigued and perplexed. Each member of the crew offered up an opinion. No one made a convincing case. The best fit: the spheres were inert objects that, in some unknown manner, were being internally or externally controlled.

Only we couldn't bring ourselves to believe it. The Square peg was refusing to fit in a round hole.

Thompson solicited my opinion, but what could a layperson contribute to this discussion? If nothing else, it wouldn't and shouldn't be anything like what was already out there.

"OK, hear me out," I said. "If the sphere is a living entity with a conscious awareness, its behavior will be nothing like ours. If its physical form is any indication, how can it be? Its view of and reaction to existence may translate into actions that are as consistent, steady, and *automatic* as a heartbeat is to us. In some sense, the spheres may not need to actively behave at all. Maybe they just *are*."

Thompson appeared to be somewhere between entertained and intrigued. I wasn't sure where, but he was about to respond when Melhaus emitted a derisive snigger. I leaned back in my chair and girded myself for another round of criticism. "You're sounding like more of a riddle than the spheres themselves," he said. Then, leaning forward to emphasize his next point, "The spheres, you need to understand, are responsible for the destruction of *Ixodes*."

Reactions to the claim—curiosity, worry, and surprise—circulated the table and landed in front of Thompson, where they were promptly absorbed. After quieting Diana, he looked out across the ocean as if seeking assurance that the spheres peacefully floating there had not appreciably moved. Then, scrutinizing Melhaus's face and apparently in no mood for equivocation, he said, "Larry, state your evidence."

"Gladly," the physicist responded. "Point by point. One: Backward extrapolation of the spheres' movement places them in the general vicinity of the sub when she was lost. Two: *Ixodes'* AI failed to confirm an internal malfunction. Three: As you have witnessed, the spheres have sufficient mass and acceleration to disable a sub. Four: The last recorded images from *Ixodes* show the presence of round objects in close proximity."

"Larry, your first three points are circumstantial," Thompson replied. "Collectively, they are not persuasive and certainly not conclusive. Regarding your last point, I've reviewed the last images from the sub. Twice, in fact. There are a few 'ghosts' caused by the optics, perhaps caused by sunlight or the sub's spotlights, but nothing more."

"You're missing it," Melhaus insisted. "I've examined the images fif…, uh, sufficiently, to determine with absolute certainty that we are not looking at image artifacts."

"I'll review them again," Thompson replied. "We all will. For the moment, let us say you are correct. Why would the spheres disable the sub?"

"No motive is necessary. Perhaps it was an accidental encounter. According to Kyle, any reason is possible."

"There is one possible explanation," I said, feeling oddly satisfied when Melhaus was temporarily thrown off-stride. Too bad I wasn't going to make Thompson's job any easier.

It also ruffled Diana's feathers. "You agree with *him*?!" she said. "What, exactly, is going on here?"

Thompson raised an eyebrow. "Kyle?"

"*Ixodes* was uninvited. It also exterminated a portion of the phytoplankton collected. That's not a good way of introducing ourselves here, is it? I kept this thought to myself because I believed the chance of the spheres acting in a hostile or protective manner was unlikely—I still do, but less so. One more thing. Some have accused me of being biased against scientific research."

"This goes a long way in confirming that opinion," Melhaus said.

"Well shit, Larry, I just can't get it right, can I?"

"No, none of you can."

"What is that supposed to mean?" Thompson asked.

"That stunt in the water proved what?"

"You're joking, right?" Diana said, turning on Melhaus.

"Information was obtained," Thompson said, motioning to Diana to be still. "I've warned against expecting easy answers. What exactly do you recommend we do, Dr. Melhaus?"

"Use the ship's cargo netting to capture one of the spheres for bifurcation and detailed study."

"I know you've lost your sense of humor," Diana exclaimed. "Have you now completely lost your mind?!"

Melhaus rose from the table, violently pushing back his chair.

"Go ahead, leave!" Diana urged. "We've tolerated enough of your bullshit!"

"We've?!"

"Who the hell haven't you pissed off?!"

"Enough!" Thompson shouted. "Larry, sit down."

When the physicist wavered, Thompson stretched out his hand, palm up, a clear and benign gesture inviting him to return to his seat. The move's physicality deftly conveyed the message and avoided an escalation of words. Melhaus reluctantly complied.

"Listen to me for a minute, Larry. *Listen*. What you suggest is unacceptable for many reasons. I'll use your argument. If you believe that the spheres are responsible for destroying *Ixodes*, wouldn't trying to capture one place all of us in considerable jeopardy?"

"It would be a small and acceptable risk. They can't reach us on land. You fail to consider how they must maintain constant contact with the ocean."

That supposed limitation had not been discussed, and it was a revelation to the rest of us that Melhaus considered it an immutable law.

"That has yet to be proven," Thompson said. "Exactly how the spheres would react is little more than guesswork. I understand we are all prepared to tolerate some risk for the sake of the mission, or we wouldn't be here. Still, you must also realize that the responsibility to evaluate and avoid unnecessary danger to the crew rests with me."

"I'll put the risk solely on myself. What I am proposing, I can, with difficulty, accomplish alone."

"I'm not surprised you'd try, given your level of dedication," Thompson said, trying to de-escalate the tension. "The only thing is, my responsibility to this mission includes intervening when a crew member voluntarily places himself in a hazardous situation. Like it or not, we're stuck with each other. An injury to one jeopardizes us all."

"That concern," Melhaus responded, "was considered when *you* planned for redundancy in our training."

"I see I fail to sway you. Have you stopped to consider that the spheres may very well be in opposition to what you are suggesting? That we would be alienating them?"

"They have few of the attributes of a life-form. Either way, we must find out."

"Isn't that a failure to respect what we don't understand?"

You, sir, ignore the immeasurable value to science this will represent. You are forgetting what is expected of this mission."

"I'm open to further discussing the ethical basis of this disagreement… when we are safely on the way home."

Thompson then made it abundantly clear that the discussion was over. A resigned, or so we thought, Dr. Larry Melhaus excused himself and went about his work.

The commander refocused on Diana. "I very rarely give second warnings. Here's yours. Keep a civil tongue, or I *will* confine you to quarters."

"You're right. I know it," Diana said petulantly. "But no more apologies. He's gone to the other side." She pointed a finger at her head and made a circling motion, the universal gesture indicating crazy.

"Maybe so. But many others would do what he's suggesting and worse."

"Can't he get it through his thick skull that I, more than anyone, would bust a gut to find out what these spheres are? There's an excellent chance they are a sophisticated life-form. Kyle instructed me not to say intelligent. Anyway, why didn't you pursue the ethical considerations?"

"Diana, I'm wondering that myself. Right or wrong, I feel words alone have little effect on people with his mindset. You either see and feel the beauty of something and respect it, or you don't. For Dr. Melhaus, beauty is exclusively found in ones and zeros, mesons, and pions. For others, it's dollars and euros or power and prestige. A perpetual fog governs their worldview that mere words won't lift. Perhaps I can be faulted for no longer trying."

I saw a faraway look in the commander's eyes, identical to when we had conversed in his cabin a few days ago. Whatever inner emotions were gripping him, they didn't hold sway.

"Kyle," he said, "your remark to Melhaus wasn't helpful."

"You're right, sorry. But it sure felt good."

Thompson shot me a menacing frown.

"Was that his first warning?" Kelly asked, straight-faced. She had been pretty quiet through all of this.

"Why are you asking?" Thompson said. "You want me to confine him to your cabin?"

"Could you?" she responded.

After Thompson left the table, Paul, who had also been silent, had a question for Diana:

"Tortoises?"

"A creep."

ORB

Many More

AS PROMISED, THOMPSON had us review the last images from *Ixodes'* onboard camera.

Diana, Kelly, and I agreed with Thompson, interpreting the appearance of the barely visible circles as artifacts caused by light refracting off multiple lenses.

Paul's opinion was more nuanced. "We're looking at images taken at a depth of seventy meters. Ambient lighting was low. *Ixodes'* lights were off. Under these conditions, why would artifacts be produced? On the other hand, the images are too indistinct to positively identify as spheres, even assuming they exist at this depth."

Our opinions didn't sit well with Melhaus. After a brief discussion, the physicist rose from the table where we were collected and muttered, "Figures." With a few short strides he disappeared inside *Desio*. In his absence, a conversation ensued among the rest of the crew.

"Is he delusional?" Diana asked.

"It fits the profile," I said.

"There's something else to worry about," Kelly added. "He's no longer taking sleep medication."

"What makes you believe so?" Thompson asked, concerned.

"I gave him ten capsules. That was eleven days ago. He has refused more."

"What's the problem?" asked Paul. "Does he believe you'd substitute another drug?"

"That's one possibility," Kelly replied. "I can think of a better reason. I suspect he doesn't want to sleep."

"I don't follow," Diana said. "Wait. I get it. Not enough time."

Kelly nodded. "Every hour spent sleeping is one less spent doing research. I'll try talking to him. Again."

Thompson wanted more. "You'll be rebuffed. He'll continue to refuse medication. Another possibility is he'll accept the capsules and feign taking them. No, I want to stay one step ahead of him. Give me something more to work with."

"I have a psychotropic that can be of some help in treating his disorder. If we ask him to take it, he will be within his rights to refuse. Unless, of course, Larry is deemed to be an active threat to himself or others. I don't…"

Kelly hesitated as Melhaus came out of *Desio*. An awkward silence ensued while he reached over her shoulder to retrieve his A.I.D. from the table where we were assembled.

"Great. Just great," Diana said after Melhaus had reentered the ship.

"Relax," Paul said, placing a hand on hers. "I don't think he overheard."

"But what if he did?"

"My advice would be the same," said Thompson. His following remark did little to put Diana at ease. "He needs to be observed. He may no longer act predictably. Couple that with his high intelligence, and we will have a potential problem."

"And you don't believe *that* meets the standard of an 'active threat'?" Diana asked.

"He's done nothing to warrant that designation," Thompson responded.

"Still want me to talk to him?" Kelly asked.

"Definitely," Thompson responded. "Advocate the new medication strongly. His refusal should be part of the medical record."

I had the distinct feeling Thompson was contemplating an additional course of action. He seemed in no mood to share what that would be.

As we considered ways to further our study of them, the spheres, en masse and heralded by a bark from Angie, drifted closer to shore. Suddenly, emulating the blue sun that each morning appeared born out of the perfectly round planet, more spheres emerged, though much smaller, the size of basketballs, popping one by one right out of the ocean. There were twelve in all, slowly peeking their glossy domes above the surface, then steadily rising until gently hovering on one tiny point upon the water.

I can only remember Kelly exclaiming, "How wonderful!"—for what happened next blurred from my memory (a rare instance when I had forgotten to turn on my pocket recorder), the other comments made, including my own.

In a bold challenge to the brightness of day, eight dozen spheres brought forth onto their surfaces the colors previously only hinted at within—vivid reds, blues, greens, and a host of other beautiful hues rarely seen before! The colors did not remain static but instead spread across their surfaces, slowly swirling and flowing like those on a glycerin soap bubble sent rising into the air by a child. Several spheres, lending a celebratory feel to the scene, began leisurely traversing back and forth, bringing themselves in close contact, as if visiting with others in the group!

I could not recall the last time I saw Diana so ecstatic, Thompson even having to deny her pleas to jump back into the ocean. I found her sitting on a stone slab, feet dangling in the water, watching in rapt fascination as the spheres cavorted while recording impressions on her A.I.D..

"They must be alive!" she insisted. "The display of colors. The excited movement. I'd stake my reputation that we're witnessing a collective response to new additions made to their group!"

Although the rest of us were unsure, we wanted it to be so. An hour after it had begun, the spheres' extraordinary display ceased, and they resumed their more staid color and motion. What, we wondered, would they have in store for us next?

Naturally, Melhaus's reaction was more subdued, reaffirming the sphere's inanimate attributes and reminding us that we were applying wishful thinking to something we did not understand.

He was right about the wishful thinking part. The human race didn't care to be alone. The universe was far too big and scary a place to occupy all by our lonesome. If life on Earth could fill every available niche, we expected the same to be true elsewhere.

So, I tended to agree with Melhaus regarding our mindset, but unlike him, I didn't rely exclusively on scientific instruments to form an opinion about the spheres. Such devices have their own bias because humans design them with specific results in mind. A rudimentary camera, for example, is a pre-chosen combination of lens, aperture, and sensor; all are compromises in creating an image that is merely a tiny slice of visual reality. The image itself is often open to different interpretations. Those produced by *Ixodes'* camera come readily to mind.

I'm only dusting off what others have said to establish why I was confident the spheres were a living entity. Absent an unbiased viewpoint, you might as well provide your own.

These thoughts occurred to me while I assisted Thompson, Melhaus, and Paul as they attempted, and failed, to modify the holo camera to detect sounds the spheres might be emitting. *Ixodes* was likely on everyone's mind, especially Melhaus's, as the missing sub had the ability to detect a wide range of frequencies above and below the water. I wondered if his interpretation of its final images was a subconscious attempt to transfer guilt from himself to the spheres. He hadn't committed to the sphere's being a life form. Still, I doubted he'd be amused if I congratulated him on being the first human in history to use an extraterrestrial as a scapegoat.

"Hey, Kyle," Thompson yelled at me, "go put pen to paper. You're no use to us here."

Nothing got by him. He could always tell when I was daydreaming. Venturing toward my cabin, I wondered where he learned the arcane expression.

Paul predicted and delivered on the approach of a fast-moving weather front. A mass of steel-gray clouds rolled in, unleashing a few hours of refreshing, late-day rain. We gleefully stood outside, letting the water wash us off and enjoying the soft sensation of raindrops tapping against bare skin. The gentleness of the rain compared to that on Earth earned an explanation from the scientists: the atmosphere here was a little denser, the gravity a little weaker.

Despite the downpour, the crew continued their work. Tents made of ultralight poles and rainproof fabrics were erected over the four science stations to protect equipment too heavy or delicate to move in and out of the ship. Like many items onboard *Desio*, the tenting was designed with multiple functions in mind—in this instance, the collection of one hundred liters of rainwater to replenish those lost by the crew when working in the warm atmosphere.

By sunset, the storm had rolled on past, leaving in its wake a tumble of puffy cumulus clouds rising in the sky. By nightfall, the sky had cleared entirely. In the partial darkness of a million dazzling suns, a mystery was solved.

The grouping of spheres had drifted further offshore but remained close enough for us to distinguish each subgroup by its blue shade. Several individuals exceeded three meters in diameter, and the overall number had multiplied from the previous evening. In sum, they threw significant radiance into the immediate atmosphere. More groups started appearing.

Many, many more.

Thousands of groups now spread themselves across the ocean. Our local group, as I said, had stayed relatively close to our island. The next nearest, its own unique shade, was a kilometer away. Beyond it, there was another, then another, and another, on and on, in every direction, out to the planet's rim.

Ignoring dinner, we sprinted to a good vantage point at the shoreline.

"Can anybody venture a guess how many?" Thompson asked as we scanned the broad ocean before us.

"Lots," Paul answered. "In the thousands. More counting those over the horizon we can't see."

"At last, one puzzle solved," Thompson said enigmatically. "Solutions have been hard to come by." "Was it not obvious that they would appear as perfect circles from orbit?" Melhaus stated. "Do you need to examine the images taken from orbit? A conservative extrapolation would place their number in the millions."

A light of recognition appeared on Paul's face. "Yes! I get it. I should have sooner. Remarkable."

"Whatever they are," Kelly said, "I certainly hope we don't do anything to antagonize them. If we haven't already, that is."

Hundreds of sphere groups in the small wedge of ocean visible to us meant exponentially more elsewhere. Similar to the spread of galaxies throughout the Universe, the spheres had dispersed across the entirety of the planet's ocean. Bending down, I picked up Angie so she could get a better view of the mysterious and beautiful phenomena we had observed from orbit.

Kelly looked at me and smiled.

"It's only fair that she get a good look," I said, ensuring everyone heard. "She seems to understand what we're dealing with better than we do."

We reluctantly returned to the table to finish our dinner. During a lull in conversation, I decided to preempt Thompson.

"I have a name for the planet. For everyone's consideration, that is."

"This should be good," Thompson warned. "Let's hear it."

"Orb."

"That's it?" said Diana, taken aback. "What, are all the two-letter names taken?"

"Let's hear the reasoning," Thompson said. "Kyle always has a reason."

"And you shall have it. I sought a name that evoked the planet's more predominant and intriguing features. The one attribute that applies to the planet and its principal occupant, the spheres, is that both are round like an orb, the Latin word for circle, sphere, or disk. There are other connotations. Magical, like the power and glow of a magician's orb; celestial, like the transparent spheres carrying the heavenly bodies in their revolutions; poetic, another word for eye. Anyway, I felt it had an air of mystery, timelessness…"

I looked around. No one commented, not even Kelly, which worried me.

"Well," Thompson began, realizing I was hanging on to his every word, "perhaps I was wrong in assigning this job to you. Two days to come up with only three letters? Hell, how long does it take you to write a complete sentence?"

"I can come up with something else—"

"I doubt we have the time. What do you think, Paul?

"I don't believe he should trouble himself."

"And you, Kelly?" Thompson asked. "Giving this job to Kyle was your idea."

"It might have been wise to seek a second opinion."

When Diana started laughing, I finally caught on. They had conspired to play me.

"You, too, Kelly?" I said. "You're in on this?"

"Sorry. Commander's orders."

"You are one sensitive SOB," Thompson said, smiling. "Anyway, I have to admit it's a fitting name for the planet."

"Glad you like it," I said. "Want me to rename that boat of yours?"

While the crew and I were enjoying ourselves, Melhaus, as usual, had remained quiet. I was tempted to share another definition for orb: a spherical *artifact* found in some digital images.

I joined Kelly in her cabin after the others (except Thompson, who continued to sleep in the open air) had gone to their quarters to rest.

"Your name for the planet is wonderful," Kelly said. "Quixotic? Wrong word. Fanciful. It somehow evokes this odd notion I have—I can't shake it—that there is more to this world than meets the eye."

"Can you be more specific?"

"No."

"Too bad," I said. "Ever since we arrived here, I've had a similar notion. It's as if we're missing something right in front of us. But then again, I'm captive to flights of imagination."

She smiled and pressed her lips against my forehead.

"That's why I lov…"

I felt her go tense. She had caught herself, but not quite in time.

"No, you can say it. Once or twice, my parents did."

"Kyle," she began, her eyes misting.

I hated myself for draining the joy out of the moment.

"Kelly," I began, trying to apologize. "What do you see in me?"

163

Recovering with a broken smile, she replied, "Do you want a list? It's rather long. Should I omit the physical stuff?"

"Will that shorten the list much?"

"Considerably." She was teasing me now.

"Not completely?"

"No."

"Tell me."

She thought for a moment and said, "I already did. Almost. A few moments ago."

I guess she had tried. Like Orb, three little letters.

Internalizing

"YOU NEVER TOLD me the details of your nightmare," Kelly said, sitting at my workstation.

After spending the night together, we prepared for day five on Orb. More accurately, she was. I was languishing on the bed, admiring her form as she passed a fine-toothed comb through the lustrous strands of her long black hair.

I remembered my rather disturbing Ice Island dream, but hadn't intended to inflict all the details on Kelly. I've always found that dreams lose much in the retelling, so I keep them to myself unless there's some compelling reason not to. Kelly seemed eager to hear mine, so I made an exception.

"Have you ever had a similar nightmare?" I asked.

"Happily, no. But then again, I don't dwell on isolation and dying quite as much."

"Don't pull any punches, Doc," I said. "I can take it."

Joining me on the bed, she placed several strands of her glossy hair over my upper lip, giving me an instant Fu Manchu mustache.

"There's more to it," she said, reflecting on my new look. "A part of you wants to be alone but not lonely."

"A seeming contradiction. I like it."

"There's something else I can't quite put my finger on."

I put a pencil-sized thickness of her hair to her lip. We sat evaluating each other.

"You look good with a mustache," she said.

"You too. Will I need therapy?"

"Yes, I'm afraid so. This goes deep. Very deep indeed. I have an hour session open this evening at twenty-two hundred."

"I can make that," I said.

At the breakfast meeting, with dozens of Orbs (that's what we were calling them now) floating offshore as a backdrop, Thompson called his crew to task, starting with me.

"Kyle," he said, with a mocking inflection and a look boring a hole clear through me, "communications major, right?"

"Last time I checked my resume," I said warily.

"I fail to believe," he went on, ratcheting up the sarcasm, "that you haven't come up with some insight, some plan of action to... what's your favorite word? Oh, yeah, *communicate* with the Orb."

"We've moved on from debating what they are?" I asked.

"Haven't we seen enough? Aren't the Orbs behaving, or if you prefer a less humanizing word, *existing* in a sentient manner?"

"Difficult to argue otherwise. That's a long way from sitting down to afternoon tea with them."

"Very well. Tell us about the obstacles we're facing; maybe they'll provide insight on how to proceed. Play the pessimist. You're good at it."

Where to begin? I looked around the table, studying the expressions on the five faces staring intently at me. Maybe that was where to start.

"Pessimism, right? Okay, then. From Communications 101. It takes two to communicate: Humans and Orb. Let's explore the human half of the equation, starting with a brief chat. Distill your impression of yesterday's weather to three words or less. How about you, Diana?"

"A bit rainy," she said, slowly counting to three on her fingers to poke fun at me.

"And you, Bruce?"

"Changeable, but sunny."

"Typical." I said, "You and Diana can't agree on anything."

But the discrepancy in their responses was precisely what I expected to hear.

"Let's try something even less subjective," I said.

I pointed to an empty, off-colored drink container on the table before me.

"Paul, what color is the container?"

"Silver."

"Kelly?"

"I thought of it as more of a blue."

"Another disagreement," I said. "What the hell is wrong with you people?"

"No, it's definitely gray," Diana volunteered. "But don't mind me."

"I won't. Tell me, did the way you perceived the container or the weather actually differ?" I didn't wait for an answer.

"Doubtful. Only the *words* you each chose to interpret your perceptions differed. And that's my point. Language, our principal form of communication, can be an inexact tool, even when we all speak the same one."

"*Mais nous ne fait pas,*" Paul said.

"Very funny. You said?"

"But we do not."

"Okay, okay. *Scusi, signore Paolo,*" I said. "*Noi esseri umani non tutti parlano la stessa lingua.* We humans don't all speak the same language. A gifted person may boast of fluency in five. Too bad. There are five thousand more. That's a lot of different ways to say silver. Or *not* to say silver if you get my meaning."

"I speak Swahili," Diana boasted.

"Good for you," I said.

"*Kweli, nasema kiswahili.*"

"Diana…" Thompson cautioned.

"Well, he didn't believe me."

I went on despite the interruptions. "When we manage to get our language in sync, we often don't understand even our most basic and innate differences, those of race, age, and sexual preference. Let's not forget gender. Diana reminded us of that when we set foot on this planet."

"Can't wait to see how that plays on Earth," she responded.

"That may depend on the culture in which it is received."

"Or one's religion," Kelly added.

"Exactly," I said. Religion and ideologies. There are thousands of them. And as many wars in their name. It often comes down to miscommunication. Principles and concepts are degraded to half-truths or lies by flashy holo images or brief sound bites. Even honest disagreements, where the truth of a matter has yet to be established, are plagued by our inability to pass along ideas without alteration, without subconsciously attaching our biases or beliefs. And what happens? Opposing ideas divide into warring camps. Even when we act with the best intentions and try to pass information faithfully from one person to another, something is lost."

Reaching across the table, I picked up the empty silver, gray, blue—take your pick—juice container and deliberately studied Melhaus, who, despite being the embodiment of what I was saying, never looked up. "Should I complete the thought?" I asked Thompson, who had been carefully watching both of us. A resigned nod indicated he knew what I was about to say.

"Humanity's failing," I continued, "is evident right here in our midst, for as smart as we are supposed to be, there is a growing divide between you, Dr. Melhaus, and the rest of the crew, which none of us seem able to bridge. I tell you sincerely that we want to. Failing so miserably at transcending the barriers we have erected between ourselves, what are our chances with the Orb?"

There was a moment's pause before the silence was broken. By Paul.

"Larry's harder."

"Say again?" I said louder, not quite sure Melhaus was getting it.

"Harder," Paul repeated, practically shouting across the table, "Larry's harder to communicate with than the Orb."

Despite the remark, the brilliant physicist remained reclusive, staying secure in his own world. The failure to even acknowledge Paul was concerning. Paul was the one person who had yet to argue with him.

Who had tried the hardest to see the world through Melhaus's eyes.

"We don't fully understand each other, do we?" I said. "How can we when we know ourselves even less?"

If he heard any of it, Melhaus was unmoved. For the first time, I began to believe, not wanting to, that we would utterly fail in our attempt to reach him. Paul felt the same way.

"Might as well go on," he said, dismayed.

Looking at Thompson, I again received unspoken confirmation. He appeared deep in thought.

"Might as well," I repeated, then began anew. "I have a few questions for you, Diana."

"Why do I feel you already know the answers?" she said, feigning a scowl. "But go right ahead anyway."

"How many species of mammals are there?"

"About four thousand and declining."

"And what is the genetic confluence between humans and other mammals?"

"In the ninety-plus percent range."

"So on our planet, with most of the genetic code in common and a ten-thousand-year head start, we've established only cursory communication with a handful of fellow mammals?"

"Somebody," Kelly said, "is a *real* slow learner."

"Good one," Diana said, laughing, then addressing Kelly, "*You* more than anyone understand just how much Kyle appreciates a responsive audience."

"You two behave yourselves," Thompson put in. Then, addressing me: "Ignore them. If you can."

"What is the genetic similarity between humans and yeast?" I continued.

"Twenty-odd percent, I believe," Diana replied.

"And humans and the Orb?"

"Zero. But, of course, you knew that. The plankton are not gene-based organisms, and neither, apparently, are the Orb."

I turned my attention back to Thompson. "And we want to communicate with the Orb in, what? The next three or four days?"

Thompson, with a crease in his brow, stared at his folded hands. My arguments had failed to shake his resolve.

"For argument's sake," he said, "I'll take an optimistic view predicated on the Orb being more adept than humans at communicating. There is some reason to believe this can be true. Consider our history, how Earth's physical features—mountain ranges, oceans, deserts—isolated us into groups, and how that isolation was the predominant cause of the cultural, racial, and language barriers you allude to. Now consider the Orb. They occupy one vast ocean with no geological barriers and therefore never developed these divisive differences."

"May I interject?" Diana requested. When she saw Thompson's skeptical expression, she added, "I'll be on point. This time, anyway."

Thompson nodded.

"There's another factor to consider," she said, "with my apologies to Darwin. Evolution, at least as we comprehend it, is not at work on this planet. The Orb are likely to have existed in their present form for untold ages, perhaps tens of millions of years. They've enjoyed an incredibly stable environment. Can you imagine how exquisitely well they have adapted, given an existence potentially a hundred times longer than our species? It's mind-boggling."

"Meaning," Thompson said, finishing the thought, "whatever form of communication they have, it must be pretty damn good."

"Yeah, I got that," I said. "I've no reason to disagree, but I was asked to play the pessimist, right?"

"Try not to overdo it," Thompson said.

"One more thought."

I grabbed the empty juice container and held it up.

"How would the Orb perceive this container? We humans have a few different ways; the Orb may have one, they may have one hundred. Do they see, feel, hear, or smell? We ask what color. Do they see color? We ask what shape. Do they consider the container as distinct from the table on which it rests? We *ask*. Do they have a concept of asking?"

"What all this leads to," Paul said, "is that we should consider ourselves the weak link. We need to transcend our own limitations to determine how and what the Orb are experiencing of the world around them."

"I agree with Kyle," Diana said, surprising me. "Expecting us to understand what the Orb think or feel is nearly impossible."

"Excuse me," Thompson responded. "So Dr. Diana Gilmore, the world-renowned biologist, is giving up. Did I set my expectations of you too high?"

"Probably too low," Diana shot back.

"You have zero idea how the Orb might communicate?"

"Ideas? Many. Want to hear them? Touch: like when two giraffes show affection by pressing their necks together; chemical: the exquisitely small quantity of sex pheromones detected by an oriental silkworm moth; sight: the dance of a honeybee directing the hive to nectar; electroreception: the platypus detecting its prey's muscular contractions; vibration:

the sound waves used by whales to communicate through a thousand kilometers of ocean. Want me to think outside the box? Magnetic fields, temperature change, molecular density changes… well, you get the idea."

"I'm pretty sure she's Dr. Gilmore," Kelly commented.

Diana *was* pretty impressive, I thought.

"I'm not asking any of you to solve this problem," Thompson said evenly. "Don't forget, I cautioned we'll leave here with many questions unanswered. What I *do* expect is for you to come up with a plan, individually or collectively, on how to proceed."

"What?" I asked, "We can't just tread water?"

I was trying to be humorous, but the remark caused Thompson to wince. He said nothing. Two days ago, he told us not to fool ourselves into believing we weren't subject to the same pressures affecting Melhaus.

Having heard enough, he was about to conclude the morning meeting when he seemed to decide on an issue on his mind.

"Larry," he said, standing.

No response.

"Dr. Melhaus," he repeated, louder and firmer. "I'm addressing you."

Melhaus glanced up.

"I'd like you and Dr. Takara to meet me in my cabin."

"Can it wait?"

"Now."

After meeting with Thompson and Melhaus, an agitated Kelly sought me in my cabin.

"From the start, the conversation did not go well," she said. "It ended worse."

"What can I do to help?" I asked, motioning for her to sit down on the bed next to Angie.

"I'm OK. It's just the adrenaline working its magic."

I sat down beside her.

"I'm afraid," she said, "nothing *can* be done."

"Sounds bad. You want to talk about it?"

"The commander made it part of the ship's record, telling Larry they already had two other conversations to no avail."

"What precipitated the meeting?"

"Late yesterday, I advised Larry to start a short regimen of a drug called Kalmbex and provided good reasons why he would do well taking it. He vehemently refused. I then asked him how well he was sleeping. He was evasive. When I strongly suggested he resume his sleep medication, he became argumentative, verbally abusive, and abruptly left. He left me no choice. I had to tell the commander."

"The meeting caught you by surprise?"

"Not exactly. Larry's demeanor this morning must have triggered the timing."

"Is the audio file available?"

"Should be."

The voice recognition in Thompson's cabin converts conversations into text form. The file, including speakers' names and voice levels, was accessible at my workstation. When necessary, the program extrapolates and brackets incomplete information. To spare Kelly from repeating an unpleasant experience, I turned off the audio portion while I read the following file:

Recording commenced 0804 hours 12-12-2232
    Melhaus(61db) Is this necessary?

Thompson(57db) Sit down, please. Do you know the purpose of this recorded meeting?

Melhaus(61db) The purpose *and* the outcome.

Thompson(56db) Truly? Have we arrived at the point where all conversation between us is useless?

Melhaus(63db) In this circumstance, yes. You presume that you know me better than I know myself.

Thompson(60db) No one can know themselves so entirely as to disregard good advice.

Melhaus(62db) Which calls into question your objectivity, would it not?

Thompson(60db) And Dr. Takara's as well?

Takara(56db) Larry, we're not presuming to judge you. We have seen changes in your behavior that are, in our reasoned opinion, an outgrowth of the extraordinary stress placed on you from any number of causes. Our opinion has been confirmed by oth[ers]…

Melhaus(66db) By whom?! By Mr. Lorenzo?! His credentials are more laughable than yours—a handful of psychology courses and, oh yes, an author of short stories. If you respect his opinion, apply his, what did he call it, [laughter] sanctuary theory to yourselves. You remember it, don't you? The undue stress you speak of could manifest itself in any member of the crew and affect their judgment, including yours.

Thompson(57db) Attempting to redirect this discussion won't work, Larry.

Melhaus(62db) So what *exactly* are you people accusing me of?

Thompson(57db) Poor choice of words.

Melhaus(62db) *My* choice of words.

Takara(58db) Rather than get into specifics, I'd prefer to generalize your behavior as alternating between argumentative and withdrawn.

Melhaus(65db) Argumentative? Is that what questioning ill-conceived decisions, and there have been several, is being called?

Thompson(57db) When have I not solicited opposing viewpoints? Few decisions were made without the entire crew's input, including yours, which I've always welcomed.

Melhaus(62db) And I have been ignored on every point. Do you have any concept of just how difficult it is to be forced into watching all of you let the scientific discovery of our age slip through our fingers?

Takara(58db) You're setting yourself apart from the crew, Larry, and you shouldn't.

Melhaus(62db) Is this retribution for what you think happened to the *Ixodes*, despite proof offered to the contrary?

Thompson(57db) You surprise me. Is that how you see it?

Melhaus(65db) That's when I started noticing what you're doing behind my back, undermining me and, in the process, the mission.

Thompson(57db) That's quite an accusation. Would you care to elaborate?

Melhaus(62db) In your absence, am I not second in command? Do you think I didn't notice when you marginalized me by putting Bertrand and Takara in charge during your escapade in the water?

Thompson(61db) If you don['t]...

Melhaus(65db) You think you had me fooled? You and the crew, afterward, when I heard you scheming behind my back?

Thompson(61db) We shouldn't interrupt one another. You only saw our concern for you based on changes in your behavior.

Takara(58db) Larry, by overhearing a fragment of a conversation, you came away with the wrong impression.

Melhaus(68db) Why lie to my face?! Isn't the purpose of this meeting to coerce me into accepting a drug I refuse to take?!

Takara(58db) I'm sorry you feel that way. Have you asked yourself why you are hostile to taking what I, as ship's doctor, strongly recommend?

Melhaus(65db) Take it on your advice? [laughter] To do so will give credence to everything you've alleged against me.

Thompson(61db) Dr. Takara's recommendation is measured and justified. As mission leader, I am asking you to comply.

Melhaus(65db) And I am within my rights to refuse. You can't invent a reason to ignore regulations; you must establish that a person is a threat to himself or the crew.

Thompson(61db) Well, then, I see no need to pursue the matter further. You are correct. The standard of proof is high, justifiably so in most situations, and I am required to follow it. That does not preclude my taking other initiatives, and I intend to do so in what I hope you see as a measured response to your intractability. I am confining you to quarters until twelve hundred hours. Take the time to reflect. Maybe that will have a positive effect on your behavior.

Melhaus(70db)   Confining me to quarters?! By doing so, you're further jeopardizing the outcome of this mission! If I refuse?!

Thompson(58db)   Consider what you say carefully, Dr. Melhaus. You risk provoking a much sterner response.

Melhaus(67db)   And you expect *what* of me when I'm released from this imprisonment?

Thompson(58db)   At a minimum, civility toward your fellow crew members.

Melhaus(04db)   You'll g[et] exactly what you [dez]…

Recording concluded 0810 hours 12-12-2232

"That was pretty intense," I said. And damn worrisome, I thought.

"The worst I've seen him."

"You handled the situation well."

"Thompson better. He went through the possible scenarios beforehand, expecting Melhaus to be confrontational. Only…"

"What? You seem a bit unsure of the outcome." Leaving the workstation, I returned to the bed and sat beside her. We leaned back together, Angie coming up to nestle tightly between us.

"Do you believe we pushed Larry even further away?" Kelly asked.

"Only time will tell. Did Thompson have another alternative?"

"Yes. To let him be."

"Keep in mind the discord among the prior crew. He'd be open to criticism for doing nothing if Larry unraveled. I see why Thompson appeared a little edgy this morning. Now, there's more to ponder over. What, if anything, to read into Larry's last statement."

A confused expression appeared on Kelly's face.

"What do you mean?"

It was my turn to be confused.

"Larry's last remark. When he responded to Thompson's demand to be civil. You didn't hear it?"

"No."

I moved off the bed and returned to the workstation.

"I assume neither you nor Thompson have had the time or inclination to play back the audio?"

Kelly shook her head, now concerned and confused in equal measure.

Setting the audio to full, I replayed the last few seconds of the file I had finished reading. Melhaus's final statement was barely audible. "Come take a look," I said.

Kelly leaned over me to read the last few sentences of the transcript, then said, "I thought he mumbled something under his breath when exiting Thompson's cabin."

"The recording system was sensitive enough to pick up Larry's voice; the ship's AI performed an incomplete conversion to text. Question is, how accurately?"

"For confirmation, I'd like to hear you repeat what he said."

"'You'll get exactly what you deserve.'"

The words had a chilling effect. Kelly turned pale as the implied threat sank in. "I should be the one," she offered, "to bring this to Thompson's attention."

"A garbled and cryptic statement said in anger. Not much for the commander to act on."

"And insufficient to use as proof positive that Larry has become a threat to others. Nevertheless, this is a cause for worry."

"Would it help any if I pointed out that Larry continues to have a very ordered and logical mind? He must realize, at least we can hope, that any hostile act adversely affecting the crew would undoubtedly affect him."

Kelly laid back and petted Angie, who was happily gnawing a rawhide bone. "Nice try, but you can't change the reality of a bad situation."

"You forget I am a fiction writer. I can change reality at will."

Angie stopped gnawing, placed her head on her paws, and gave me a curious look. "My two favorites," I said, joining them on the bed.

"Why did you major in communications?" Kelly asked, the sudden change of topic catching me off-guard.

"Are you searching for one more piece of the jigsaw puzzle named Kyle?"

"I want to know everything about you. Every one of the thousand little pieces."

"Nine hundred ninety-nine. One's missing from the box."

"Tell me. Why communications?"

The answer to the question, never put into words, wasn't exactly a tale of woe, but it wasn't that pleasant to me either.

"Please."

Something inside me wanted to tell her, and I realized that my willingness to tell her was more important than the story itself.

"OK," I said, watching her eyes brighten. "You'll settle for the short version of my *deformative* years?"

"I'm happy to hear any version."

"I was fourteen when my brother left for college, leaving me alone with two incompatible and argumentative people, namely, my parents. I remember most vividly the three of us sitting at the dinner table. How eerily quiet it was."

"But I thought you said they argued...?"

"Oh, my parents argued, but only sporadically, and when they did, I intently listened. I remember thinking to myself, as words were exchanged in anger, why can't they understand each other's point of view?

"Some of the arguments had a logical basis, money, for example; other times, it was a simple matter of not understanding one another's feelings. They rarely got through to each other. So, what did they do to resolve the impasse? Nothing. My mom would cook dinner, as always, and we'd sit, the three of us, evenly separated at the small round table, in the small square kitchen, in the small suburban house, and the dreaded silence would descend."

"That's awful. No talking at all?"

"Virtually none. Only the minimum words for any three people, even strangers, to coexist. My parents were too stubborn to speak, and I was a teenager stranded in the middle."

"This went on until the next day, the next argument?"

"Oh, no, the silence would drag on, quite literally, for several weeks at a time. More noticeable, much more, when I was with them at the dinner table."

"I'm sorry."

"They say never argue in front of the children. There were times when my parents turned that adage into an art form. After two years of this, college was on the horizon. Although it wasn't a conscious decision on my part, you can see why communications, plus a smattering of psych for good measure, would be an outgrowth of what went on before."

Kelly looked troubled, the story affecting her more than me. "You're aware that the effect this abuse had, and that's what it was, was on more than your choice of study."

"I've given it some attention. I imagine living through that whole silent treatment thing made me introspective."

"And nothing else?"

"You want *more*?" I said with exaggerated astonishment. "A catharsis?"

"Come on, you can do it…!" Kelly, half serious and half joking, urged me to further revelation.

I played along. It was the most serious playacting I would ever do. "Internalizing? That's it! I internalize my emotions!"

"*Veir merkink gutten progress, ja?*"

"Not bad," I said. "Affectation of a German accent, in English, by a native of Japan raised in Los Angeles."

"Another first on Orb," Kelly responded, suddenly rising from the bed. "To be continued. I must immediately see Thompson. Any message?"

I scanned the floor and spotted what I was searching for—something resembling a slightly damp bunched rag in the corner.

"No," I said. "But can you return this T-shirt Angie stole off his bed?"

As Kelly turned to leave, I kissed her, saying, "Don't worry about Dr. Melhaus. He's all of our responsibility, but more so Thompson's. I feel confident he's up to the challenge."

I leaned against the open doorway and watched her head off down the narrow hall.

Amazing how someone that sensitive wanted to be with the likes of me.

There was a low sound of whining down at my feet, and there was Angie, staring up at me with her beady little eyes and mouth crammed full of a stuffed toy rabbit. I sat with my back against the bulkhead opposite the open doorway and threw the rabbit down the hall.

Play began.

My little dog had straightforward, uncomplicated needs: food, space to live and breathe, time to play and romp. Most importantly, she needed affection. Call these things simple, but that sounds condescending, for they are very much our exact needs, only reduced to their uncomplicated essence. With a bark, a meaningful stare, or a nuzzling, she nearly always received or gave what was wanted.

By comparison, two doors down, in a soundproof cabin, sat Doctor Larry Melhaus.

Not nearly as satisfied or communicative.

ORB

Ambassador

KELLY AND I postponed a visit to the cove to be present when Melhaus emerged from his confinement at 1200 hours. At precisely 1300 hours, he appeared, looking like nothing had happened. I attributed the extra hour to pride. He could damn well stay in his cabin as long as *he* wished to do so.

At 1305, I approached Thompson, asking: "Did Melhaus see his shadow when he came out?"

"I do believe he did," Thompson responded, playing along.

"Damn," I said. "Six more weeks of winter."

As the afternoon progressed, the physicist engaged in minimal and constrained conversation with the crew. Sufficient, and no more, to satisfy Thompson's requirement for civil conduct.

Logic dictated that with so little time left on the planet, the physicist would not jeopardize his research by behaving in a manner that would precipitate another confinement. As for the implied threat he had made—if that's what it had been—Thompson decided to let it go.

Or did he? I remembered him saying, "Onboard *Desio*, my duty is to ensure nothing gets by me." I had this uneasy feeling that he and Melhaus were playing a grandmaster's chess game in which something as slight as the position of a pawn affords a significant advantage.

Our apprehension about Melhaus's state of mind worsened when we attempted to evaluate his potential threat to the mission. In the most draconian scenario we could conceive of, he sabotaged *Desio's* crucial operating systems—life support, propulsion, navigation—essentially marooning himself on Orb along with crewmates. There would be an unlimited supply of purified water, but after four months—six or seven with rationing—our food stores would be depleted. We would then have two choices: starvation or the little blue L-pill.

We increased our watchfulness and looked for suspicious behavior on his part. At first, we did this sporadically, even unconsciously. Motivated by our own feelings of isolation and paranoia, we began to steal more frequent glances in his direction. Thompson continued to see nothing sufficiently alarming to warrant placing one of Earth's top scientists under constant confinement. Nor did he consider the humiliating step of ordering one of us to accompany Melhaus when not in his cabin.

The near-term consequence of this decision permitted the physicist to conduct his research unhindered and, ironically, probably more disturbed by the insult of our ill-disguised scrutiny.

With the possibility of being stranded on Orb fresh on our minds, I attempted to amuse myself at Diana's expense, asking, "Do plankton living in the ocean of Orb have any nutritional value?"

It took no time for her to answer: "No, but you do... Yum."

"Not what I wanted to hear," I said, making room for myself on the stone slab she was sitting on. "I concede the crew might be *mentally* quicker. Do I have to worry they are *physically* quicker, too?"

"Well, Kyle, it would be survival of the fittest. Looks like we'll have Darwin here with us after all."

"He'd be the first invited for dinner. By the way, have you seen Angie lately?"

"Last seen, she was sniffing by the water's edge." We squinted at the glistening water and the Orbs basking in the brilliance of late afternoon sunshine.

"So," she said, gesturing toward wherever *they* were. "Have you devised a plan to communicate? Thompson wants a plan. A plan, a plan, a plan." The repetition was her way of venting frustration.

"Perhaps," I said. "An embarrassingly simple one. I was going to get Kelly's opinion first. It involves her anyway, and she'll be less insulting about it than Thompson. And you?"

"Will I be any less insulting?"

"No," I said, frowning. "I know that answer. I mean, do you have any new ideas?"

"Yes and no. I asked Melhaus to conduct a test to see if the Orbs have magnetic fields and if they were fluctuating in any definable way. He was way ahead of me on this;

electromagnetic waves and the forces associated with them being solidly within his field of expertise. He began explaining his results, but quickly lost patience when I failed to appreciate the subtleties of advanced particle physics. I grasped that the planet's magnetosphere interferes with obtaining readings on the Orb. He is not sure why, and he's mired in his usual funk about it. I can commiserate with him. One more challenge to his intellect, one more question unanswered."

"At least he spoke with you."

"*At me* is a better description."

"Where does that leave you?"

"A long way from home."

"You're not giving up?"

"You know better. Besides, I have a secret weapon."

"Namely?"

"Paul. Do I have to tell you how smart he is?"

"No."

"I'll tell you anyway. In some ways, smarter than Larry. His approach is just low key. I can't tell you how often he's had a clarifying insight that helped put me on the right path. But what about you? Are you as pessimistic about communicating as you sounded?"

"Depends on my mood. I may have exaggerated humanity's failure to communicate with other species." I smiled. "And there is Angie."

"Maybe we both overstated the problem. Consider the silkworm moth I alluded to the other day. A few years ago, I became fascinated with the creature. Did you know the male moth can detect one pheromone molecule per hundred quadrillion air molecules and then triangulate to find the source? From ten kilometers away. Pretty amazing. Here's something more amazing: Humans have developed the means to send a perfectly accurate virtual image thirty thousand times as far in one second. Humans have either found a substitute or copied and improved almost any form of communication in nature."

"Maybe the point isn't just the type and speed of the message, but what we do with the information when we get it." I pointed to my head. "We're still limited by what's in here."

"Yes, but do you know what Paul would say?"

"I have a pretty good idea…"

"We're overthinking the problem."

"Maybe *you* are. I've seldom been accused of overthinking anything." There were notable exceptions, I thought to myself.

"I accuse you now," Diana said. It took me a second to see she wanted to goad me into talking about Kelly. It worked.

"I'll tell you what I told the commander. This adventure is a way of stepping outside the confines of the box I put myself in. Maybe I haven't stepped outside, but it's grown larger."

"Large enough to let someone wriggle in there with you?"

"I'm still in the process of overthinking that."

"Less thinking, more feeling."

I looked again toward the ocean, the sun's glare partially blinding my view. Between me and the water was the ship. Not far away was the rest of the crew, working their experiments. I heard Angie bark once or twice, her paws in the water, standing on one of the small stone slabs that inclined into the ocean. Hovering out on that ocean, closer to shore than when I last looked, were several Orbs. A large one appeared unusually close, which is why Angie had barked.

"My pooch needs dinner," I said and headed away.

In the time it took to utter those words, the Orb had moved next to Angie, towering over her, intention unknown.

Concerned for her safety, I broke into a run. Unafraid, she stood still, only her short tail vibrating in excitement. I called out, "Angie, come!" and again, louder, "Angie, come!"—but to no avail. She stood transfixed.

What transpired next sent a surge of adrenaline through me.

I heard a small yelp, though not an expression of pain, and in one swift motion, Angie was utterly enveloped within the Orb, passing through its solid surface with no more difficulty than putting your hand into the ocean! As she disappeared from view, I reflexively yelled, "Angie!" while continuing to run, intent on rescuing her. I'd use my body as a weapon, hurling myself full force against the surface of the Orb, disregarding whatever perilous consequences might ensue. Would I, too, be trapped inside?

As I ran past *Desio*, I caught Thompson out of the corner of my eye, rapidly closing the gap between us. I assumed he was coming to my assistance. He was yelling, "Somebody throw something!"

The next instant, a second shout came from behind me— "Kyle! Stop!"—and suddenly, inexplicably, I stumbled and fell, sent sprawling face forward onto the hard stone. Frantic, trying to rise, I discovered I was prevented by Thompson pinning me down, his full weight on my back. Half-crazed, I desperately struggled to free myself, fighting against his superior position and forcing him to use all his strength to keep me down. He won out, even as I resorted to yelling, "Get off me, you fucking bastard!" my chin scraping the rough ground in the process.

"Wait, damn you!" I heard in return, but the command, uttered by a voice stretched thin with exertion and anxiety, only incited me to renew my futile struggle. In the end, I remained helpless, forced to watch as the solitary Orb threatened the life of my little dog.

There was a moment of complete silence. Then, exploding from within, the Orb's surface erupted into a shimmering tapestry of sparkling silver flecks alternating with multicolored, ribbon-like bands that fluctuated in width as they traveled longitudinally. Each band flowed in opposition to the next, causing them to interlace or pool into spiraling eddies. The closest analogy to this colorful spectacle, Jupiter's atmosphere seen outbound from Earth, was a poor comparison rendered wholly inadequate by what happened next. The entire Orb began vibrating like a struck gong, then faster, like the plucked strings of a violin, the motion sending concentric ripples radiating outward that (Could it be?) were absorbed by other Orbs in the group!

In those few seconds, as all this unraveled, the situation became too much for Kelly to bear without intervening. She would have, too, except that as she advanced, brandishing a tent pole as a makeshift weapon, the Orb, still quivering, still in full display, spontaneously and entirely of its own accord, retreated oceanward, leaving Angie, from all appearances, completely unscathed!

Only then did Thompson agree to release me, cautiously retreating two steps backward, surmising that my late liberation might motivate me to swing at him. I wasn't that foolish, but quickly retrieving Angie, I shot him a look of contempt, which, judging by his pained expression, distressed him more.

I was on my feet, bruised and scraped from my hard fall. Angie spotted me and, bursting with unbridled joy, came running. Together with Kelly, Paul, and Diana, we crouched to welcome her with affection. It was impossible to tell if she was excited from the attention we lavished or contact with the Orb, but her happiness was contagious. For a brief moment, the problems confronting us faded into the background.

In that background, watching quietly, stood Melhaus and Thompson. And beyond them, the Orb.

"They may initiate even more threatening action against us," Melhaus remarked.

Thompson said nothing in response. Meanwhile, the retreating entity, its vibrations and colors fading, rejoined the others.

"What the hell just happened!?" Diana exclaimed.

"Can what happened... happen?" Paul added, visibly stunned.

I paid little attention. My concern was for Angie. Had the contact affected her in any way?

"She *appears* unharmed," I said to Kelly as we knelt to examine her together. I winced as my knees, scraped raw from my fall, touched the stone.

"Your injuries need treatment," Kelly remarked, but she stayed beside me to perform a cursory physical examination of Angie for signs of trauma.

"Nothing presents itself," she advised. "No broken bones, no evidence of tenderness or pain. I can do more inside the ship. Let's go."

"In a moment, Doctor," Thompson said, stepping forward. "If you please."

"What do you have in mind?" I said, more as an accusation than an inquiry.

"You've taught Angie a few commands, right?" Thompson said, ignoring my hostile attitude. "Run through some of them. Let's see how well she does."

The request was sensible. Angie was a clever dog; during the last few years, she learned verbal commands such as sit, paw, come, roll over, and play dead. I had devised a few more challenges, such as retrieving hidden objects. I went through several of them, which she performed flawlessly.

"She did exceptionally well," Thompson commented, looking to me for confirmation.

"Never better," I responded. It was a poor choice of words. I received five inquisitive stares.

"Better than ever?" Paul asked.

"A little faster. But she's pretty wound up."

More stares.

"May I?" Paul inquired.

"Be my guest," I said.

"Angie, bark!"

"I didn't teach her that," I said, frowning.

"I know," Paul said, looking down, waiting.

Angie looked up at him, happy, tail vibrating. And quiet.

"Damn," Paul said, laughing.

"Yeah, damn," echoed Diana.

"Satisfied?" I asked Thompson.

"Yes," he answered, then to Kelly, "How long do you need to dress Kyle's wounds?"

"Ten minutes."

"Meeting, everyone, in twenty." Thompson paused. "Hopefully before something else happens."

Paul and Diana walked in as Kelly was treating my superficial injuries in the exam room.

"So when are you going to apologize to Thompson?" Diana asked me.

"What the hell for?" I snapped back, aggravated.

"For giving him shit when he did what anybody in his position would have done."

"Screw that. He practically threw Angie to the wolves."

"You prefer that he had a double standard? Did you forget what he said when Larry wanted to place himself at risk? The commander has to make tough decisions based on the good of all."

"I was under the impression Angie was considered an important member of the crew. She's boosted morale and alerted us to the Orbs' presence. Hell, she probably just made first contact. Aren't we supposed to watch out for each other?"

"You think Thompson hasn't considered her worth?"

"Dispassionately, maybe. As a valuable but expendable asset. Hard to judge otherwise based on what just happened."

"You're wrong. Let me tell you a story to set you straight. Think back to several months ago when you formally requested that Angie be part of the ship's roster. Do you recall what happened?"

"They took a couple of days to decide, but they caved."

"Do you have any idea why?"

"I told them where she goes, I go."

"And you were both going nowhere if not for Thompson."

"News to me," I said, staring at Diana in disbelief. "Care to explain?"

"We were all granted permission to bring a few personal objects onboard. Angie, however, was quite another matter— the microbial problem, food and water requirements, the additional waste products—it just wasn't going to happen.

When Thompson was apprised of CSA's decision, he put his ass on the line by intervening on your... no, yours *and* Angie's behalf, by personally arguing your case. When they refused to budge, the commander said losing you was unacceptable, claiming that your alternate was insufficiently trained and, under the circumstances, would be forced to reconsider his participation in the mission. Everyone realized your alternate was up to speed. Thompson saying otherwise, and the threat he made, gave the Committee justification to reverse their decision without losing face."

"Shit."

"Yeah, shit," Diana echoed.

"Why was this kept from me?"

"Hard to tell. One possibility is that Thompson didn't want you, or any crewmember for that matter, to set themself above anyone else. Hell, I only found out by accident. A snippet of conversation overheard in a hallway."

"I bet."

"OK, maybe I lingered a little longer than necessary. But what I heard, I kept to myself."

"And I shall do the same."

I looked at Kelly, who had finished treating my scrapes. "Looks like I have a wound to mend," I said.

She nodded in agreement.

Thompson would have been disappointed if I had made my apology too sappy. No sense lying to him either. "I respect what you did," I said. "I'll show you even more respect if we're confronted with a similar situation and you try again to stop me."

"You're a hard man to pin down," he answered, pleased. But, as we took our places at the table, I noticed he was slightly favoring his right shoulder, in all likelihood having wrenched it tackling me and trying to keep me down. Kelly took note, too. She'd insist he take treatment after the meeting.

"If you hadn't been so upset," Paul said to me, "you could have passed off what happened with Angie as your idea on how to open communication with the Orb."

Thompson jumped on the remark. "Is that your take on what happened?" he asked.

"Yes," Paul answered quickly.

"Why?"

"Thirty minutes ago, a weak but defensible argument could have been made that Orb movements are unmotivated. No longer. There is a virtual certainty that the entity wanted to make contact with Angie. During the contact, something indefinable passed between them. I'm unable to say more."

"Diana?" Thompson said, asking for her opinion. She, too, answered with conviction.

"On two occasions, the Orb have displayed the most stunning colors I have ever seen. It closely resembles how an octopus shows emotion by triggering chromatophore cells. I believe the entity can experience something akin to excitement. I am less certain to what extent Angie experienced similar sensations. She appeared happy and excited, but then again, she usually is."

"Anybody disagree?" Thompson asked.

There were no takers. We did not presume Dr. Melhaus agreed.

"Let's get into particulars then," Thompson said. "Paul, did the cameras capture any of what happened?"

"Unfortunately, no. The activity was outside the field of view."

"Larry, one of the more difficult questions falls within your expertise. You've anticipated it, I presume?"

"Of course. Elementary particles can pass through matter. If you ask how the Orb accomplished this remarkable phenomenon, add it to the growing list of questions posed to me while disallowing the means of finding answers."

"Let's not go there again," Thompson cautioned.

"The entity manipulates matter! Has it not dawned on any of you," Melhaus uttered, his face flushing red, a throbbing temple vein betraying his repressed anger, "that I am striving to connect seemingly unrelated phenomena into one construct that may promote physics a hundred years?!"

"Dr. Melhaus," Thompson responded, "it is true we may not have appreciated the magnitude of the problems you are working on. How could we since you are describing it to us for the first time and we, in kind, are preoccupied with groundbreaking research in our respective fields? So I ask: Do you have something definitive to propose?"

Melhaus had his response already scripted. "Attach a minicam and microsensors to the dog."

"You mean to use Angie as bait?" I said, more than a little surprised by the suggestion. I girded myself for yet another conversation doomed to have an unhappy conclusion.

"It wouldn't be the first time an animal had been used to advance science," Melhaus insisted.

"Larry, didn't I overhear you say to the commander— what was it exactly?—something to the effect that the Orb may take more threatening actions?"

"All the more reason to acquire additional information concerning them."

"And if the Orb feel threatened by the instrumentation?" (To keep the peace, I choose not to mention Melhaus's belief that the Orb were responsible for *Ixodes'* demise.)

"And so you refuse?"

197

"I didn't say either way. I want to give the idea some consideration." I glanced at my crewmates. They remained noncommittal, in effect leaving the decision up to me. There was only Thompson's opinion to worry about. Melhaus, increasingly exasperated, turned to him.

"I'm requesting that you order Mr. Lorenzo to comply."

"I shall not do so," Thompson said flatly.

"Your justification?"

"Angie is not property, and we should not be guilty of treating her as such. The bond between her, Kyle, and others in the crew has grown strong for a reason. The world I want to live in requires respecting this. I suggest we all pause before what is important races us by."

Thompson never stood up in the middle of a crew meeting, but he did so now, stepping away from the table, searching out to sea with a stern, steady gaze. In the stillness the Orb hovered gracefully, as if waiting for what he had to say. Beyond them, countless more. Further on, nearly impossible to conceptualize, billions of galaxies spinning through the infinity of space.

"Life drawn to life," Thompson said, his back to us, his voice so low I thought he momentarily forgot we were present. I had the feeling the short distance from us gave him the perspective he seemed to need.

A few long seconds later, he returned to us. "We've been ignoring one fundamental question. Why did the Orb single out Angie? Why not one of us? The opportunity was there. Every time we were in the water."

To me, the reasons were apparent. "Angie acknowledged the entity's presence before we did, and they don't need to wade through as many layers of bullshit to get through to her. She's better adjusted than we are." I knew my next remark would not go over well. "Don't you see the humor, the cosmic irony, if the Orb viewed Angie as the higher life form?"

"More Kylesqian logic," Melhaus said, seething but not raising his voice.

"I'll take that as a compliment. Listen, I'm not predisposed to your idea, but I haven't decided. Can't you accept that for now?"

"Four days," Melhaus said, scowling, calling attention to our time left on the planet. "You will be held accountable."

"Time is one thing that has never been on our side," Thompson responded, addressing us all. "This morning, you were asked to develop a plan to communicate with the entity. Consider the request retracted. Continue to collect data and record observations. Come to me with ideas if you have any. If none, fine. I can ask no more, no less."

"May I inquire," Kelly said, taken aback, "why the sudden change of heart?"

"What happened to Angie is a game-changer. The Orbs were telling us something. Our erratic behavior told me the rest. The stress of trying to find the solution to so many riddles in so short a time has become counterproductive. Individually and collectively, we should take a deep breath, step back, and relax. It's within us to do so. Make it your choice." Thompson concluded the meeting and headed off with Kelly to have his shoulder treated.

Paul and Diana continued their research.

Before Melhaus and I went our separate ways, he said the following, for my ears only: "And you still maintain that you're not opposed to science?"

ORB

OceanOrb

DAY SIX.

Angie has shown no signs of being worse off from her contact with the entity. With her moist nose constantly sniffing at the water's edge and her puffy tail vibrating expectantly, she appears ready and eager for a repeat encounter.

What occurred inside the entity is open to conjecture. Neither party was talking in any way we could comprehend, but speculation became fair game for discussion. The most sensible explanation was that Angie became excited from being subjected to the overwhelming colors and physical stimulations. That failed to explain what prompted the encounter and what caused the Orb to respond to Angie in the manner in which it did. I was the most vocal in insisting that something was shared and that some form of communication was involved.

Whatever the nature of the encounter, and as non-threatening as it seemed to Angie, I nevertheless decided against allowing an encore performance—at least not until we had a better understanding of the entity. My misgivings partly stemmed from being wary of the monitoring conditions Melhaus had proposed. I didn't consider it wise to resurrect the demise of *Ixodes*; instead, I voiced misgivings about human technology interfacing with the Orb. Thompson did not take issue with my decision.

A mid-afternoon downpour was followed by the sun's emergence from behind a retreating layer of fast-moving, low-hanging clouds. The temperature rapidly rose to a sultry thirty-two degrees.

The crew had worked several hours straight without taking more than a five-minute lunch break, so when the commander recommended we visit the cove, emphasizing that the interlude would clear our minds, he received no argument. When we tried to coax him into coming with us, he demurred, promising to break up his work regimen with several short, cooling plunges in the waters lapping onto the Square. Except for several short excursions to his spires, he preferred keeping the Orb, *Desio*, and Melhaus in sight.

As for the sullen scientist (my covert name for Melhaus), he maintained his adamant refusal to dip even a proverbial toe in the refreshing waters of the planet. Attempting civility, we each tried to convince him to join us. Paul received the politest response: "I have no time to waste."

And so the five of us (Angie included) sprinted to the cove and dove in. When the laughter and ensuing splash fight ended, Kelly came up behind me, draping her arms around my neck and clasping her legs around my waist. Wet skin pressed tightly to mine, I carried her through the water onto the shore, where I gently laid her down, drinking in the sight of her, the sparkling water, the sun and sky, until a rush, a feeling of euphoria, passed clean through me. As I leaned over, she stared up at me and said, "These are moments that stay with you for a lifetime."

"I could stay with you a lifetime." The words, without any thinking, had come pouring out of me.

"Are you worried you said too much?" Kelly responded. She put a finger to my lips. "No, don't answer... but don't be."

Paul and Diana joined us. With Angie, we lay side by side on a blanket-covered rock, basking in the blue-tinged light of the sun. We had precious little time before heading back.

"There is something intrusive about the summer sun," I said. "The intense brightness seeps deep into you, then draws you out into the world."

"The ever-contemplative Kyle," Diana observed.

"A clumsy way to start a conversation," I said, somewhat apologetically.

"No, I like it," Diana remarked. "Appreciably, we *are* drawn out. Being sixty percent water, a part of us evaporates into the sky."

I reclined and let Kelly lean back into my chest and the crook of my arm.

"Sixty percent?" I inquired. "That helps explain why I've always had an affinity for the water."

"What about the other forty percent?" Paul said distractedly. He was lying on his stomach at the edge of the slab, one arm lazily moving back and forth in the water. He appeared fascinated by the subtle colors that occasionally appeared in the swirls he produced.

"The other forty percent," I said, "is along for the joyride."

"Tell me, Paul," Kelly said, wiping away the beads of sweat on her upper lip, "does the temperature get much hotter?" When Paul failed to respond, the question was repeated. When he still didn't answer, Kelly simply said, "Paul?"

"His mind went elsewhere," Diana noted. Curious as to why, she sat up to study him. Under the weight of our stares, he finally responded to Kelly's inquiry.

"Sorry. I'm listening. More than you know, I am listening. For some reason, the conversation reminded me of one Kyle and I had. In any event, a day like today is about as hot as it gets. The ocean moderates the temperature nicely."

"And yet, fifteen months from now, there'll be several meters of ice," Diana said, still watching Paul. "I wonder where the Orb go during the winter?"

"A warmer planet?" I said, earning a good-natured elbowing from Kelly.

"No, really," Diana persisted. "There are *millions* of them. Perhaps they stay submerged, keeping far below the ice. Another indication of how intimate their connection to the ocean must be…"

Diana was interrupted by the sudden motion of Paul standing upright, his eyes wide in astonishment, fixated on the horizon. Startled, expecting to see advancing Orbs, we followed his gaze outward.

What we saw, and for the last time, was only ocean.

"Can it be?" Paul whispered, nearly speechless, repeatedly shaking his head side to side to mean *no*, but really meaning *yes*. *But yes to what?*

"Paul, what is it?!" Diana entreated, attempting to coax him out of his reverie. He had her full attention. He had all our attention. Paul wasn't prone to false alarms.

"The ocean…" he stammered, "…the ocean *is* the Orb!"

The three of us exchanged confused glances. Diana came to understand first, eyes widening, jaw dropping open. Temporarily at a loss for words, she, too, began to shake her head.

"You understand?" Paul asked.

"Yes," she managed to reply, looking out over the water.

"Kyle," Paul said, giddy with exhilaration, striving to make me comprehend, "try to phrase it correctly…the Ocean is the Orb, the Ocean are the Orb, the Orb is an Ocean…"

The wave of comprehension that smacked into Paul, then Diana, washed over me. I grasped what Paul had accomplished: the complex made beautiful and simple. But was it true? I looked to Kelly, seeing her eyes welling with tears. As she blinked in disbelief, one drop of water fell onto her cheek, telling me that she, too, understood. "Kyle," she said in a gasp, "your name for the planet. It's as if you suspected all along."

I could not claim this was so. No, this was Paul's giant leap, his vision, and we were enthralled by it, the three of us standing beside him, perched at the end of the slab, seeing the ocean as if for the first time.

Ocean? How crudely expressed, for this vast *body* was no more defined as water than you and I. No, an entity, a life form, or a collective organism were more apt descriptions, even as I sought in vain for a better one, for a word yet to be devised.

As I searched for mere words, the scientist in Diana excitedly sought proof, haphazardly retracing the steps Paul had likely taken to arrive at his brilliant insight.

"So much now seems to fit together. It makes perfect sense. There's some form of intimate relationship where individual Orbs—they're not exactly individual, are they?—are bound to the main body, the ocean. I must refrain from calling it an ocean. There's the intimacy of Orb-water contact we've never seen broken. The nearly identical chemical composition between the two. The confusing magnetic readings. The like colors, yes, the colors, swirls, and ripples—you were fascinated with them, weren't you, my love? And what about the excitement Angie felt after contact and, lesser, the way *we* feel in the water? *Water?* Damn, I did it again. Kyle, can we say the OceanOrb? Let's, thát'll work for now. But how is the perfect roundness explained? And where does the phytoplankton fit in? Are we assuming too much? There are still loose ends..."

We let Diana's stream of consciousness wander an irregular course until it slowed enough for her to say, "We must immediately inform Thompson. And Larry! *He* couldn't make the connection. I can't wait to see his face, Paul. To see the reaction to your doing what he couldn't!"

"The credit, and it remains to be proved any is due, is by no means mine alone," Paul said, gently admonishing her. "Consciously or not, you are all partly responsible; you led me to this conclusion."

I wasn't sure what he meant, but he was sincere—anyone else I'd have accused of false modesty.

"The implications inherent in *your* insight," Diana insisted, "are mind-boggling. Forget I once said tens of millions of years. The Orb and OceanOrb may be *hundreds* of millions of years old. Perhaps nearly as old as the planet itself. Try to wrap your mind around *that* concept."

"I, for one," Kelly said, "am still working on the fact that we swam in it! To it, we're the size of a bacterium. Less; a virus. What does that mean?"

"What does it mean to us?" Diana asked. "Maybe nothing more than a slight feeling of euphoria."

"And to the OceanOrb?"

"It's too premature to say. Maybe it's largely unaware of our presence. Or maybe we inadvertently established a rudimentary form of communication."

"The Orb was pretty stimulated by contact with Angie," I reminded.

"True," Diana said. "Responsiveness may be intensified by contact with individual Orbs. Maybe the OceanOrb spins off individuals for that very reason, to become semi-autonomous. They can sensate more intensely when they are orders of magnitude less in volume than the parent entity. I didn't express that well. Let me try again in reverse. When we are in the ocean, the Orb may experience us in a diluted way."

"Do you think all the individuals emerge from the OceanOrb?" Kelly asked.

"That's one of two possibilities I can imagine," Paul ventured. "The other is that they are the progeny of larger individual Orbs. If either or both of those possibilities are true, it helps confirm our impression that the emergence of the smaller Orbs generated excitement."

"And are the individuals ever reabsorbed?" I asked.

"Remains to be observed."

"How do individuals die?" Kelly asked.

"Do they die?" Diana wondered. "If the individuals are reabsorbed, then death, at least as we define it, seems uncertain."

"Incredible," Kelly responded.

"Yeah."

"We've repeatedly observed them banding together," I commented, formulating an idea.

"Yes, there's that," Diana added. "And they appear to congregate in groups of twelve, and please don't ask me why."

"They are, in some capacity, behaving as a society?"

"In my estimation, yes," Diana responded.

"Analogous," I continued, "to humans procreating, establishing family and social groups?"

"The comparison may be apt," Diana responded. "Although Orb society is, as Thompson suggested, far more homogeneous than ours."

"Meaning," I said, "that the Orb, untold millions of them, can conceivably communicate instantaneously among themselves."

"Logic would dictate so," Diana agreed. "The individual Orbs may respond to us instantly and in unison if they choose to. Given their amazing interconnectivity, we should consider the likelihood of a heightened intimacy, a shared understanding we could only dream of."

"Therefore," Kelly said, "we should exercise caution in dealing with them."

"I agree," Paul said. "This may provide our first clue into their mindset, one that we might cultivate, or attempt to emulate, to get through to them… or it."

"I have to ask," Kelly began, "does any of this increase the chance *Ixodes* was destroyed by, or should I say, within the Orb?"

"Do you mean to suggest that Larry could have been right?" Diana asked, holding back her annoyance.

"No. Yes. Certainly a greater chance of that," Kelly responded. "I'm not going to be his defender, but maybe, just maybe, the sub was considered a viral threat."

"There's something to that," Paul said. "Before the arrival of humans, the Orb may have never come into contact with technology. It may be more alien to them than we are. On the other hand, given their perfect shape, metalloid composition, and inexplicable movement, I could just as easily say they have incorporated a technology far superior to ours into themselves. After all, they've had a few hundred million years to do so."

"The holy grail of technology," I protested. "An assumption we humans like to cultivate, that higher life forms unavoidably develop sophisticated technology. Not necessarily so, as seems to be the case here, when there is no compelling reason to."

"Or maybe they can't," Diana said, holding up one hand and flexing her fingers. "No opposable thumbs."

"You keep a straight face," I said, smiling. "Haven't decided if you're joking?"

"No."

"Without technology, they can't explore other worlds," Kelly remarked.

"When you have one hundred million years to wait," I replied, "why not sit back and let everybody come to you?"

"We can be welcomed either as visitors or intruders," Paul said. "Other than the mystery of what happened to *Ixodes*, we seem to be well tolerated. By implementing Thompson's idea, we were allowed contact, briefly, with two individual Orbs. All of us except Larry have physically entered the OceanOrb, apparently with no ill effects. Quite the contrary. Pretty considerate of them, no?"

"And, still," Diana said, "Angie appears to have had the most significant contact. Why? Why? Why?"

"For every scientific discovery, one question resolved, two more—"

Interrupting Paul were three piercing notes from his communicator. The tonal pattern signaled high priority.

"Put me on speaker," we heard Thompson say with uncharacteristic urgency.

"Go ahead," Paul responded.

"Return immediately. If for any reason I don't meet you at the edge of the Square, don't approach any closer than one hundred meters of *Desio*."

"Why?" Paul asked, grabbing his clothes.

"Melhaus has commandeered the ship."

Thompson let the ramifications of his message sink in. Diana reacted first.

"What in hell does he possibly hope to accomplish?!" she shouted. "Has he gone *completely* insane?!"

"What he has done is reconfigured the turret laser and threatens to burn a hole clear through anyone approaching."

"Can he do what he says?" I asked.

"The laser is quite lethal. Better keep Angie on a short leash when you approach."

"We're on our way," Paul said.

We dressed quickly. Collecting our gear, we exchanged worried glances, hoping to find some measure of assurance in each other, wondering what was in store for us, fearful that our lives were in the hands of a person we thought we had come to know but who was a total stranger in many ways.

During the trip back, the feeling that we could have done more to prevent Melhaus's breakdown was replaced by anger that one man, one ego, could hold us hostage. I returned to where I typically sought refuge, the lonely inner sanctum where my justification for avoiding people resided.

I couldn't reside there long, for a contradictory thought intruded. An idea of how to communicate with the Orb. That, unencumbered by words, Kelly was best suited to give voice to what humanity can aspire to—simply through the unambiguous harmonic vibrations and evocative chords of her violin.

A part of me said the idea was misleading when, drowning out all we might represent individually and collectively as a species, might be replaced by the strident sound of one of our own, at his worst moment, bringing to the fore *our* worst moments.

Then I realized how we live most of our lives between these extremes.

I told Kelly everything privately, and she implored me to share my idea with Paul and Diana. I did so, ignoring misgivings about the timing, for Kelly had convinced me there might not be a better opportunity.

The idea was well received, with Diana proclaiming that Kelly would soon play on a high promontory.

High enough, quite literally, for a whole world to hear.

And to feel.

Larry Melhaus

APPROACHING THE EDGE of the Square, I gathered Angie in my arms. Up ahead was Thompson, waiting for us, as promised.

"*What the hell?*" Paul said, addressing the mission leader.

"Yeah, what the bloody hell," Thompson acknowledged.

"I'm going to punch that son-of-a-bitch's lights out," Diana declared, balling her hand into a fist, then waiting to be chastised. Thompson did just the opposite.

"Diana, when the opportunity presents itself, I'm going to let you."

That remark, together with Thompson's assured manner, helped to break the palpable tension. Despite all his concerns, there was something else Thompson did that I was particularly appreciative of, and deserves mentioning. He had found the time to take a cord from the tent covering his geology equipment and used it to fashion a serviceable leash and slip collar.

"Something for Angie," he said, handing it to me. "To keep her out of trouble."

Placing one looped end onto Angie's neck and securing the leash around my wrist was all that was necessary. I thanked him by paraphrasing his words from a week ago.

"As you've said, nothing gets by you."

"Not exactly," he replied, regarding *Desio* in the distance. "Something apparently did."

That statement—more of a challenge to himself—was just like Thompson. He was shouldering the blame for this mess, just as he would view the problem as an affront to his leadership to be faced head-on. He was two pawns down to someone the world had designated a genius. But Thompson was not the type to be overawed by Melhaus's intellect. Brilliant in his own right, he had all the attributes that make a good leader, including quiet self-assurance. In large measure, his self-confidence was infectious. We followed him to a cluster of rocks to discuss the worrisome development.

"Melhaus used the opportunity of my brief absence to his best advantage," Thompson began. "I was collecting a core sample among the spires, gone ten minutes tops, when I heard the echoes of an unmistakable sound. Returning, my fears were confirmed. He was at the ready, standing in front of *Desio* with a controller in hand, loudly shouting that if I approached much closer, it would be at my peril. Half-seriously, I yelled back, "Just how close is that, Dr. Melhaus?" He responded by redirecting my attention to your lab station, Diana, which you had set up nearer to the ocean and the ship."

The damage was visible even at a distance. All that was once Diana's science equipment was now metal, glass, and plastics fused into twisted and blackened shapes. I watched her eyes harden and her body stiffen. She said nothing, which was more disturbing than if she had screamed in anger. Paul, sitting nearby, placed one hand over hers.

"I'm sorry, Diana," said Thompson. "I trust a good deal of your research has already been stored?"

"And *where* is it stored?" she said bitterly. The answer, of course, was *Desio*, where Dr. Melhaus held sway over the invaluable data from lab tests, experiments, and samples that the scientists meticulously archived for future study.

"For the moment," Thompson responded, "let's not presume he'll go into the system files and start selectively deleting. There isn't any reason."

"Reason? *Reason?*!" Diana snickered, refusing to accept any association between the word and Melhaus's actions.

"Despite his deranged state of mind, he is planning well ahead. Judge for yourself." Thompson reached into his shirt pocket and pulled out a device the size of a pack of cards, only half as thin. "Kyle's not the only one who carries a voice recorder. Returning from the spires, I recalled that I had the one I routinely use for field observations. I activated it without Larry noticing. Here's our brief exchange, recorded just after the damage to the biology station."

Thompson studied our reactions as the encounter with Melhaus played out:

"I'm a bit surprised, Larry, that you, of all people, would show so little respect for another scientist's research."

"I have paid the same respect as was shown to mine."

"And if I choose to ignore your advice and decide to approach?"

215

"Go ahead. If you're able to deflect three point two megawatts of laser."

"Larry, we both know the laser wasn't designed to—"

"Adjusting the laser to auto-activate on human heat and motion signatures was child's play. The manual control is in my hand. I accomplished this right under Kyle's nose, only he was too stupid to realize."

"When did you attempt this?"

"Attempt?! Underestimating me still. Three days ago. When I modified the spectroscopy equipment. It became clear then that every one of my recommendations would be ignored, and I was to be blamed for what happened to Ixodes."

There were several seconds of silence before the resumption of Thompson's voice:

"Whatever mischief you're contemplating is a grave mistake. You will regret this, I can assure you."

"You can cut the bullshit. Now call back the others from their playtime so I can make my intentions plain. I won't waste time repeating myself."

Thompson turned off the recorder and slipped it back into his pocket. He turned to Kelly. "That's all of it. Melhaus hasn't exited *Desio* since."

"He sounded pretty cogent," she said. "I wish I had been better able to diagnose the severity of his illness. To predict this behavior."

"Who could have predicted this? You and Kyle did well enough. Recommendations?"

"He harbors a deep resentment toward us, yet has all his mental faculties. There's still a chance he can be reasoned with. That's not very helpful, I'm afraid."

"I was in my cabin, writing, when Melhaus was reconfiguring the spectroscopic equipment," I said. "He must have used the opportunity to tamper with the laser. Once or twice, the ship's lights flickered. At the time, I figured that was normal."

"Anything else?" Thompson asked.

There was. "Won't make you feel any better," I said.

"Let's hear it anyway."

"Leaving my cabin, I ran into him coming down from the command and control compartment. He had an uneasy look, which I attributed to his usual impatience with my casual manner. I didn't think much about it. It was three days ago. Before our concerns about him intensified. Sorry. I should have put two and two together."

"Leave the math to us scientists," Thompson remarked. "And don't kick yourself about it."

"No, let me do it," Diana said.

"So Melhaus can follow through with his threats?" Paul asked, seeking confirmation from Thompson.

"The laser was strategically mounted on a turret and designed to rotate three hundred sixty degrees, so all possible approaches are covered. If he's reprogrammed acquisition and firing parameters, our body heat, motion, or a combination of both will instantaneously signal the weapon to fire. Once fired—unless he's altered this too—a five-centimeter diameter laser beam will activate for several seconds. Whatever or whoever is unlucky enough to be in its path will be sporting a hole or have been sliced through. The weapon is capable of burning a cavity ten centimeters deep into the toughest metal alloys. So, yes, he can keep us at bay."

"Indefinitely?" Paul asked.

"Long enough," Thompson responded, although I detected in his voice, or imagined, the slightest trace of hesitation. Whatever I heard was insufficient for me to pursue.

"You haven't explained how he could stand outside mouthing off," Diana said.

"That small, handheld device he was holding. I'm not sure how it works, but if I had to guess, it was programmed with a second, overriding set of acquisition parameters."

"Why doesn't he avoid us altogether?" Kelly asked. "He's capable of solo piloting to another island."

"Four possible reasons," Thompson said. "The nearby islands have fewer viable landing sites; why would he leave a location where the Orb has acknowledged our presence; he has some need of our assistance; and, lastly, this…"

Thompson unfastened the flap of a security pouch on his belt. Reaching in, he took out and held up an object roughly the size and shape of a walnut for our inspection.

"Without this reactor shunt, he's going nowhere. I'm not sure he's aware of that just yet."

"Oh, I *so* hope he isn't," Diana said with great pleasure, "because I'd sure like to be around when he finds out. But when did you…?"

"Two days ago," Thompson replied, "when I had misgivings about his mental state. I also entered numerous programming codes to alert me if unauthorized alterations were made to *Desio's* operating systems—including the laser. Unfortunately, at some point in advance of my actions, Melhaus wrote and installed ghost programming that prevented me from realizing I was wasting my time. His programming skills are more sophisticated than mine."

"His programming skills are par excellence," Paul commented.

"But he's not well-versed in engineering," Thompson added, returning the shunt to his belt pouch.

218

"So, two possibilities lie ahead," I ventured. The two I assumed all along. "We all leave this planet together, or we leave it not at all."

I couldn't tell if Thompson agreed with my simplified assessment of our situation. Again, I had a vague feeling he was holding something back. Diana, however, did not hold back.

"And what the hell are we supposed to do in the meantime?" she blurted out. "Eat rocks?"

"We need to hear what Larry has to say," Kelly said. "Isn't he waiting for us?"

"Let him wait," Thompson said. "If we jump when he tells us, he'll presume to tell us how high."

"There's something important that I think you should know first," Diana said. "Paul, tell him."

"Yes, of course," Paul replied. "We have come to the tentative conclusion that the entirety of the planet's ocean *is* the Orb and gives rise to millions of Orbs."

Spoken with his usual understated delivery and modesty, Paul summarized the available supporting evidence. Despite our grave situation, I enjoyed watching Thompson's face change from placid stoicism to bewilderment to comprehension and, lastly, to an expression of shock, or at least as close to that emotion as I'd likely ever see in him. His eyes were drawn to what used to be the ocean and to the Orbs serenely floating thereon.

"Don't let him try to fool you," Diana proudly informed Thompson. "The revelation is exclusively Paul's."

"And this occurred where?" Thompson, collecting himself, inquired of Paul.

"At the cove."

Where else, I thought, since it was evident we had just returned from there. Then I realized why Thompson wanted confirmation of the location. The time we spent at the cove relaxing or in contemplation, encouraged by him, was now justified a hundredfold.

"Beautiful work, Paul," Thompson said. "Well done, all of you."

"Can we go rub Melhaus's face in this?" Diana asked.

The commander had other ideas. "For the immediate future, we'll keep it from him."

"Why?" Diana complained.

"Any knowledge we possess, and he doesn't, may assist us somehow."

As if on cue, Melhaus exited *Desio*. "You don't want to keep me waiting any longer," he angrily shouted across the Square. "Not if you expect food and water."

"What the hell," Diana, teeth clenched, muttered under her breath. "He's treating us like animals in a zoo."

We approached the ship, keeping a prudent distance. Thompson positioned himself slightly ahead of us. He attempted to grab the initiative.

"We're all together, Larry. What do you have to say for yourself?"

"I see the dog's kept on leash," he observed, ignoring Thompson. "Still no ill effects from the encounter?"

I chose not to answer, fearing I'd worsen a bad situation. Melhaus, acting as if I had responded, said, "Very well. I will have use for her tomorrow."

"And what would that be?" Thompson demanded.

"In good time, in good time. And Kelly, have you nothing to say? Not peddling your pills today?"

"Maybe you've forgotten," Kelly responded, "that a laser stands between me and the drugs you need."

"That is an impediment," Melhaus affirmed, laughing. "Oh, yes, I shall share one other impediment with you. I destroyed a good deal of your pharmacopeia."

"Not *all*, I trust?" Kelly said, suppressing alarm.

"'Trust' is an interesting word coming from any of you."

"We're wasting our time here," Thompson said suddenly, turning his back on Melhaus to face us. My heart began to race, contemplating how the physicist might react.

I didn't have long to wait.

Faster than the eye could follow, *Desio's* turret rotated and emitted a streak of purple light that instantly intersected with Thompson's geology equipment. A blinding cascade of orange sparks radiated outward, followed by several rapid popping sounds as metal and glass components exploded and burned, sending black smoke skyward. Beneath a sagging equipment table, a molten patch of rock glowed deep red.

The purple light vanished as fast as it began, as did a low hum originating from the ship's interior.

The destruction was unnerving, but Thompson's face also had a resigned look of satisfaction. He had deliberately provoked Melhaus to discover the capabilities of the laser controller being held tightly in the physicist's hand.

"So, Larry," Thompson said, "your little toy works as advertised."

"Proven at the expense of your equipment," Melhaus responded.

"A small price to pay."

"The next price will be higher. You can't afford it."

"Harm any member of my crew," Thompson said flatly, "and chances are you'll never leave the planet."

"A strange threat considering the circumstances."

"Anyone of us, and that includes Angie," Thompson repeated. "You've been warned. Do not presume you can anticipate the outcome of your actions with absolute certainty."

"Empty talk," Melhaus said dismissively.

"No, Larry," Thompson said in a voice so low and sorrowful that only a fool would have completely misread his sincerity.

But Melhaus was unmoved, and judging him so, Thompson removed the reactor shunt from his belt and held it up for the physicist to see.

"The reactor shunt, Larry. Without it, *Desio* goes nowhere."

The effect of the pronouncement, a disturbingly shrill and forced laugh, was less than Thompson had hoped for.

"Ha! You still believe the future rotates around you or me?!" Melhaus said, wildly gesturing toward the distant Orb. "It's discovering what *they* are! There's nothing to lose." Entering *Desio*, the physicist turned back and said, "No, you will assist me tomorrow. Unable to leave the planet? If you fail me, we'll remain here until hell and the planet freeze over!"

In an uncharacteristic burst of anger, Paul shouted a warning after him. "Assist you?! Unlikely. You'll find us quite unwilling without water, food, and bedding."

The physicist paused momentarily, muttered something, and disappeared from view.

I looked at Thompson and, with an awkward attempt at humor, said, "That went well."

We crossed the Square to a secluded semicircle of boulders where Thompson spent nights gazing at the stars and sleeping. He had created a minicamp using a bedroll, a small table, a solar-powered lamp, and a few personal effects.

"Make ourselves at home?" Diana inquired, critically evaluating our accommodations for the evening, if not considerably longer.

"Right," Thompson replied, "help yourself to a cold one in the fridge."

"We may be the cold ones in the fridge," Paul said, picking up on the remark. "And it won't be imaginary."

Our sense of humor may have been intact, but we were avoiding the inevitable discussion, starting with the question, "What the hell do we do now?"

Diana met and held Thompson's eyes, giving her words a touching emphasis. "Your research. Your equipment. I am sorry, Bruce. Such an incredible waste."

"Diana," Thompson responded, "I have much of my research archived onboard *Desio*. I'm confident we'll recover the bulk of the rest. Want to know the worst of it?" He pointed to the enigmatic stone formations that had consumed much of his attention. "Unless I'm favored by one of Paul's insights, I may need to rely on whatever twisted logic Kyle might use to explain those spires."

"Rest easy," I said, "I don't have a credible explanation. *Yet*. Too many damn distractions."

What passed for idle conversation gave us time to regroup mentally and steady our nerves. Subtly, it brought us closer together, Thompson letting us ramble on and occasionally joining in. Over their polite objections, he convinced Diana and Paul to sit on his bedding while he found a less comfortable place on one of the boulders ringing our little enclave.

Kelly and I sat on the bare ground, counterbalancing each other by leaning back to back. Angie, still on the leash for safety, crawled onto my lap. Her body was facing forward, but she twisted her neck and head around to give me a pathetic look, and I realized it was well past the hour she expected to be fed. When her stare went ignored for several minutes, she began to whine softly, but she settled when I issued a "quiet" command. Soon enough, the rest of us would be hungry, too. Unlike Angie, however, we understood the reason why. Or did we, for how well did we understand what led to the mental decline of our fellow crewmate? Not sufficiently well, that was apparent.

Collectively and individually, however, we were not the type to let the universe just happen to us. This was especially true of Thompson. As darkness enveloped us, he said, not in an offhanded way, "Tomorrow, the sun will come up."

"I beg your pardon?" Diana said as if she hadn't heard him.

"Tomorrow, the sun will rise; of that, we can be reasonably sure. Since we are sure of one thing, we go about our days predisposed to seeking the same assurance, even when it does not exist, in all we see and do. That was our error when we expected rational behavior from our colleague. By trying to help him, he became a casualty of our better nature.

"His desire to find an answer to this planet's riddles has consumed him," Thompson continued. "Tomorrow, I anticipate he'll want to attach instrumentation to Angie and use her to draw the Orb closer. This is not acceptable to me. You understand the possible consequences of what Melhaus proposes? Are they permissible to you?"

"Yes," I said, stopping Thompson cold. I felt Kelly tense behind me.

"I appreciate the gesture," Thompson began, believing I had decided to offer up Angie. He was partially correct.

"There's a twist," I said.

"Namely?"

"I'll be holding her."

The remark caught everyone, including Thompson, off guard. "Say again?" he asked.

"I'll be holding Angie in my arms. You asked for ideas on communicating with the Orb. Well, that's mine. Is there a better way?"

Thompson took less time than I imagined to ponder the idea.

"I'll allow it," he said.

"No, Bruce!" Kelly exclaimed. "You can't!" She never expected my proposal (I should have warned her) or the Commander's response. Paul and Diana were about to join in with their own objections.

"Hold on," Thompson said. "Do any of you truly believe the offer will sate Melhaus? It will not. So I will permit you to suggest it to him with one non-negotiable condition. He must first relinquish control of *Desio*."

"But he doesn't trust us," I said. "He won't expect us to follow through."

"Nor do I trust him. The significant difference is that he has threatened us. I will not misjudge him twice."

"But if he agrees?" Kelly asked, standing in front of Thompson, still very much concerned. "I seem to remember you were the one trying to stop Kyle…"

"Since then, there have been two significant developments. We all agreed that Angie's contact left her completely unharmed. And by Paul's estimation, the five of us have, on multiple occasions, been enveloped in the Orb."

"It's not the same thing," Paul objected. "And I didn't intend what is unproven to justify what Kyle is suggesting."

"No, you didn't, but the idea is out there anyway. Do you foresee that great a risk?"

"What standard shall I apply?" Paul asked. "The risk is unquantifiable."

Thompson faced me.

"He's right, you know."

"He always is," I said. "Sure, I'll be taking a risk. We all took a risk when we boarded *Desio* three months ago. I'm asking to do this. Besides, as you've said, Larry may not agree to your condition."

"Neither may the Orb," Thompson said, then turned to the one person not heard from.

"Diana? What say you?"

"I'd do it myself if you'd let me."

Thompson glanced at Kelly, expecting further dissent. She looked worried but, seeing my resolve, remained silent.

"We'll float the idea to Melhaus," Thompson said, finalizing his decision.

Paul reluctantly came to accept my proposal and had one of his own.

"I'd like permission to discuss the Orb being one entity," he said. "Seeing the potential danger, Melhaus might reconsider whatever he is planning. There's little chance of turning him off the destructive path he's on, but I'd like to give it a try."

"Of course," Thompson responded. "If anyone can do it, it's you."

"Who are we fooling?" Diana said, irritated. "Larry won't accept any of this. Is there no way to circumvent the laser?"

"None I'm aware of," Thompson answered.

"What if we all simultaneously rush him?"

"You're fast, Diana, but not that fast. The turret servo operates magnetically and with blinding speed."

"We're at the mercy of a madman. What's 'Plan B'? There's *always* a 'Plan B.'"

"I was coming to that."

Thompson's face showed a pained expression reminiscent of one I noted after he hurt his shoulder. No, that was not quite it. The cause was something other than physical pain, something I couldn't put my finger on.

"I'll be back shortly," he said, quickly disappearing from view, leaving us wondering aloud where he was going and why. As we waited, Kelly activated the solar lamp, situated it centrally, and sat close beside Angie and me. The orange glow of the lamplight on our faces reminded me of a rare camping trip I went on as a boy and, rarer still, the campfire I enjoyed.

Back in the disappearing forests of Earth.

A distant memory in so many ways.

I would have to go back a thousand years more, tap into genetic memory, to conjure up anything resembling the next image: Thompson emerging out of the darkness, navigating a path through boulders to stand in the center of the enclave, his sturdy features set in relief by light and shadow, his weathered hands clutching a weapon. While I had no problem identifying the San bow, I had difficulty accepting the incongruity, the primitiveness.

What I alone immediately grasped was the weapon's potentially life-saving lethality.

I said—and instantly regretted— "Is *this* what you meant by 'our better nature'?" Then, quickly and contritely, "I'm sorry. The remark was uncalled for."

"No," said Thompson, visibly stung by my offhand comment. "I'd be disappointed if one of you hadn't said it."

Those few words measured the sum and substance of the man. More than anyone, I understood him by learning about his tragic encounter with the San.

There was, however, a lot more he'd need to explain to my crewmates. Diana would see to it that he did.

"The artifact from your cabin," she said, staring. "What do you possibly hope to accomplish with that relic?"

"I assure you, I know how to use it."

"Have you used it?"

"Yes. To hunt."

"You'd use it on Melhaus?"

"If I have to."

"Wait a minute!" Kelly said. "You apparently hid the bow. When? Why?"

"A few days ago. I'm not sure why. A feeling."

"A *feeling*? Diana said with strained humor. "Like, uh, maybe a feeling of hunger? Or, better yet, I feel like hunting today?"

I imagined that this remark, too, hurt Thompson.

"Larry was on a downhill slide," he said. Considering his intellect, I wanted a fallback position—something he'd never contemplate. Does that answer satisfy you? Possibly, it's true, I can't really say."

"You obviously don't want him to know you have this weapon," Kelly said. "He'd defend against it. What if he breaks into your cabin and sees it missing? If, like me, he believed the bow to be only ornamental, he'd still have to wonder why you took it down."

"I'm guessing it's the one item in my cabin he's paid no attention to. If he realizes it's gone, we're no worse off than if I hadn't removed it."

Kelly examined the unstrung bow and the quiver of animal hide secured lengthwise along its limb. She carefully withdrew one of the two wood arrows, its point expertly fashioned from bone. With Thompson watching, she used the meat of her thumb to test the point's sharpness. I couldn't read her expression in the darkness, but it prompted Thompson to say, "Kelly, I did my best. On two occasions warning him."

Kelly nodded. "I have limited resources to treat him," she said. "He very likely could die from loss of blood alone. You're aware of this?" Then, with compassion for what he might be compelled to do, "Sorry. I'd be remiss if I said nothing."

"The bow is not a sure thing," Thompson responded. "Far from it."

During the grilling of Thompson that followed, I kept quiet, preferring not to prolong a conversation I knew to be difficult for him. I waited for somebody to ask how he came into possession of the bow. That didn't happen, but an ill-timed remark must have evoked the painful memory of killing a man. It was said to Paul as he headed across the Square on the chance that Melhaus had left out food or bedding:

"Why not take the bow?" Diana asked. "Never mind. We're hunter-gatherers with nothing to hunt or gather."

Paul emerged from the darkness triumphantly holding one bedroll and four meal packets, which were insufficient for our needs, though more than expected.

Diana's explanation, the easiest to believe, was that Melhaus was responding to the last thing he heard from us, which was Paul's threat.

Paul objected, claiming that Melhaus's behavior was not always predictable and not exclusively mean-spirited. Moreover, some of the contentious points the physicist had raised since touching down on the planet contained a modicum of truth, like it or not.

I wondered aloud if our opinions were more often driven by our personalities rather than facts, and what that might say about objective reality.

It was an admittedly dangerous idea to suggest to scientists. Thompson would have none of the conversation. Adamantly refusing a meal packet or bedding but agreeing to use my towel for a pillow, he succumbed to a shallow, restless sleep.

Kelly, Angie, and I separated from Paul and Diana. Guided by the firmament's silvery light, we located level ground on the far side of the enclave, where we unfurled a bedroll and whispered without being overheard.

Kelly was quieter than usual, and her body language—the slight stiffness of her movements—prompted me to speak.

"You need to hear this," I said. "Tomorrow, Melhaus was going to compel Bruce to relinquish Angie. He has decided not to allow it, no matter the consequences. Entering the Orb with Angie is the only way to unburden the commander of making an impossible decision."

I shared with her the story of the bow, violating no confidence by doing so. I finished by describing, or trying to, how Thompson remained troubled by what he had done.

Kelly took a few moments to reexamine the last few hours in context with the story. "On the face of it, he's holding up well." Sadness entered her eyes. "If only I could take back some of my words to him—sentiments that could have been better expressed."

"When the opportunity arises, I'll explain to Diana and Paul."

"Yes. Please."

The day's tension subdued our appetites, but we ate anyway, breaking off small portions of our meal and feeding them to Angie.

"We probably should try to get some sleep," I said.

We lay back, with Angie curled up and nestled between us.

"How did we get into this mess?" Kelly whispered.

"We never left it."

"Is that what you had hoped to do?"

"Writers can be dreamers," I admitted.

"Tonight, we shall dream together," she said, kissing me.

The night was sultry and cloudless. Above, stars beyond counting crowded the sky. A breeze sent delicate strands of Kelly's hair to tickle my face.

"Scheherazade," I mumbled, my mind wandering.

Sleep overtook us, ending our waking dreams.

ORB

"But We Must Try"

I TRAVELED IN and out of sleep. Somewhere off in the distance, I heard several stilted yips of joy. Angie, ears flapping, tongue hanging, bounding toward me across a sunlit-dappled field of bright green grass! My little dog. Our example. We are fools in our failure to emulate such unbridled happiness.

More little yelps and yips, much closer. My eyes opened. Next to me, Angie, still dreaming, emitting the sounds I had heard, her head and one small paw softly resting on Kelly's gently rising breast as she, too, slept.

And in that touching image, in that singular reprieve from the trials that lay ahead, my oft-times foolish heart was gladdened, and I was encouraged to face the coming day. As stars scurried into hiding from the approach of the bullying sun, I carefully rose and left the enclave. I spotted Thompson alone in the distance, standing steady as a stone, staring at the horizon.

Anticipating the sun.

I approached. Standing shoulder to shoulder, we passed several seconds quietly contemplating the dawn.

"You were right," I said.

"About?"

"The sun rising. Just as you predicted."

We watched as a blue sliver of light cut into the sky.

"As Paul would say, it is a *fait accompli*."

In the distance were several dozen Orb groups, their colors gradually softening with the first signs of light; nearer in, one group drifted aimlessly.

"We're not sure what they are, are we?" I said.

"Not even close."

"Will we ever be? *Can* we ever be?" I asked.

"We like to think so, don't we?"

"When I consider the Orb—what little we know of them, or it—I wonder if we humans have everything backward."

"How so?"

"We're so damned proficient at complicating our lives with material possessions and technology, with confusing social relationships, personalities, and emotions. Would the Orb view these aspects of humanity as wonderful diversity or pure folly? Has it accomplished the opposite? Has it simplified itself to the extreme?"

Thompson took a long time to reflect and said: "Simplicity often connotes innocence and vulnerability—in which case, the Orb may soon require protection from Larry and others like him who will follow. On the other hand, it can also impart unity of purpose and action. In that case, we should not expect the Orb to indulge our ignorance if and when it defends itself."

"Six people occupying an entire planet and, shit, we can't even get that right."

"No," Thompson said, "But we must try."

By divining little clues acquired through our growing friendship, I sensed that Thompson was looking inward, lifting and searching under stones to find support for his beliefs.

"I've studied more earthquakes than I can count," he said, "finding as much fascination in their political and sociological implications as their geological cause and effect. Did you know that in 464 B.C., a major quake destroyed the city-state of Sparta, decimating the population and precipitating a slave revolt? Soldiers sent by Athens to assist Sparta in crushing the uprising were turned away, increasing the mistrust between the two city-states. Hostilities escalated, and the Peloponnesian Wars ensued. Although the subsequent history is convoluted, the Golden Age of Greek culture resulted from the conflicts. The influence of Greek culture on Western civilization has been profound. It is interesting, in retrospect, how one specific event, an earthquake, was the catalyst for so much that followed. They may be rare, but sometimes defining moments in human history can be identified *precisely* when they happen—as when Armstrong touched the moon."

"Are we approaching a defining moment?"

"I'm constrained to act as if we are."

"You won't be alone," I said. "Although you may often feel that way today."

Our eyes were drawn to a minuscule detail within the larger tableau: on the black, polished fuselage of *Desio*, a glint of reflected sunlight had appeared and was beginning to grow. "Have you ever stopped and considered," Thompson said, "that often the direction of a person's life can also be traced to one defining moment, one event, one action? Perhaps one solitary word? How often do we have the luxury —or the burden—of knowing when that moment is at hand? If we are granted that awareness, and we make a choice, and somebody is made to suffer the consequences…"

"When you faced such a moment," I said, "at least you had the courage and conviction to act. Recently, I had neither."

"I guess you mean Kelly?" Thompson said.

I had not believed my words and feelings to be so transparent. My response, a quick turn of the head, was sufficient for Thompson to look at me and say, "Your mistake, *if* you so choose, can yet be rectified. At best, I can only atone for mine."

"You're too hard on yourself," I said. "You know something else about history, and this includes personal history? It is often rewritten. You made no mistake, then, with the San; you'll make no mistake, now, with Larry."

Angie, tugging on Kelly, approached to greet us; trailing behind them were Paul and Diana. His attention drawn, Thompson's demeanor changed to one of concern. When they were still out of earshot, with determination and resignation, he said, "Today, our colleague, Larry, will also make a personal choice. If it's the wrong choice, he'll be damned by it."

Thompson's words deliberately conveyed what he felt I needed to hear. His personal demons would not hinder him from taking action.

"Anyone for breakfast?" Diana said in greeting. "May I recommend two eggs, lasered side up? Or, perhaps, an order of eggs Benedict Arnold?"

"I'm glad to see you in fine fettle this morning, Diana," Thompson replied. "The question is, will you be retaining your sense of humor by the end of the day?"

"The end of the day? Ha!" Diana replied. "At the end of the day, I'm sure of only one thing."

"What's that?"

"The sun will set," she said it with confidence, though still turned to Thompson for assurance. "It will, won't it? You seem to know about these things."

The distraction of their conversation allowed Kelly to hug me and, while doing so, whispered "told them" in my ear. I was glad that Diana and Paul, especially Paul, could put the choices confronting Thompson in context with the past; if Thompson decided to use lethal force, the last thing he needed was us judging him harshly. He was doing that quite adequately by himself.

Upon returning to the enclave, Thompson said, "If there are any new ideas, I'll hear them now."

"Are we again going to take the initiative?" I asked. "Approach Melhaus before being summoned?"

"Yes," Thompson responded. "Diana, Kelly, and Angie will remain behind. Paul, as requested, you get the first crack at altering Larry's thinking. Take the time you must. Kyle, barring a change in Melhaus's behavior, you'll present your proposal. I will tell him of the condition on which it rests."

"What about us?" Diana asked. "Doing nothing isn't what Kelly and I had in mind."

"I'm quite sure of that," Thompson remarked, "but let's keep Larry's attention focused on the ideas presented. Why should he expect to have all of us at his disposal?"

Thompson, Paul, and I immediately headed out across the Square. "Be safe, gentlemen," Kelly called after us. We looked back to acknowledge the sentiment, and there she was, a brave smile on her face, holding up one of Angie's paws as if to wave goodbye.

Reaching the last position of safety from the laser, Thompson shouted out to alert Melhaus of our presence. Responding to a second, much louder shout, the physicist, tired and disheveled, emerged from *Desio*.

"By the looks of you," Thompson chided, "I should have been worried you'd forget the laser override. If you had accidentally blasted yourself, we'd all be in trouble, wouldn't we?"

"Your concern for my welfare is touching," Melhaus responded. "You're early. What do you want? Where are the others?"

"I'd like you to hear what Paul has to say about the Orb," Thompson responded. "You'll find it quite informative."

There was a tremendous amount of pressure on Paul to dissuade Melhaus from traveling down the path he was on. He had to convince the physicist of a radically different depiction of the Orb and the risk of engaging in any act involving an entity that spanned the entirety of the planet. Five crew members had embraced the idea; however, Melhaus's mind was a fortress yet to be breached.

Lost in thought, Paul absently began walking forward into laser range before being stopped by the firm grip of Thompson's hand on his shoulder.

"Sorry," Paul muttered, retreating a step. "Careless of me."

"Be forewarned," Melhaus said, "I am increasingly intolerant of the mundane. Waste my time, and I'll use your climatology equipment as a test target. The laser's output was increased overnight."

"Given the present circumstances," Paul answered, "the destruction of my work is the least of my concerns. What I say won't bore you. Whether you choose to believe it is quite another matter."

"Get on with it," Melhaus ordered.

"I'll begin by making an assertion, then work backward through the supporting evidence. The entirety of this planet's ocean and the millions of Orbs populating it is one single, semi-homogeneous entity." Paul paused to let the message sink in. "Shall I proceed?"

Melhaus hesitated, then, in a sarcastic voice, said, "By all means, I am intrigued. Yes, yes, continue."

Ten minutes later, I thought that Paul, as persuasive as I'd ever heard, had gained entrance inside Larry's fortress walls. My optimism was short-lived.

"You do yourselves credit, you and Kyle," Melhaus said, mouthing the words through the condescending chuckle he worked to annoying perfection. "Together, you have fabricated a most wonderful and inventive yarn! No, no, no, not boring at all! Especially diverting was the part where you wove aspects of my findings into your own story. Kyle, there is a glimmer of hope for your waning career."

"I'll ask you to write the foreword for my next novel," I muttered, though the distance probably prevented my being heard. I was at the point of not caring as I watched a dejected Paul rejoin Thompson and me.

"He *appeared* attentive," Paul lamented. "He's fixated on seeing only the parts, not the whole."

"Don't beat yourself up, Paul," Thompson said, turning to me. "Still think your idea has a chance?" he asked. Although skeptical, the commander showed no inclination to stop me.

I considered abandoning my idea and walking away, but we had to take every road not ending in violence. "Is there anything left to lose?" I said, realizing there was plenty.

Thompson advanced toward *Desio*. "Larry," he said, "since we are doing such a stellar job of entertaining you, perhaps you'll indulge Kyle. He has a proposal for you to consider. I wouldn't waste your time, or mine, if I didn't believe the idea had merit."

"Here's what…" I began, stepping forward.

"Careful," Melhaus interrupted. "Wander into your fantasyland, and I will cut you off at the knees."

"Better be brief," Thompson advised.

"Here's what I propose, Larry," I said. "I'll wear whatever monitors you want. I'll hold onto Angie. Assuming the Orb wishes to repeat an encounter, you will have both the instrument readings and my firsthand account of the experience."

I retraced a half step and addressed Thompson. "Succinct enough?" I said.

Looking past me, Melhaus gave Thompson a menacing scowl. "And?" he demanded. "I assume there are conditions."

"They are reasonable and non-negotiable. Disarm the laser and relinquish control of the ship. Do so, and you have my word we shall implement Kyle's proposition." Then, almost as an afterthought: "One more thing. I will erase from the record any mention of wrongdoing for the demise of *Ixodes*. That only leaves the incident in Kyle's narrative."

I'd have to erase a lot more than what happened to *Ixodes* to make Melhaus look good, I thought to myself. "Gone," I lied. "Like the words were never written, a mere figment of my overactive imagination. I'll substitute something about the mysteries of the ocean deep or the relationship between a man and his dog."

Altering the mission record would give Melhaus a way out of his mess, handing it to him on a silver platter. Or is the platter to be perceived as gray? Or maybe bluish?

Or, in the mind of Dr. Larry Melhaus, vivid red with fucking green stripes.

I would do what's necessary.

"And here is what shall be," he countered. "I shall not relinquish control of *Desio*. Return to me in one hour. I need time to prepare the devices Kyle will be wearing and additional monitors to fit a seven-kilogram dog."

"Don't waste your time," Thompson said, suppressing anger.

"One hour," Melhaus repeated.

"You demand the impossible. We refuse." Thompson turned to Paul and me. "We're finished here, let's go."

All we could do was walk away. As the distance between Melhaus and us increased, so did his anger.

"Thompson! Are you prepared to suffer the consequences? I shall remind you of what they are! Without food from me, you'll all starve! Do you hear, starve! And you'll be responsible, Thompson! You, alone! You'll get *nothing* from me! Not even an L-capsule to put an end to your pitiful little lives, do you hear ?!"

"The downfall of a brilliant mind," a subdued Kelly remarked as we regrouped. Melhaus's outburst—after which he had disappeared inside *Desio*—had carried loud and clear across the Square.

"What in hell would he have us do!?" Diana exclaimed, becoming increasingly exasperated as Paul informed her of everything that transpired.

"That's the point," Thompson emphasized. "It's useless to appease him. He will make demands until he understands the composition and physics of the Orb—even if it takes three days, three weeks, or three months."

"Great! Just great!" Diana said. "In three days, the opportunity to return to Earth is lost. Three weeks and we'll watch each other starve. Three months, Earth prepares a hero's welcome. Only we won't be there to enjoy it, will we?"

"How long can he last by himself?" Kelly asked.

"He'd live off our supplies," Thompson said. "Assuming no life support and power malfunction—perhaps a year or more."

"That's well short of a rescue expedition arriving," Kelly said. "He knows that. Perhaps he's bluffing."

"Didn't you hear him rant?" Diana asked. "He's certifiable."

"Anyone care to speculate on what he'll do next?" Kelly asked.

"Although he has control of *Desio*, the options are limited," Thompson responded. "He can't go anywhere. The laser protects him, but only in sight of the ship. If he strays too far, he risks us ambushing him. He'll look for a way to use the laser offensively and in a manner that induces our cooperation. Exactly how is a good deal less certain."

"We're about to find out!" Kelly shouted, pointing toward *Desio*. Melhaus, the controller in hand, had come bounding out.

A purple streak of light instantly appeared overhead, rapidly followed by two more. Simultaneously, three ear-splitting peals cracked the air. Behind us, high up on the spires, were corresponding explosions, the sounds of laser-superheated moisture violently expelled from inside solid rock. Unable to withstand the internal pressure, the rock shattered and spalled, sending a cascade of deadly shards downward.

"Move!" Thompson screamed. "Move!" He was first to grasp the danger, moving behind us, spreading his arms wide, corralling us in an attempt to push us further away. "Damn it, move!" he repeated, shoving until we began running, some of us stumbling and dragged along by others in our retreat.

Reaching safety, I realized that Angie, shaking in fear, was being tightly held in my arms. I couldn't recall how she got there. Last I remembered, Kelly had been holding her.

"I had to release her as I fell," Kelly said, "or she would have been crushed beneath me."

"Is everyone OK?" Thompson asked, looking at each of us.

"You're not," Kelly said. "You're bleeding."

Thompson's hand went to his temple. "A glancing blow," he said, examining the trace of red on his fingers.

While Kelly tended to the commander's superficial wound and her own scraped palms, a high-pitched voice crossed the fractured plateau of the Square to insult and provoke us.

"Thompson! Do you hear me, Thompson?! Is that what you meant by unforeseen consequences?!"

"Glad to see you're acquiring a sense of humor, Doctor," Diana yelled back.

"Best leave off with that for now," Thompson advised. "As for my counter? He'll have it soon."

While dismissive of his wound, Thompson was not nearly as obliging concerning the injury to his spires. Three magnificent formations, including the two tallest, were now marred by disfiguring scars. The peak of one spire was partly missing, and irregular holes bored in the others. The damage was sobering, a symbol of humanity's desire to destroy.

After returning to the relative safety of our enclave, an opportunity arose for Kelly and me to spend a few minutes alone. Taking full advantage, I suddenly grabbed her arm, drew her close, and urgently kissed her.

"What's this for?" she asked.

"I needed a reminder."

"Of?"

"Of something in this universe that's good. Of how you feel. How much I need you. I'm being selfish."

"Don't you understand by now that I can be selfish, too?"

She was about to kiss me when there was a gentle tug on the leash.

"Our little ambassador to the Orb," Kelly said.

We crouched down to put Angie between us.

"There's a silver lining on today's black cloud," I said. "No longer is there a chance Angie will be at the mercy of Dr. Melhaus."

"Listening to Thompson," Kelly said, "I doubt there ever was."

The Unthinkable

"I WANTED TO spare him. To give him, and therefore us, every possible chance." So said Thompson, his back against one of the large stones ringing the enclave, contemplating and flexing the fingers of his weathered hands.

There was, in Thompson's declaration, a more profound meaning beneath the obvious desire to save the life of a person in his charge: he needed us to realize that the taking of a life meant shouldering a burden that would haunt us for a lifetime. He would try to bear much of the burden, but not all, for there was no denying we had acted as a group.

At his instruction, we again agonized over every conceivable alternative only to return to where we started: to avoid acting based on the mistaken belief Melhaus would relent placed us in greater peril. When Thompson finally decided he had to use violence, he did so with great reluctance.

We collectively agreed out of desperation and fear and were surprised to feel complicity and sorrow.

After hearing what Thompson said next, we better understood why.

"It would be wrong to shield from you something weighing heavily on my mind," he said. "Although I am accomplished with the bow, the shot will be extremely difficult. But something troubles me more than the consequences of failing. Succeeding. The taking of a life made even more grievous because it will be the first taken beyond the bounds of Earth, a symbol of humanity's flawed nature for all to see. An extension of ourselves into the universe that shatters the hope that we could somehow start anew. Inevitable, you may say, is this failure of ours, and you would be right, for the only way to prove you wrong is for each person to renounce violence."

"Larry has not," Diana said, "so how can we?"

"Larry? Larry?" Thompson declared in despair. "Recall your physics! Are we not the observer affecting the observed? I would beg forgiveness, but who shall I ask it of?"

Standing alone, transfixed, he seemed to withdraw from us and maybe a part of himself. When Diana gently reached out and touched his hand, he came back. Seeing her, seeing our concerned stares, he said, "Not to worry. We… I will play the part."

And with that, he went off to retrieve the bow from the place it was hidden.

Paul's gaze followed Thompson until he disappeared among the blocks. "Do we need better proof of why he is our leader?"

"None," I said. "I'd go so far as to call him my superior."

"To his face?" Diana asked.

"Don't push it."

"You understand him better than any of us," Kelly said. "Do you think he's wavering?"

"Not a chance in hell," I responded.

I had learned to pay close attention to Angie's body language. Watching now, I noticed a change in posture: body upright and tense; ears perked and twitching; tail erect and vibrating as if she was trying to decide whether to be alert or excited. When Thompson returned, I mentioned my observation. In response, he told us to leave the seclusion of the enclave and look out toward the horizon.

Compared to an hour ago, twice as many Orb groups were visible. One group had drifted significantly closer to shore. Angie pointed her snout in the air and started emitting a low whine.

"What do you think is happening?" I asked. "Trouble?"

"Not sure," Thompson remarked, squatting down to pet Angie. "Nor is she."

"I don't like this," Paul said.

"Agreed," Thompson said, his face turning grave.

"You think Larry is up to something?" Kelly asked. When neither answered, she turned to Thompson. "If that's so, what?"

"He's devised a way, maybe ultrasound, to lure the Orb closer."

"To do…?"

"The unthinkable."

"What?" Kelly asked again. "Wait. You don't think he'd use the laser on the Orb?!"

The distraught faces of Thompson and Paul stared back at her.

"Are you shitting me?!" Diana screamed. "What does he hope to... No, don't tell me. A physics experiment. He wants to measure the Orbs' reaction!"

Still no confirmation from either Thompson or Paul.

Diana's eyes widened in disbelief. She took a step toward *Desio*. "It's worse than that, isn't it? Isn't it? He wants to split one open like it's an egg. Like it's some kind of giant fucking piñata!"

The perverse humor of her remark startled Diana, and she began laughing, but the laughter was born out of frustration and rage and could only end in an expression of sorrow. "All the Orb are doing is floating out there peacefully," she said, "while we act like idiots and scar its planet."

Thompson became all business now.

"I'll need to establish a position just out of laser range but as close to the ship as possible without being observed. Do you see that boulder over there?" Thompson pointed out a rectangular block wide enough, no more, to shield two people in a crouching position.

"Appears we can make it partway there following that crevice," I said.

Thompson gave me a hard stare. "We? Not happening."

"I said you wouldn't be alone."

"And how, *exactly*, do you hope to assist me?"

Except for the word *exactly*, I had a ready reply. "Thompson's Law of Unintended Consequences. Can you predict how events will unfold?"

"Lame."

"Yeah."

"That cinches it then," he said, examining his bow and deliberately catching me off guard. "You're coming with me. If the situation arises, there may be one small task you can do."

Stringing a bow requires substantial upper-body strength. Thompson had plenty. He wedged the tip with the bowstring attached between the ground and his instep while holding the opposite end. His free hand firmly gripped the bow's center. Applying pressure, the bow was forced into a "U" shape, allowing the loose bowstring to be fastened. Thompson made it look easy. Kelly caught him flinching.

"Shoulder bothering you?" she asked.

"Shouldn't matter."

Like hell, I thought. Drawing back a tight bowstring and then holding the tension steady while aiming an arrow is difficult. If Thompson's shoulder was bothering him...

Kelly, too, appeared skeptical. "A few more treatments, and you would have been healed." She gestured toward *Desio*. "You know where they are, right?"

"Let me guess."

"You'll get them for me, won't you?"

"Only a fool would deny you, Kelly," Thompson replied. Then, as he moved to grab his quiver, "Right, Kyle?"

We prepared to leave our hidden location. There was little risk of being spotted if Melhaus stayed inside *Desio*. Diana asked what to do if he decided to come out. Would there be circumstances where a diversion might draw attention away from Thompson and me?

"That would be a good idea," Thompson replied, "but Melhaus is clever enough to suspect the underlying motivation."

"Well then," she said, trying to mask her nervous tension. "Better get your asses in gear."

"And try keeping them out of trouble," Paul added.

Kelly was quiet. She had picked up Angie. There was a strange commonality in their expressions. "You both look worried," I said. Then, with the slightest grin, I said the opposite of what most people would expect. "Is it any wonder?"

Kelly touched my cheek. "Be safe," she said, and Thompson pulled me away.

We jogged across a flat expanse to the start of a narrow, shallow crevice that would shelter us partway to the boulder, our final destination. Crouching, we followed the crevice's meandering course to its end. The last leg of the journey was two hundred meters of open terrain, leaving us exposed and vulnerable. We were preparing to sprint the distance when Melhaus emerged from the ship.

"Bloody bad timing," Thompson whispered.

Peering over the crevice gave us an unhindered view of *Desio*, the Orb groups close to shore, and Melhaus. His posture and direction indicated that the closest group was the focus of attention. He placed his A.I.D on a nearby table but kept the laser controller tightly in hand.

Behind me, I heard Angie barking what sounded like a warning.

"What's he up to?" I whispered.

"Can't be good," Thompson answered.

A low hum emanated from inside *Desio*, and the laser turret slowly started rotating, aligning the weapon's nozzle with the closest Orb. The holocam was pointing in the same orientation as the turret, leaving no doubt that Melhaus wanted a visual record of what he was about to do: fire at the Orb. Our inability to prevent him was infuriating. I did not have to imagine how Diana felt. Looking back toward the enclave, I saw Paul and Kelly struggling to restrain her.

Thompson weighed the possibilities. "If we move, he'll see us in his peripheral vision."

"Maybe it's a chance worth taking. If he sees us, we might elude the laser by retreating into the crevice." I hung this idea out there without complete confidence.

"True enough, but he'll figure out where we were heading. He won't know exactly why if I manage to keep the bow hidden behind me, but we'll certainly lose the advantage of the boulder. There is no alternate place to reach him. Not within bowshot."

"A bad chance is better than none at all," I said. "We can't let him fire at the Orb."

"If we move now and we are seen, all is lost. Melhaus gets to run amok for a year. No, we wait."

"You're right, of course."

"Don't want to play devil's advocate?"

"Don't believe in the devil."

"Don't need to," Thompson said, drawing my attention to the bow. "He believes in us."

Given no choice, we waited. The air hung down on us, still and warm. Angie stopped barking. In the silence, trivial observations commanded my attention: a tiny gouge in the bow, the odd shape of a rock, the drop of sweat falling onto my knee. Thompson and I exchanged a wide-eyed look of recognition. The type two people share when they realize something disastrous is about to happen.

Melhaus fired his laser.

A purple line of light intersected the closest Orb. For the duration of firing, a widening circle identical to that of the laser's tracer beam appeared, then faded, on the Orb's surface.

Consequences immediately followed. The Orb abruptly halted all movement; Melhaus, who had been calm, grew visibly agitated and began talking to himself.

We were close enough to make out some of the words and numbers the physicist strung together. "Totally unanticipated. Time. Five point seven four seconds. Megawatts. Point six eight three. Joules. One point one eight eight four two. Remarkable. Need to double. Yes, double…"

While he continued to rant, I whispered to Thompson, "You get any of that?"

"Some. He was performing calculations in his head. He unleashed more than a million joules of energy in the area the size of an orange onto the surface of the Orb."

"Translation?"

"The bastard expected to burn a hole or get a measurable reaction. Instead, it was barely noticed."

"Damn. What's the laser's limitation?"

"Much more than anything we've witnessed. I remember him saying something about the output being boosted. Let's assume six megawatts. He can lengthen the beam duration, possibly generate twenty megajoules. By controlling the beam aperture, he can… Wait—he's firing again."

A louder hum came from *Desio*, again followed by a bright line of purple light intersecting the Orb, but for a longer duration and at greater power.

If Melhaus wanted a reaction, he got it—twelvefold.

The area targeted again mirrored the color of the beam, but the purple smudge began spreading, deepening in hue, until one-third of the entity's surface was affected. Then, possibly to avoid the intense heat generated, it went skimming at high velocity across the OceanOrb, colliding like a struck billiard ball with a like-sized member of its group, transferring its momentum, whereby *it* continued on, collided with yet another, and so on until all twelve members of the group had been similarly impacted. Upon completing this bizarre activity, as if to demonstrate unity, the motion of all twelve Orbs promptly ceased.

Any person in their right mind would have been sobered by what we just saw. Thompson's scientific assessment of the situation seemed fitting: "They seem to be transferring the energy among themselves."

I had another view. "Or, sensing hostility, they are communicating a way to reply."

"Something to think about," Thompson agreed. "And with further provocation, will that reply have an end?"

But the Orbs remained docile, neither advancing nor retreating, leaving an easy target for Melhaus's laser. I found myself wishing they'd initiate a more aggressive response. I confessed as much to Thompson.

"Understandable," he commented.

"At least you didn't say that I'm acting human."

"I was being charitable."

The results of the second attack on the Orb baffled and frustrated Melhaus. Failing to open a portal into the entity, he resumed talking to himself or, more accurately, to the Orb (which had reverted to its original uniform coloration), addressing it as if an adversary.

"Three million joules. You remain unaffected. Shall I try six? No answer? Six, then. Six it shall be."

A loud telltale hum emanated from *Desio*.

"The damn fool! He's firing again!" I shouted, cringing because I had raised my voice above the noise.

A smooth, shimmering, manhole-sized indentation appeared on the Orb's surface, slowly radiating outward from the laser's impingement.

"Round! You're not perfectly round *now*, are you?!" Melhaus cackled, the childish petulance of the remark sending a shiver up my spine.

In response, the Orb began vibrating and, at last, moving. Good, I thought, protect yourself, distance yourself from the bastard. That would make sense and conform to my expectations. But, once again, I was wrong.

Nearby, a second and third Orb began to move.

Then the entire group of twelve was in motion, drawing closer together, tighter and tighter, until, like giant beads of mercury, they began to merge, one absorbing into another, all merging into one dynamic and perfectly round entity dwarfing all we had seen before!

Melhaus was momentarily stunned, utterly confounded by his obsession.

"Get ready to act," I heard a tense Thompson say. He was beside me, but sounded far away. I felt a shove and an urgent "Follow me. *Low. Keep low.*"

We ran for what seemed an eternity to the protection of the boulder. Backs against stone, we collapsed, our hearts pounding in our ears, afraid to move for fear of being detected.

Abruptly came the voice of Dr. Melhaus: "So you think you can defy me?"

I flashed Thompson a look of panic. A muscle in his jaw tightened, and a light in his eyes flickered, but he relaxed, grimaced, and said, "We're safe. He's talking to his Orb."

"Shit," I said, forcing a smile.

Thompson peered around his side of the boulder, then asked, "You good with determining distances?"

"Yes."

"How far?"

I took a long look from around my side of the boulder. "From where he is now, thirty-five to forty meters."

"That's what I estimate." But Thompson looked again.

"What do you think?" I said.

"Wish to hell I had a couple of practice shots. There's no wind. That's good. Air resistance is slightly more than Earth's. Gravity is less. The trajectory will be altered. The arrow will carry farther."

"Sounds like physics. Should I get Melhaus's opinion?"

"Sure… if you think you two can… what's that damn word again?"

"Communicate?" I said.

"Yeah, that's it."

"Now what's he doing?" I asked.

Peering around the boulder allowed an oblique view of a haggard man, face drawn, appearance wild and unkempt from days without eating or sleeping. He was hastily tapping entries on the controller.

"The device regulates the laser's power supply," Thompson said. "But look there! Look what's happening in the distance."

There was movement along the horizon, which I had not noticed—the continued merging of Orb groups into progressively larger and larger entities. Their concerted activity was the clearest signal yet that what affected one group affected all.

Didn't Melhaus see this? Was it not a warning for him to stop his madness? If he saw, he chose not to care.

"I have your undivided attention, do I? I see *everybody* is watching!"

I whispered to Thompson, "Who is he talking to, us or the Orb?"

Thompson shook his head. "We're running out of time. I don't want to see what happens if he fires again." He reached for the quiver, withdrew two arrows, and handed one to me. I looked at him questioningly. "In due time," he said. "You're nervous enough."

As Melhaus entered commands to boost and discharge *Desio*'s laser, the Orb group he had been harassing sank below the OceanOrb, disappearing without a ripple. It was the last thing he wanted to happen. With his invented nemesis gone, together with hopes of a revelation in physics, he began venting his frustration by repeatedly discharging the laser on the calm surface of what he still believed was water. To the sky, he shouted something resembling "test your theory" or "at best a story." No, it was both. He was mocking Paul and me.

What happened next had me doubting my sanity.

The OceanOrb came to life in a roil, upwell, and tumble. Deep within the turbulence, iridescent cords of color emerged, twisted, and intertwined, then brightened as they reached sunlight. The affected area, the size of a ballfield but circular, far exceeded that disturbed by laser energy. Melhaus, realizing this, ceased firing—but as soon as the phenomenon captivated his scientific interest, the troubled area reverted to a tranquil, perfectly flat sheen.

The world, in anticipation, went dead calm.

"Be ready," Thompson said.

Suddenly, a large circular area of the OceanOrb smoothly concaved, then heaved and undulated, sending a ripple crashing onto the rocky shore. Where the upwelling had been, a glistening dome broke the surface.

Slowly, rising like a second sun, colossal as a giant oak, the Orb rose. Defying a watery birth, not a drop of liquid clung to its textureless surface; defying gravity, it balanced on one tiny point as if light as a feather. In front of this mammoth stood Melhaus, diminutive, pathetically so, gazing in astonishment at what he presumed to have wrought.

Thompson was moved to action. He was standing next to me, bow in hand. Drawing back, he let an arrow fly.

An arc, a blur, went whooshing through the air. There was a loud clanging sound as the arrow, whizzing past Melhaus's shoulder, shattered against the metal shell of *Desio*.

A large splinter came to rest at the physicist's feet. Shaken from his trance, he looked down, trying to make sense of a wooden stick with some feathers stuck to it.

"Arrow," I heard Thompson say from above me.

The bewildered look on Melhaus's face was replaced by recognition. And fear.

"Arrow," I heard Thompson repeat. "Missed high."

"What?" I said. But I reflexively did as he bid.

Melhaus, realizing his danger, began wildly entering laser commands.

Thompson, exposed, remained standing. Ice water in his veins, he pulled the bowstring back until it rested against his jaw, sighted, held steady, and released.

When I resumed breathing, I noticed an arrow protruding from the side of Melhaus's chest near the shoulder. All he could do was look at it in utter disbelief. His hand involuntarily opened, sending the controller clanking against a rock. His eyes glazed and rolled to the back of his head as he slumped.

Thompson reached him first and began immediately applying pressure to the wound to stem the loss of blood.

Anguish in his eyes, he turned to me. "He has a fighting chance. The tip has come completely through."

Our other pressing concern was the Orb, but by the time our crewmates arrived, every last one had disappeared over the horizon or beneath the surface. No, all were gone save one—the constant, unfathomable OceanOrb.

"You saved our lives!" Diana said, addressing Thompson, although he likely never heard her. His attention was on Kelly. She took over.

"Hypovolemic shock," she said, quickly examining Melhaus's injury. "Keep applying pressure. The amount and color of blood indicate no major artery damage or lung penetration. He has a chance."

"Make the most of it," Thompson said, as if his words could make it so. "Sorry. I know you will."

Kelly entered *Desio*, emerging with a medical kit and wound dressings. She removed a flexible, thick metal band from the kit and clamped it to Melhaus's wrist. A screen on the kit's lid instantly flashed biometric measurements. "Fourteen percent blood loss. Manageable. We have some time."

A long tube protected by a sterilized wrapper was removed from the kit. "Break off the arrow shaft and pull back his shirt," Kelly commanded. With a steady hand, she removed the arrow and inserted the surgical tube deep into the bleeding wound. As the tube was withdrawn, its contents were deposited along the entire length of the injury. "Crude but effective," she said.

"What's in the liquid?" Paul asked.

"Biochems. A sterilizing agent, an anticoagulant, and a new drug that promotes rapid healing."

"Do you have his consent?" Diana asked. When Kelly frowned, Diana affectionately touched her shoulder and said, "You have mine."

A surgical dressing was applied to the wound, and an AI-regulated IV was started. "Let's make him comfortable here," Kelly ordered. "We can move him inside before nightfall. It's as sterile out here as inside the ship."

"Prognosis?" Thompson asked. His hands, yet to be washed, were stained red with blood.

"Let me ask you a question," Kelly responded. "Did you deliberately aim for part of the anatomy that would cause the least trauma?"

"That, doctor, would be absurd," Thompson remarked.

"For the record," I remarked, "not a complete answer."

"Uh-huh," Kelly said, sharing my skepticism. "If there are no complications, he'll do fine physically. That's only half the battle, of course."

We waited expectantly for Melhaus, who had remained unconscious during Kelly's expert care, to open his eyes. Our concern was for his welfare, but we were also curious about what he might say, if anything, concerning his actions.

Eventually, with a moan and a fluttering of eyelids, he gazed up at five crewmates staring at him. Slowly, he grasped that he was flat on his back, somehow injured but very much alive.

"Good to have you still with us, Dr. Melhaus," Thompson said.

"Thompson... I can't believe you shot me... with, with... an arrow...?"

"My apologies," Thompson responded, "for not being a bit more high-tech."

Diana leaned in and, with a conspiratorial voice, said, "Larry, I know what you think of drugs. I told Dr. Takara to go easy on the pain medication."

Melhaus rasped out a laugh or a cough, grimacing from the effort. The last thing he said before Kelly ushered us away was, "Paul, about the Orb, you were right. You were right."

Nobody believed this more than Thompson. I noted with interest that he washed the blood from his hands inside *Desio*, not at the shoreline, which would have been much more convenient.

Heartfelt

THOMPSON ORDERED A thorough inspection of *Desio* to determine if it was in any way damaged or sabotaged.

"Nothing amiss in my cabin," I reported.

"I'm surprised," Kelly said. She had just completed inventorying her ransacked drug supply. "You're lucky Larry did not destroy your mission chronicle."

"Lucky?" I said with mock chagrin. "I'm rather offended."

"Offended?" Paul and Kelly simultaneously asked.

"Very much so," I replied. "But I do have a theory…"

"Here he goes again," Diana teased.

"…that Larry didn't consider my work worthy of reading. At least you scientists had *your* work judged sufficiently valuable to be threatened."

"You realize," Paul said, "there is an uncanny logic to what he's been saying."

"You bet there is," I said, persisting with my argument. "Even Bruce thought enough of my work to offer it to Larry for sacrifice."

"Whoa," Thompson interrupted, "That was an act of sheer desperation. I wouldn't let it go to your head."

"Larry *did* reject the offer," Paul emphasized. "Almost instantly, as I seem to recall."

"See? There you have it," I said. "I rest my case."

"Yes, there we have it," Thompson echoed. "Finally, with a little help, a theory you have proven. Bravo!"

I graciously accepted the honor for what it was worth.

The inspection of *Desio* revealed several clever changes to the laser power supply and firing circuitry. One surprise: the ultrasonic humidifier was now in serious need of repair. Melhaus had removed the unit's piezoelectric transducer and installed it in a high-frequency sound-emitting device of his creation. With it, he had attracted the Orb. Or so we believed. Another example of his warped brilliance. For all the right reasons, further use of the invention was not considered.

In a bit of good news, none of the collected samples, onboard experiments, or saved files were compromised. Better yet, there had been no tampering with the ship's operating systems. We could leave for home if we could manage to get through one more day without misadventure.

Because of this, and despite the other setbacks and damage done, we were in a buoyant mood, nobody more so than Dr. Diana Gilmore.

"I may not have to pummel Melhaus into another dimension after all," she said, not caring that he was recuperating close by and might be listening.

Once again, we dined at the outside table, enjoying the processed food displayed in front of us. We had only missed one day's meals, but weren't accustomed to such ill-treatment. Angie was the hungriest of us, and I spoiled her with an extra portion of her favorite dry food. Having eaten her fill, she was now spread out across my lap, belly up and legs spread apart, looking very much like a spatchcocked chicken.

"And so, tell me, commander," Kelly prodded. "You stood there realizing that in the blink of an eye you could be toasted by the laser, an Orb the size of a building looming nearby, an absurdly difficult shot to make, all the while facing the dire consequence of failure. Seriously, what planet did you come from to pull that off?"

"I can't take full responsibility for my actions," Thompson contended. "I forced all that into submission, telling myself I was taking practice shots at an archery range."

"Oh, great," Diana said, unsatisfied. "You held our lives in the balance predicated on the mere pretense of target shooting?"

"Afraid so."

"You reckless SOB," Diana hissed, staring hard at Thompson and sounding indignant. In the next breath, she said, "Gutsiest damn thing I ever saw."

"You both were brave," Kelly said, draping her arms around my neck and leaning over to peck my cheek.

"Was I there?" I said. "Just what the hell was I thinking?"

"May I join the chorus of praise?" Paul said. "You both have our *undying* gratitude."

The groans got worse when I complimented Paul on his deadpan delivery.

"How big was the Orb, in your estimation?" Kelly asked.

"Upwards of fifty meters in diameter," Thompson ventured. "Born right before our eyes out of the maelstrom."

"That matches our estimates from further away," Paul stated. "Amazing. And I assume you observed the Orbs skimming along the surface, combining into ever-larger entities?"

"Remarkable, was it not?" Thompson understated. "There were, however, two things we did not see, and one may depend on the other. Despite repeated provocation, the Orb never acted overtly aggressively. And merged ones, no matter how large, never left contact with the OceanOrb."

"And just how large can they become?" I asked.

"Oberon."

I choked on the reconstituted grape juice I was drinking. The unlikely utterance came from Melhaus. I was familiar with only one Oberon.

"As big as the King of the Fairies?" I said, having a pretty good idea that's not what he meant.

"I don't follow," Melhaus remarked.

"Oberon," I said. "A whimsical character in *A Midsummer Night's Dream*. King of *all* the fairies. Not very big, though."

"The Oberon I refer to is much more massive." Melhaus's deadpan delivery was completely unintentional.

"How much more massive?"

"Oberon is a moon orbiting Uranus. It has a diameter of fifteen hundred twenty-six kilometers."

"That *is* bigger than Shakespeare's Oberon," I replied, glancing at Thompson. I recalled the day he told me he was an avid reader of the Bard. He was having difficulty suppressing his laughter. Melhaus, however, was oblivious.

"The volume of Oberon," Melhaus continued, "when rounding off, is one point nine billion cubic kilometers."

"A very big number," I commented.

"A number," Melhaus insisted, "that compares favorably to the volume of water contained by this planet's ocean."

"Are you claiming one Orb can reach that size?" He certainly had captivated our attention, but when he didn't respond immediately, I assumed I had lost his. This was not so, for he was carefully considering a reply.

"It is theoretically possible. The entity can bend the laws of physics to its advantage, rapidly changing its molecular density. It explains the perfectly round shape, textureless surface, laser resistance, and how they can merge at will. By controlling its density, the entity can overcome the size limitations we typically associate with Earth organisms. I doubt the Orb are restricted by anything but the total volume of water in what, through force of habit, I will call the ocean. As Paul astutely pointed out, the entity is the ocean."

"You must concede this much, Kyle," Thompson interjected, "imagining an Orb as immense as the Uranian moon Oberon is as phantasmagorical as anything found in the plays of Shakespeare. It strains the imagination."

"You'll get no argument from me," I replied, "'The lunatic, the lover, and the poet are of imagination all compact.' I submit that if the Bard were alive, he would amend his words and add a scientist to the group."

"It certainly does appear all four types are represented on this voyage," Thompson responded.

By now, Melhaus had dropped out of the conversation, too exhausted to continue. "Seems like we have put him to sleep," Diana said as Kelly monitored her patient's vitals.

"But he," I said, "has started me thinking."

"Oh shit," Diana said, grinning.

"If you remember," I continued, unfazed, "that I was criticized for suggesting the plankton were seeded here by an alien race to transform the planet into a habitable world for their subsequent arrival. Now I understand exactly how the plankton arrived on this planet: they got a free ride from the Orb."

"This is your fault for encouraging him, Bruce," Diana complained.

"Diana," I persisted, "it was you who said the phytoplankton were out of place, that they shouldn't exist here all by themselves. Yet they produce the entire planet's oxygen. *Melhaus* believes the entity can bend the laws of physics to its advantage. That would be key in accomplishing the journey. Paul and Bruce agree that this planet is very young and incredibly stable. Is there a better place to begin a new world? Considering all this, is it so far-fetched that in the distant past, the Orb, a moon unto itself, carried the phytoplankton to this eminently suitable ball of rock and now calls it home?"

"He has somehow managed to implicate us all," Diana admitted. "I guess we are all to blame."

"The thing is, I believe the idea may have some merit," Thompson remarked.

"Hey," I said, with an elaborate show of modesty, "I'm only standing on the shoulders of giants."

As I pushed back from the table, I spied Kelly, smiling and enjoying the fun I was having. Her patient was doing well, at least physically, due to her care. She had been adamant about letting him convalesce outside in the bright, palliative sunlight. In deference to her and the logic of the circumstances, Thompson did not object.

Over and above the draining effects of his injury, there was a markedly subdued aspect to Melhaus's manner. He was, in part, pitiable. The compassion we showed, however, was not without bounds. We were, after all, only human and could never forget the threats that were made to our lives. Only Angie completely forgave, bringing him her stuffed duck as if the whole affair never happened. I guess she saw him as ready and willing to play, sitting there helpless, his back to the exterior bulkhead, legs sticking straight out in front. Immobile.

The measured compassion Thompson felt, and I'm convinced he was saddened to see one in his charge brought so low, had to make his duty tougher. He issued strict orders that Melhaus, for his protection and ours, would be under constant visual surveillance or confined within electronically monitored quarters. In three months, Thompson would offer him up to the appropriate authorities who, for good or ill, would be in a position to judge him more dispassionately.

As the day progressed, the horizon stayed empty of Orbs, and the high we felt from stepping back from the brink of disaster began to dissipate slowly.

"Will they ever return," Diana lamented, "so we can somehow use the opportunity to make amends?"

She had touched on the one subject troubling us most: how dreadful the entity's perception of us must be.

When Thompson heard Diana, he turned to me and said, "Let's grab some tools. There's something that needs fixing."

A moment later, I clutched the servicing footholds and handholds built into *Desio*'s metallic skin, following Thompson to the laser turret.

"A laser doesn't belong on this ship, never did," Thompson remarked. "You and I are going to dismantle it."

"And when we return to Earth? Don't we need protection from orbiting pirates and space junk?"

Thompson scowled. "Conversations with other ship commanders have led me to believe the presence of space pirates is a rumor started by certain multinational companies to foster the militarization of space." Thompson's scowl deepened. "Space junk? What in hell would a laser do except create numerous smaller pieces, each harder to detect, each more dangerous."

We tackled the laser's mechanical connections by removing old-fashioned nuts and bolts, trading insults as the weapon began to come free of its mount. One of the things I appreciated about Thompson was how easily conversation went back and forth between the inane and the sublime—sometimes mixing the two.

"Your shoulder ready for this?" I asked Thompson.

"Shoulder's fine. Kelly treated it. What about you? Still afraid of heights?"

"You're kidding, right? We're not that far off the ground." I moved closer to the edge and balanced on one leg to prove my point. "Does this look like I'm afraid of heights?"

"I meant Kelly."

"Shithead," I said, moving back from the edge. Over his shoulder, I watched as three delicate and precious rose-colored crystals were removed from their secure housing. "Our weapons have come a long way from the bow and arrow. Too bad our sensibilities haven't kept pace."

"The so-called primitive San used the bow primarily as a means to hunt. To survive as a people."

"Some good came of your encounter with them," I said. "You brought away their bow and, with it, an appreciation of their culture, a small part of their way of life. Think about this:

268

without your use of their bow, Melhaus would have continued provoking the Orb, and we would likely have all perished here. Help me out. Is this an example of irony or Thompson's Law of Unintended Consequences?"

"The most stellar example of an unintended consequence in all of recorded history."

We continued working. Eventually, I held the offending laser weapon in my arms. "What do we do with this?"

"Let's deposit it near the shore."

"For the Orb to see?"

Thompson nodded. "A token gesture that likely will never be seen. But it makes me feel better."

"You want a more demonstrative gesture and gratification?" I asked. "Melhaus is below us. How about I drop the laser on him?"

Thompson laughed. "Anywhere *but* him is okay."

I made sure nobody was in harm's way, yelled a general warning to expect a loud noise, and heaved the laser as far out as my strength would allow. There was a satisfying crash followed by a resonating echo bouncing off the spires. We climbed down, picked up the laser, and carried it to the shoreline. Thompson hurried off to examine the spire rubble while Angie and I headed into *Desio*.

I needed to catch up on my writing. Halfway done, and Kelly popped her head in.

"You're busy," she said from the doorway. "Come back later?"

"Please. But if you don't return," I warned, "I'm going to send Angie out looking for you."

I had promised myself, and often it was a promise kept, to chronicle mission events contemporaneously. Most of my work involved adding comments and insights to the raw text file stored on my voice-activated personal recorder. At regular intervals, completed work was archived to my A.I.D. and workstation. Now, catching up, I found the writing more difficult than usual. One word kept tripping me up.

Ocean.

In the course of my life, and after the numerous times I spent on or immersed in the ocean (I have been in all seven, but they are connected; they are one), I presumed to know what I was looking at. Because the oceans of Earth are its most prominent physical feature, logic dictated that the same word applied to Orb. In Spanish, *Océano.* In Chinese, *Hai Yang.* In Arabic, *Moheet.* In any language, who would have otherwise labeled what covers this strange and beautiful world?

There must be another way to describe what we observe here.

The mind and the written word strain to embrace the concept of an OceanOrb. A fundamental problem occurs when you are compelled to take a lifelong assumption and toss it out the window. When that window is open, what else flies out? Revisit the ocean of Earth. Does the vast and breathtakingly beautiful biodiversity within, and dependent on, that ocean make it any less wondrous a living entity than the 'ocean' of Orb?

I've posed and answered this question for myself. You can spend a lifetime looking at something, believing it is one thing when it's really something else.

There was another word giving me trouble.

I laid the writing aside to play with my sorely neglected pooch, quietly waiting at my feet with her mouth chock-full of toy duck. By acknowledging her stare, playtime became as inevitable as Thompson's sunrise. I cleared a space for her to run, opened my cabin door, and flung that silly little toy into the hallway. A sparkle came into her eyes, followed by several delighted little yips that carried on the warm air to beckon Kelly. An excited little dog, tail vibrating, duck in mouth, peered up at her expectantly.

"Can I play, too?" Kelly pleaded, affecting a child's voice.

The duck was deposited at her feet. We humans do not catch on right away. To rule out a mistake on our part (as a species, we had made a bunch lately), Angie stared down at the duck and up at Kelly while increasing the speed of her oscillating tail.

"Come," I said to Kelly, motioning and making room. "Sit beside me." The space was tight, but I didn't mind. We were dressed in shorts and T-shirts. The bare skin of our arms and legs touched, and a feeling not unlike touching the Orb passed between us.

"How's your patient?" I asked.

"Serious but stable. Resting comfortably. How's the writing?"

"I guess about the same as your patient."

"We only have one more day here," Kelly said. There was more in those words than the obvious.

"Yes, one more day."

I threw the duck. As it pirouetted through the air, Angie bounded into the hall. She rotated and leaped in one supple and athletic motion, snatching the toy mid-air. Funny-strange how, for every toss, the toy was alternately returned to Kelly, then to me. At last tired, Angie collapsed on her back, front paws folded up on her thorax like the forelegs of a praying mantis. The triangular shape of her head, formed by her snout and protruding ears, did nothing to dispel the image.

My heart raced with apprehension. I turned to face Kelly. "I love you."

Stunned, she stared at me, her black and gold eyes widening, searching, questioning.

"I love you. I'll say the words once for each star in the night sky until you believe me."

Before I knew what was happening, she was sitting astride my lap, her whole weight preventing my escape. Her stare penetrated me. She needed to know, to discover, that I was telling the truth.

To her. To myself.

There was a moment of solemnity, that wondrous sadness that often precedes utter joy. She was deliriously happy, laughing at her justifiable need for assurance that I had finally found a way to break my abject silence.

She kissed me feverishly and said, "More than anything, I believe you. I believe you because I believe in you. I love you."

We made promises and commitments as lovers do until Angie, feeling left out, nuzzled her way between us and began licking the tips of our noses. This was the scene Diana interrupted when she appeared in the doorway of my cabin.

"Thought I'd find you two… uh, three, in here playing kissy-face." The smiles we beamed up at her temporarily derailed what she had come to say. Scrutinizing our faces, she said, "Something is up here. *Isn't there*, Kelly? Anyway, come quick. You need to see what's happening outside."

Expecting the return of the Orb, we untangled ourselves and followed Diana. We were disappointed to see Thompson and Paul staring intently at an empty horizon—the direction a freshening breeze seemed to be originating. Responding to a Thompson inquiry, Paul said, "Not with any certainty, but it will be here soon. Very soon."

A sudden gust of wind cleared several empty juice containers from our outside table.

"Paul?" I said.

"Feel that wind?" he said, not taking his eyes off the horizon. "My instruments are registering an intense storm approaching. Look—look there!" He pointed to a thin black line off in the distance. "That's the leading edge of a front. Only it can't be. Not by any meteorological definition that I'm aware of. We're missing a key ingredient: two air masses with different densities."

"Any idea how severe?" Thompson asked.

"No," Paul answered.

Thompson frowned. "I need ten minutes to get *Desio* above the storm. Do I have them?"

"Not a chance. This is happening fast. The wind has increased to a fresh gale while we've talked."

"Get everything that wasn't damaged inside. Fast!" Thompson ordered. "Kelly—"

"I'm on it! Kyle, Paul, help me with Larry."

With our help, Kelly quickly got the physicist standing. Getting him onto *Desio*'s landing, then through the narrow hatchway and into his cabin, was much more difficult. Once he was safely inside, we helped Thompson secure the undamaged remains of the geology and marine biology stations. With nothing left for the wind to turn into a dangerous projectile, Paul prepared to launch a small weather balloon. The rest of us watched the advancing storm.

The features of the advancing front were becoming clear: a sheer, billowing wall of dark green and black clouds rising angrily from a starting point five hundred meters above the OceanOrb and then extending high into the troposphere. Between the clouds and OceanOrb, wind-driven rain fell in wavy, dark gray sheets. An ominous darkness descended as the storm's leading edge obscured the late afternoon sun. A fierce wind whipped through the spires, producing an eerie, high-pitched howl.

"Won't be long now!" Thompson said, shouting to be heard. "Another minute, and we're going to be slammed. Be prepared to duck inside!"

"Bruce!" Diana yelled. "How much wind can *Desio* withstand?!"

"With her reduced weight on Orb, I'd start worrying at two hundred kilometers per hour!"

"I'll start worrying now, if you don't mind!"

"Velocity is half that!" Paul said, glancing at his anemometer. "But where's the lightning?!"

"You *want* lightning?!" Kelly asked, hooking her arm in mine. I grabbed Angie, who, nose twitching, faced the wind. She appeared unafraid. Perhaps she sensed what would happen next.

"Look at that!" Paul cried out.

A V-shaped indentation appeared at the center of the ominous wall of churning clouds. Initially a minor feature, the V-cleft deepened and widened until a massive split was created in the towering column.

"What's happening?!" Thompson shouted.

"*That's* happening!" was all Paul could say, pointing to what was now a kilometer-wide rift in the storm, frustrated that his command of all things meteorological could not explain the phenomenon.

The front was moving fast. Suddenly, we found ourselves in the mouth of the V, gazing up at cloud banks dramatically parting to both sides. It was as if the tiny island we inhabited could cleave the storm in two or that some unnatural force, conceding our puny presence, had decided to spare us the worst of the tempest.

The wind slackened to fluctuating gusts as the storm passed to each side. Straight above, the blue-gray sky was partially obscured by curtains of rain driven laterally into the divide we occupied. Drenched to the bone, we stubbornly refused to move. The strange and magnificent canyon of black clouds was too awe-inspiring to miss; the bands of large, warm droplets too refreshing for us to seek cover.

We played. Kelly squeezed a stream of water from a handful of her shiny black hair. Diana tilted her head up, letting the rain fall freely on her face and catching liquid refreshment with her tongue. I put Angie down, and she shook her coat, whipping spray outward. It eventually occurred to Paul that he needed to release the tethered weather balloon, which, buffeted by gusts, floated high into the air and disappeared.

Thompson, looking at his wet crew, shook his head and laughed.

The rain stopped. The retreating storm's wall, which had split entirely in two, dissipated quickly. Puffs of clouds gathered on the horizon. The giant blue sun poked out, scattering soft beams of light into the mist-filled air. In the saturated atmosphere, an overarching rainbow appeared.

"It seems we're the subject of some attention," Thompson said.

"*Do you think?*" Diana said, making fun of Thompson, pointing out what, to her, was evident.

"Paul?" Thompson said, looking to the meteorologist for a possible explanation.

"Trillions of liters of OceanOrb evaporate into the atmosphere each day. I should have guessed that the entity could influence local weather, possibly the entire planet's climate." Paul paused, troubled. "Or, is my thinking too constrained? As the Orb is the Ocean, the same may be true for the atmosphere, for the two are intrinsically linked. I come to this problem humbly admitting I don't know how the storm originated or split in half like a bifurcating amoeba. Not a clue. Not yet."

"Did anybody notice how calm the OceanOrb stayed?" Kelly asked.

Our blank expressions confirmed we had failed to make the observation.

"Undisturbed in a gale-force wind," Thompson commented, annoyed with himself. "Of all of us, I should have taken note."

"Under the circumstances, it's understandable," Kelly said. "But I'll tell you what needs no clarification: We just witnessed a demonstration of exactly who is benevolently in charge here."

Thompson agreed. "The Orb showed us that we are vulnerable on land, removing any doubt about strict physical limitations to its domain."

With an hour of usable sunlight left in the day, I asked leave of Thompson to visit the cove, betting on the off-chance that the Orb might return to the location where they were first spotted. If the entity sought to avoid contact, it would go where we were not. Human logic and emotion were holding sway, but those were the imperfect tools I had to work with.

Granting my request, Thompson said, "Nothing to lose." With everyone else preoccupied, Angie and I set off by ourselves.

At the cove, I resisted the urge to swim and instead climbed to the highest accessible vantage point. I gazed out into the distance, first with the unaided eye and then with the binoculars Diana had thrust upon me while leaving the Square.

Not a single Orb was visible. Their absence saddened me. My obsession with scanning the distance almost caused me to overlook an object nearby that should have claimed my immediate attention.

Ixodes.

Or what remained of it. The visible half of the submersible, mangled and indented, was tilting above the surface, inconveniently wedged between two jagged boulders.

Determining how the sub met its fate was crucial. I considered swimming out to the wreckage for a closer look, but reconsidered because the sunlight was fading fast. I activated the binoculars' image retention function for later upload to the crew's A.I.D.. Ideas about what happened could then be offered, parsed, and weighed.

My already formulated opinion would quite conceivably be mangled worse than the *Ixodes.*

"The hull is rated for one thousand atmospheres," Thompson informed the crew (minus Melhaus, who was recovering) as he studied the images. "Some of the damage—see how the tubular manipulator arms are crushed—must have been inflicted by twice the sub's working pressure. We're talking ocean depths of twenty thousand meters. No way could she sink to that level and return to the surface under her own power."

"Orbs, however, can make their exteriors as molecularly dense as they want," Paul said. "They can withstand virtually unlimited pressure. As for the OceanOrb, pressure isn't even a consideration."

"So you agree with the premise?"

"Yes. The planet is devoid of tides. The recent storm produced no coincidental wave disturbance. Yet these images show the submersible in a partially elevated position, attainable only through the direct action of an individual Orb or the influence of the OceanOrb. Barring further evidence, I'd consider either conclusive proof.

"In effect, this proves Melhaus right," Diana was forced to admit. "Good thing you dismantled the laser. I'd be tempted to use it on myself rather than see his reaction to this piece of news."

"There's something else to think about, Diana," Kelly said. "One reason for Larry's behavior was the belief that a discovery in his field was slipping through his hands. But we shouldn't forget—how could we?—how badly he reacted to being held accountable for *Ixodes*' destruction."

"Maybe he wasn't correct," I said, disturbing the lull produced by Kelly's sobering remark. "Perhaps the Orb resurrected it from the depths *after* it malfunctioned and went to the bottom."

"Why?" Kelly asked.

"We can't prove exactly when it was deposited on those rocks, but what if it was after we discarded the laser at the shoreline?"

"You mean the sub was brought to the cove as a signal?"

"Maybe," I said, replying to Kelly but staring at Diana. "Or not. *Ixodes* was indiscriminately collecting phyto-plankton."

"That again?" Diana said, this time without the smirk I was getting used to. She was pleased that I had supplied a plausible alternative to Melhaus's vindication and a glimmer of hope that the entity would return.

After listening for a few more minutes, Thompson distilled the conversation to its essence.

"Possibility one: *Ixodes* was destroyed and then stranded by the Orb. Possibility two: It malfunctioned and was subsequently stranded by the Orb. Is there a possibility three?"

There were no takers. "Well?" Thompson persisted. "Is there a possibility that does *not* involve the Orb?"

Still no takers. Well, almost.

"The King of the Fairies?" I said.

After dinner, Kelly, Angie, and I sat side-by-side on our favorite boulder. As the last light retreated and the first stars revealed themselves, we discussed our lives on Earth—lives that would intertwine in ways yet to be discovered, drawing us closer together and widening our circle of family, friends, and associates.

I felt a constricting aspect to this socialization, an implied expectation (though never by Kelly) for me to "fit in." Just one more small part in the machine that has run amok on the planet for six thousand years, destroying nature and ravaging resources.

If you will, call this fear a phobia.

I own it.

Tell me that I'm fooling myself, for when you're a citizen of planet Earth, like it or not, you're a cog in that machine.

See you when I get back.

When I sought help with these feelings, Kelly volunteered her best palliative advice. "At first," she said, "take your medicine in small doses."

"Like my participation in this expedition?"

"Do you see any signs of a cure?"

"Four out of five, one especially, will be friends for life."

But as I fought against the idea of inclusion, a pang of loneliness washed over me. I expressed this to Kelly the best way I knew how. "My father repeatedly said to believe in nothing and no one other than yourself. I've lived most of my life that way."

"Bringing you to this point. To me. You see those paired stars over there, the red and the blue? They *appear* close together, but in all likelihood, they are hundreds of light-years apart. That, my love, will never be us."

I took her hand in mine and began to tell her something she already guessed. "There is something I need to do. If the Orb return, I want to reiterate my proposition to Thompson and the others. With help from our little ambassador, I want to attempt contact."

"Can I tell you I'm afraid?" Kelly said. "Afraid of losing you. We have no idea what could happen. What if you're changed in some way?"

"Perhaps I already am—thanks to you and the others, and even, strangely enough, to Melhaus. I must do this. For many reasons. How often does a person get to perform a selfish act that is selfless at the same time?"

Later that evening, in a sign that championed my idea, a thousand colored lights reappeared to regale us from a distance.

D Major op. 61

ALTHOUGH THE MASSIVE BLUE sun rose over the eastern horizon, our attention was drawn to the Orb flotilla gracefully tracing meandering paths among themselves. The radiant colors displayed during the prior evening had reverted to muted tones of pearlescent gray in the brightness of day.

"Do you think they'll come any closer?" Diana repeated for the third time, speaking to no one in particular. Her face had been hidden behind binoculars for the last several minutes.

"If wishing would make it so, yes," Thompson replied. "But even if an Orb sits in your lap, what then?"

"Hey, at least it would be a sign that they've forgiven us for being total jerks."

On that, we all agreed. Four of us stood beside Diana, squinting in the early morning sunlight. Melhaus was convalescing within his secured cabin.

"Couldn't sleep," Paul said. "I was looking for a way for us to make amends. Nothing presented itself, and we're running out of time."

"A cynic would say the impression we're leaving is the correct one," Thompson replied. "So why try to change it?"

Kelly and I exchanged glances. She gave me a nervous smile, then turned to Thompson and said:

"Commander, with your permission, I'd like to use the bow."

"On Melhaus?" Thompson replied, believing he was being toyed with. "As the ship's physician, I'd expect you to find a better way to make amends. Besides, both arrows were broken."

There were good reasons Thompson would be the last to understand the real intent of Kelly's words. Unlike Diana and Paul, he was absent when I suggested that Kelly play the violin to attract the Orb. Concluding that four of his crew knew something he didn't, he focused on Kelly. "Okay, Takara, you have something in mind. Spill it."

"It's been suggested that I play for them. I agreed."

Thompson caught on immediately. "Vibrations. It seems innocuous enough. Good idea."

"Kyle thought of it."

"Uh-huh," Thompson responded. "Why do I think there's much more to this?"

"Maybe I should explain," I said.

"Yes, why don't you."

"I previously mentioned to Kelly—she voiced her misgivings—that I wanted an opportunity to contact the Orb.

I never connected it to her playing the violin. I probably should have, since that might bring the Orb closer."

Thompson decided to bring Paul and Diana into the conversation.

"And what do you two know about this?"

"Only the part about the violin," Diana responded. "Kyle mentioned it two days ago. Back when you wanted ideas on how to make contact."

"Let me get this straight," Thompson said, his attention returning to Kelly. "You play the violin... I suppose you have a specific selection in mind—"

"As a matter of fact, I do," Kelly responded, although the commander's voice indicated he wasn't seeking or expecting a response. "I thought Beethoven was appropriate for the occasion. *Opus 61 in D Major Concerto for Violin and Orchestra.* Second movement. Sans orchestra, of course."

"Of course," Thompson said, undeterred. "And while playing—like you're some kind of modern-day Pied Piper— the Orb are drawn closer." It was plain that Thompson was immensely enjoying himself. I wasn't spared scrutiny. "Meanwhile, you, Kyle, squat on a submerged boulder, waiting. Waiting for what? To be swallowed whole like some modern-day Jonah?"

"That pretty much sums it up," I said. "You did, however, leave out one character, our little ambassador, Angie. Where I go, she goes. Or should I say where she has gone, I hope to go. She may be the only reason this idea can work."

Angie's inclusion captured Thompson's imagination. He turned more serious, soliciting Paul and Diana's opinion. "What do you think of this?"

"Dangerous," Paul volunteered. "Is it outlandish? No more farfetched than a perfectly round planet that harbors a perfectly round entity that…"

"I get it," Thompson interrupted. "Diana?"

"Why Kyle? Why not someone with a science background? Like myself."

"Hold on," Paul said. "We're getting ahead of ourselves here, subjugating personal safety for the theoretical chance, and that's all this is, that it will make amends for how we've behaved as a species."

"I suppose we are," Thompson responded. "But the idea has merit."

"Does this mean you approve?" I asked.

"No," Thompson responded. "This needs airing out." He gestured at the work table. "While we're sitting down."

Once seated, Thompson said, "Someone's missing. Get Melhaus out here."

"Why bring him into this?" Diana complained. "He's the cause of this discussion."

"Should we deny him the example of our better conduct?" Thompson countered. "I refuse to accept that he's irredeemable given what he said when informed that the Orb were the probable cause of *Ixodes'* demise."

"And that was?" Diana asked, doubting it could make a difference.

"He took some personal responsibility, saying that ignoring my order was contributory."

"Said with an ulterior motive."

"Could be," Thompson acknowledged.

Melhaus was retrieved from *Desio*. After being made comfortable near the table, Thompson addressed him.

"Thanks almost entirely to your reckless actions, Doctor, the Orb may see us as a hostile threat. Nevertheless, I invite you to assist us in evaluating what Kyle has proposed in this regard."

"I shall furnish my best advice."

"Like a well-worn sofa. Isn't that comforting," Diana said to me in a whisper. I grinned but agreed with Thompson regarding Melhaus. Society would exact punishment on him soon enough, but until that day arrived, including him in our society might have a positive effect. There was no downside other than Diana's objection, and much of that was an affectation.

I've had more enjoyable experiences than the debate that ensued. Most of it centered on what might happen when entering the Orb, including (singly or in combination) being captured, crushed, stranded, altered (mentally, molecularly, or, as Diana said, sexually), drowned, electrocuted, asphyxiated, and irradiated. Unfortunately, Kelly was also obliged to endure this ordeal.

I pointed out that since Angie had emerged unscathed, so would I. Nor would I allow anybody to go in my place if she was involved. No one successfully argued that point.

Paul added that some benefit might be conveyed if the Orb felt the strong emotional bond between Angie and me. They also displayed no hostility before or after the laser provocation. The remarkable weather phenomenon was, in all likelihood, a demonstration of ability—a warning to behave.

As to what befell *Ixodes*, two ideas presented themselves: the entity was protecting the phytoplankton; the sub had been viewed as something akin to an intrusive virus. Both ideas were speculative, making my next words to Thompson problematic.

"Bruce, I realize you have a tough decision to make, but I strongly believe that our technology is far more alien to the Orb than the life-form we represent. It is either incomprehensible or rejected for reasons unclear to us. Humanity has become wholly dependent on material things. The opposite may be true of the Orb, an entity conceivably hundreds of millions of years old but apparently without material possessions. Sorry, commander, I don't wish to make this harder on you."

"If I understand correctly, you don't want any form of monitoring?"

"Afraid so."

"Dr. Melhaus, what do you think about this?"

I was surprised that Thompson sought Melhaus's opinion first. If he was looking for a counterpoint to mine, he didn't find it.

"There is no monitoring device or communicator signal capable of penetrating the Orb. Unless facilitated by the entity, that is. *Nothing* can penetrate the Orb. There is a potential danger in attempting to do so."

"Spoken from personal experience," Diana said.

We expected an argument to ensue. Melhaus simply nodded. Diana seemed disappointed. I leaned into her and, in what I hoped was a low voice, said, "Too bad. Fun's all gone."

Thompson told us to shut up, then sought Paul's opinion about the matter at hand.

"I reluctantly agree with Kyle and Larry."

"Change of heart?" Thompson asked.

"Not really."

"Let's hear it."

"It's what you said previously. If we are doing this to make amends and to impart a better sense of what we humans are all about, then collecting scientific data must be subordinated. No monitoring."

"What about you, Diana?" Thompson asked.

"Sure, Kyle and Angie are inseparable. I also understand his arguments for not bringing instrumentation. But this is a scientific expedition. As such, wouldn't a scientist be better able to evaluate the information gathered by the best instruments of all, those of our five senses? I should go."

Thompson withheld his response. "Kelly? We haven't heard from you. I'll give you a pass if you feel personal feelings would compromise your advice."

Tough spot, I thought. And I had put her there.

"No, I have something to add," she responded. "It would be a big mistake to send anybody but Kyle! Can't you see, Commander? The scientific methods, with their successes and failures, have been tried. They have their place. But not in this. We need to try something else."

"And exactly what would that be?" Thompson asked.

"I'm not sure I can name it. I remember what Kyle shared with me after we flew over what we then assumed was an ocean. He said he felt something intangible was down there. It took Paul's genius to solidify that feeling into a concept our minds could accept. But have we? Kyle will come the closest if there is any chance of doing so."

If I needed further proof of Kelly's devotion, well, there it was, hitting me right between the eyes.

"No dissension," Thompson commented. "Except for Diana's point that a scientist should attempt this. But I have to agree with Kelly. Can we anticipate what will happen if the encounter takes place? It may be incomprehensible to our experience as scientists. Beyond our capacity to imagine. I'm also forced to consider what Kyle constantly tells us: True communication requires information to flow both ways. Who among us is better suited to the task?"

"Was it merely a coincidence that Kyle saw, or almost as important, *imagined* he saw the Orb before any of us? Or that the name he chose for the planet so aptly describes it? Remember, he was selected among a group of accomplished candidates to provide a perspective that differed from that of scientists. Well, he's done that often enough, hasn't he— sometimes to the point of annoyance."

Thompson looked down at his hands, then stared at the far horizon. Out there in the serenity was the promise of a better understanding. And a decision.

"You see," Thompson said, glancing around the table, then settling on Diana, "how I'm tending to view this? Sorry, but you'll have to be content with grilling him after."

"You can count on it," Diana replied.

"We will proceed," Thompson said. "But for our edification, Kyle, what *exactly* is compelling you to do this? What is your motivation?"

"Curiosity," I said, but my crewmates deserved better from me. "I joined this mission hoping to climb out of the emotional box I put myself in. What better way than stepping into a perfectly round sphere?"

"From where we sit," Thompson said, glancing at Kelly, "you're out already." He then pointed to the spires as we rose to make preparations. "One more thing. If you get into the Orb and don't get an answer to what formed those, don't bother coming back out."

Someone needed to make entries in my mission chronicle during the interval I might be inside the Orb. My first inclination was to ask Kelly, but I sought someone with a more detached perspective.

I invited Paul to join me in my cabin.

"Would you object to adding your observations and impressions to my work when I am indisposed?"

"Not at all."

"I can't think of anyone who'd do it better. Do you need my recorder? The file name is *Orb*. The password is *Aishiteru*." I spelled it.

"Japanese?"

"Yes." I told him the definition. Then I told him the meaning.

"I'd say your proverbial box is exploding from within."

"Stand back. Wouldn't want to get any on you."

"Too late for that."

"Am I alone, Paul, thinking humanity is too preoccupied with hurling itself across the cosmos? Ultimately, what will we discover? That the journey outward has distracted us from facing inward?"

"That generalization may apply to humanity. I doubt it describes everyone in this crew. I'm certain it does not apply to you."

"The problem is how critically I view myself transfers to others. The compassion I have for a specific few—present company included—is sadly lacking toward people in general."

"Ah, *mon ami*," Paul said, rising, "the proper wording of a problem often helps define the solution. I must be off. Thompson wants the holocam repositioned."

With Angie in tow, I headed straight for Kelly's cabin.

She was sitting on her bed. Spread out beside her were old-fashioned pages of sheet music. I leaned against the frame of the open doorway, watching as she tuned her violin, first tightening the bow by turning its small tensioning screw, then measuring the distance between hair and stick until there was a pinky's width between the two. Next, she tuned the four strings, plucking and adjusting each until an acceptable tone was produced. When finished, she played each string with the bow, appearing satisfied with the resulting sound. All was done by ear, a difficult skill to master.

Funny strange. At that moment, I thought of Thompson stringing *his* bow.

Kelly put the violin aside. With a worried look, she stared straight ahead.

I left the doorway and knelt before her, folding my arms in her lap. I looked up into her black and gold eyes. "Don't be afraid for me," I pleaded. "Do you know why I will be safe? Your music. It is more than vibrations. It's you discovering the emotional intent of the composer and expressing the same within yourself—a form of empathy. Deep inside me, I believe something similar will occur within the Orb. They will hear *you*. Without words, nothing can be misinterpreted. Not your music, not Angie, and not me."

Bending forward, she placed her lips against the top of my head. I was in a darkened space, safely hidden within the drapings of her sweet-smelling hair.

"Am I in the Orb?" I said, getting her to laugh.

"Am I in your heart?"

"You are a part of me. The missing jigsaw piece."

Angie, wanting to be included, jumped onto the bed. I moved to prevent her from lying across the pages of music.

"It's all right," Kelly said, petting her. "There's no harm done. I have the music here and here." She pointed to her heart and head.

"The three of us make a good team."

"I won't be there with you two."

"Not physically."

"Do me a favor?"

"Anything."

"At one point, think of me."

"Always."

I wasn't sure why, but I wanted to speak with Melhaus. I found him outside, propped up in a position to view the coming show.

"How are you feeling?" I asked.

"Sore. I'm a bit tired. Kelly's taking good care of me. You probably think it's much better care than I deserve."

"No, not true, Doctor. I have not written you off. And suffice it to say that the only person who has been more stressed on this voyage than yourself was Thompson when he decided to hold your life in his hands."

Melhaus's eyes turned glassy. "I once spent several months blackboarding an equation that solved a difficult physics problem. When I finished, I stood back and reviewed my work, delighted with myself until I realized there was a simpler, more elegant solution. If only I had seen it earlier…"

The uncharacteristic depth of introspection took me by surprise. "Larry, if *I* look back at what happened, I also see a possibility. This crew, like the prior one, experienced extraordinarily high stress. The only difference is that you and that prior crew never benefited from entering the OceanOrb."

"The Orb and your sanctuary theory exonerate me? Ah, if it were only that simple."

I wasn't prepared to argue that point. Instead, I asked, "Do you have any last-minute advice?"

There was a short pause followed by an enigmatic, "Be yourself."

All was ready.

I walked over to the shoreline and stared out. Flat as a board. The mere hint of a breeze.

And a vague sense of expectation emanating from somewhere. Everywhere.

What is waiting for me out there?

Not far away, Kelly sought the perfect promontory overlooking the Orb armada. Taking Angie in my arms, I grabbed one paw and used it to wave. Exactly as Kelly once did for me.

Thompson, Diana, and Paul came up beside me.

"Nervous?" Diana asked.

"Should I be?" I responded, half in jest.

"Only a fool wouldn't be," she answered back.

"Then he's definitely not nervous," Thompson remarked.

"Cool as a cucumber," Diana added.

"As temperate as a summer's eve," Paul said. Then to me, "Sorry. Had to contribute."

Diana punched me in the shoulder. "Be well," she said.

I was touched by how concerned they were for my welfare. Reluctantly, they withdrew to a nearby vantage point. Melhaus was ordered to stay out of sight.

I sat in a modified lotus position in a shallow pool thirty meters out from dry land. In my lap, Angie, cradled to keep her partly immersed in the OceanOrb. She happily gave me an affectionate lick on the nose.

The violin is a remarkably expressive musical instrument, perhaps the closest to duplicating the singing human voice. In the hands of a master, its sound can elevate us above the turmoil we've created as a species—a promise of release from all things mundane and material. I have seen people overwhelmed by emotion. I've seen Paul wipe a tear away while hearing Kelly play.

And as she played, my heart missed a beat. Every Orb, and there were hundreds, ceased movement.

"Maestro," I heard Thompson exclaim, "you have an audience. Play on!"

A minute later, Diana shouted, "Here they come!"

Incredibly, the Orb were steadily progressing toward our little island! Twelve, approaching slowly at first, then with greater speed. I wondered if they would overrun me when they suddenly and simultaneously halted.

The smallest Orb was a meter in diameter; the largest was taller than I. All had transformed to radiant blue with an overlay of light blue circular shapes traversing across their surfaces. Was there a correlation between the ebb and flow of the colored shapes and the cadence of the music? There was no denying that they were drawn to the vibrations, perhaps to the underlying emotion. At Thompson's request, Kelly stopped playing.

In an instant, Angie and I became the new center of attention, with twelve Orbs forming a semicircle around us. The largest Orb broke ranks and approached. My heart raced.

This is what I wanted.

Account of Kyle Lorenzo's and Angie's Acceptance into the Orb. Related Matters.
Paul Bertrand, Ph.D.

My first thought? This can't be happening.

Kyle reflectively lowered his head and tucked in his shoulders as the Orb (an estimated three meters in diameter) moved forward from the group to envelope him and Angie. The entity's external appearance, which had regressed to a uniform blue with the cessation of music, became embedded with silver flecks. Instantly doubling in diameter, it withdrew rapidly, disappearing over a cloudless horizon. Kyle and Angie were gone.

Diana attempted to console Kelly. It cannot be overstated how immensely troubled we were by this development. Although it was one of the many potential risks discussed, it was considered unlikely during prior conversations. At that time, we decided that *Desio* should not be used to follow after Kyle. To do so would almost certainly be futile and perhaps counterproductive. In light of the present reality, the idea was reconsidered. Thompson, however, resolved to do what we agreed to when calmer heads prevailed.

The resumption of violin playing, in the desperate hope of summoning the Orb, only managed to captivate the attention of the others remaining offshore. Still, Kelly had to try. Our hopes were further dampened when they began retreating as the sun reached its zenith. Within ten minutes, all had vanished. All we could do was watch the horizon and halfheartedly resume the vital work of the mission.

And trust, as Kyle did, in the benevolence of the Orb.

I witnessed Kelly standing knee-deep in the OceanOrb. An hour later, she was still there, staring into the distance. The image is hard to forget.

Diana and I went to Thompson, who had been watching all along. Together, we waded out to join our crewmate. When Thompson was beside Kelly, he gently touched her arm and said, "Let's go find him."

"No need. He's all right."

"Kelly…" Thompson began, unsure what to say next.

"No. I believe," Kelly assured him. "Please. All of you. Continue your work."

My logical mind told me that this was false hope. A part of me felt otherwise. My crewmates and I exchanged glances and stepped away.

Not long afterward, Diana cried out, "I see something!"

Advancing at tremendous speed out of the blue-gray distance was a solitary Orb. Kelly splashed her way over to where it finally came to rest. She attempted to peer down through its impenetrable surface, then rushed forward as the Orb sped away. But not until it had returned Kyle and Angie to the precise location from where they had been taken, apparently unharmed.

Kelly hugged and kissed them both.

I received a bewildered look from Kyle when I said, "We have to know if you're okay. Kyle! Bark!"

Thompson, laughing with us, said, "Give it up. He wasn't taught that."

Imagining the Unimaginable

IN THE PEREGRINATION of human experience, objective reality remains an elusive destination. Although what reaches our senses is incomplete, it is nevertheless assimilated and, with bias, judged.

I claimed no immunity from bias when embarking on this journey. From the start, I never purported to be other than an honest first filter chronicling what was to be the remarkable, hard-to-believe events of this mission. In this light, the relative merit (for absolute truth is elusive) of my accounting can best be evaluated in context with what I have revealed about myself. For this reason, there are passages within the body of this work that are highly personal.

I may have earned your confidence. You may choose to believe me when I write that on a worktable I once saw an empty juice container and had judged its color to be metallic silver. But if I compound the problem, if my description of the container color were to unexpectedly stray from the norm (perhaps the color had changed in the light of a blue sun), your acceptance might not necessarily follow.

In this uncertainty, I can only try to avoid letting words form an additional barrier between you and me.

But what if the artificial construct we've accepted as reality completely breaks down? What if it disintegrates and becomes altogether indistinguishable from our imagination and dreams?

What then?

Then, if we temporarily suspend disbelief, we take one small step on a journey to understanding something other than ourselves.

We take a step toward understanding the Orb.

In truth, there is no other way for you to accept the following.

Contact With the Orb. Summary of Verbal Report Submitted to Mission Leader Bruce Thompson and the Crew of *Desio*:

It happened in the blink of an eye. My vision briefly pixelated as Angie and I passed through and into the Orb. I chose to remain in the modified lotus position, as there was little room to stand. Angie stayed calm and alert.

A feeling of tension gave way to one of mild elation. Encompassing and confining us was the unexpectedly *transparent* concavity of the Orb. I waved to my crewmates, signaling that we were unharmed. No response. I could only assume the entity was using its remarkable command of molecular manipulation to maintain its opaque appearance.

Without forewarning, the space I inhabited began enlarging, uniformly expanding several meters. Simultaneously, there was rapid lateral movement. I did not feel apprehensive as I watched the shoreline and my crewmates recede into the distance.

What was inside the Orb?

Angie and me.

I shall repeat myself:

The inside of the Orb was Angie and I. Our bodies, my clothing, the air—the fleeting, infinitesimally small particles making up these physicalities were, of course, also present— and yet what was really occupying the interior was the *beingness* of Angie and me, essentially filling the space more entirely and utterly than air molecules filling an inflated balloon or neutrons packing a collapsed star. How I came to this exquisite sentience, I do not know, but an undeniable feeling of expansiveness, a projection of the conscious self, radiated outward from my being. The sensation was euphoric, and I realized that this *ethereality* was a pathway by which the Orb could somehow sense and respond to Angie's and my intrinsic nature. With conviction, I offer this unlikely thought because I was aware of, and could intensely feel, Angie's mood—an exuberant and delightful mix of anticipation and happiness.

As you will see, I would soon experience a startling extrapolation of this ability, this greater self.

Concerning the interior of the Orb, there is little to describe except that, unlike its unyielding, hard exterior, the surface Angie and I rested on had the forgiving density of a soft rubber mat but with the transparency of lightly tinted glass. The composition of this unusual material is probably unknown to us, but I considered it bad manners to attempt to gouge out a chunk for later analysis. I can tell you that the material's clarity facilitated an unimpeded view in *every* direction—up into the bright sky and down into the bottomless depths of the OceanOrb—thereby greatly accentuating the floating sensation. The panoramic vista, the feeling of perfectly filling the space occupied, led me to believe that I was inseparable from the Orb as we gracefully slid across the planetary surface. It was easy to accommodate this exhilarating feeling, this indefinable connection to that which I desired to understand.

The nearly undetectable fluidity of our movement made gauging travel velocity impossible. Some indeterminate time elapsed before I noticed that all motion had ceased. By this juncture, all points of reference—the occasional stray cloud, a passing island, groups of Orbs—were long gone. I was left to speculate why we had been transported from the shoreline to the edge of nowhere so quickly and inexplicably. I doubted the Orb was avoiding, as I so fondly remembered, the threat of being battered by Kelly with a tent pole. A more generalized wariness of anything human was a distinct possibility, but this explanation seemed implausible upon further reflection. I realized that from the OceanOrb's unique perspective, we could never be on the edge of nowhere. How could we be when an entity occupying the entirety of a perfectly round planet placed us at the exact center of its everywhere? Whatever the reason for our relocation and whatever was intended for us, I had no alternative but to lie back and wait.

And wait. The long period of inactivity was troubling. I felt the need to mark the passage of time. The sun was immediately overhead, meaning approximately two hours had elapsed. I resolutely hung on to the belief that the Orb would do no intentional harm. But what if the entity had a different concept of time than I? Or, more worrisome, none whatsoever? In that continuum that I partitioned into something called 'tomorrow,' I'd have an unhindered view of *Desio* leaving the atmosphere with Angie and me left behind. I was made well aware of the many risks of attempting contact, but as time passed, I started believing that I had better and brighter ideas in my life.

Ironically, as you shall see, this prolonged period when nothing *appeared* to be happening was the one occasion I talked myself into feeling apprehensive. And not just for Angie and me. I was worried that my crewmates would be increasingly concerned for my welfare.

What to do? I decided it was a great time to use an object formerly classified by the mission engineers as "nonessential mass." And, just like a particular violin and hunting bow, they could not have been more mistaken. Only Kelly, smiling, had spotted the stuffed duck protruding from my side pocket. I now held the toy up for Angie to see and immediately felt her happiness and excitement surge. There was, however, a small problem. Although the Orb had initially been accommodating by expanding to three times my height, our play area was limited. Nothing, however, could discourage us.

Nor was it an obstacle to the Orb. After a dozen duck tosses, I started to see and feel the diameter of the Orb slowly expanding! After twelve more tosses, we had a satisfactory space in which to play. Funny-strange, this synchronicity of Angie, Orb, and me.

From nowhere, an idea entered my head. I paused to contemplate the nature of time and began to see it differently. For me, the simple and endlessly enjoyable act of tossing the duck could define time's passage more satisfactorily than minutes and hours. For an entity five hundred million years old, our play could be more meaningful than the planet's spin and solar sweep. My worries began to subside.

What was happening to me?

Who can say? Perhaps not only *I* was happening to me, and wasn't that so much the better? Attempting, as if 'I' could, to maintain greater objectivity during my contact with the Orb seemed futile and would have been unproductive. Everything bringing me to this juncture—the strengths and weaknesses of my personality, the insights of my fellow crewmates, all that we collectively observed and surmised and wildly guessed about the Orb—all this cried out to me that the opposite approach was essential. Acting emotionally was the only idea that made sense to me as a nonscientist. As a *human*. How else can we communicate with an entity whose principal open channel, at least thus far, appeared to be a form of two-way empathy? There were no precedents, no set ways to proceed. The rules get invented as you go. I mention this as an introduction to and support of what follows.

I let myself fall asleep.

How could I permit that to happen?

Considering where I was and what I hoped to accomplish, this feat was easier than imagined.

Playtime with Angie had ended. I had lain back to relax, letting her settle in beside me. The temperature within our space had remained surprisingly comfortable. The wall encompassing us, judged at least one meter thick, had taken on a blue-gray opacity. The soothing quality of light within the interior and a gentle swaying and bobbing motion produced a lulling effect. The only sound was my own quiet, rhythmic breathing. The Orb had no objection to my dozing off. In all probability, it actively encouraged me to attain a peaceful and open mind.

Sleep may not be the best description of what I experienced, and I'm not sure what is. Waking dreams? A type of unfettered daydreaming? Call it what you will. A flood of memories burst into my consciousness, one following in the wake of another, every image and every word recalled with startling clarity and detail. I am convinced this *experiencing* was intentionally induced so that I, and therefore the Orb, could examine and *feel* the recent moments of my life. You will see that this was all too easy to do, for there were strongly felt emotions in every memory:

Hate: "You mean to use Angie as bait?"

Ecstasy: "Did I hurt you? I don't ever want to hurt you."

Rage: "Get off me, you fucking bastard!"

Fascination: "Did you see that!?" A flash of color when I swirled the water."

Guilt: I'm feeling guilty. Have we been gone too long?"

Hopelessness: 'We don't fully understand each other, do we? How can we when we know ourselves even less?"

Amazement: "Kyle, try to phrase it correctly… the Ocean is the Orb, the Ocean are the Orb, the Orb is an Ocean…"

Loneliness: As the tide rolls out and only the memory of this experience remains, not the feeling itself, a lifetime of questions is strewn like pebbles on the shore: Does life have any meaning? Why do I feel so alone?"

And love, the strongest emotion of all: "I love you. I'll say the words once for each star in the night sky until you believe me."

I am glad to see, Diana, that I have made you smile.

Do you see how the strength of my recollection speaks to the intensity of those relived moments? Some are again receding into the background. If need be, I could recount others: Sorrow, alarm, disgust, fear, surprise, loathing, and more, all experienced on Orb. Every member of the crew seems to have been involved.

What was the purpose of this catharsis? By absorbing all these disparate emotions, the Orb could identify a point of reference between us and prepare me for what was to follow. This shall become clearer, but I'll offer this much: as all visible colors comprise white light, so, to the Orb, all emotions marry to become one. The point of our commonality. Joy.

Joy. Happiness. Euphoria.

And when I arrived at this point, all my recent memories, every last one inspired by a caress, a caring look, a laugh, all the encouraging words spoken by, or to, me—every small encounter that prompted this welcome feeling came cascading out:

"What do you dream about, my faithful dog?"

"It's delightful! Nearly as warm as the Caribbean."

" *"Il est presque aussi belle que vous, mon amour!"*

"Incredibly refreshing. I feel euphoric."

"I could stay with you a lifetime."

There were more. Let me impress upon you that not a word needed to be spoken. For example, I recalled watching Kelly sleeping peacefully while Angie, dreaming, lay with her head and one twitching paw across her breast. I remembered all these things, and when the succession of memories finally ended, the pervasive feeling of joy did not. I did not want it to. How could I let it?

Something then prompted me to investigate the region below the entity's saucer-sized point of contact with the greater OceanOrb. Previously, I had seen nothing notable. Now, there was a shimmering disturbance resembling waves of heat rising above a desert floor or, a better analogy, the thermoclines that often appear while diving. These translucent waves spiraled downward and outward until they blended into and disappeared within the abyss. They seemed to have no tangible substance of their own.

Had I previously overlooked these emanations?

Perhaps they had been obscured in the brighter light of full sun.

I placed my hand over the saucer-shaped point of contact. An inviting tingling sensation rapidly spread across my flattened palm. I had the opportunity to remove my hand from the spot. I did not. The sensation raced up my arm and through me. Completely. Utterly.

Suddenly, I was outside the Orb.

How is this possible?

I left my body behind.

Or should I say the Orb left my body behind, for I had entered the OceanOrb—slowly at first, along the nebulous pathway I've described; lifelines thousands of meters long providing a welcome and also a means of returning to a reality I knew and could more readily accept. I looked back and saw Angie resting contentedly. I made my choice.

I let go.

Diana, do you recall what you told me about the silkworm moth detecting one pheromone molecule per hundred quadrillion of air? Well, I went sailing beyond that corporeal limitation into the space around me, billowing out like one solitary drop of dye, diluting into, but never lost, within a vast ocean. Once again, I have no explanation for what appears fantastical other than offering up that most profound of mysteries, an unsolved riddle: that each of us is both the sum and more than the sum of every elusive particle constituting our mind and body. This was made manifest to me within the ubiquitous OceanOrb, where not one drop, molecule, atom, boson, or lepton goes unaccounted for or can be willingly separated from another. Is it so great a leap to believe that when I was in touch with one part of the OceanOrb, I was in touch with all?

That without moving, I could travel?

That, like in a vivid dream, my eyes were not necessary to see?

And as I viewed this new world, I perceived things. Incredible things.

I ventured upon a grouping of tiny Orbs playfully bumping into others a thousand times larger. The smaller Orbs' excited behavior reminding me of frantic little tugboats as they went about nudging their much larger companions this way and that. The participants were engaged in some mutually enjoyable game because the huge Orbs returned repeatedly for more, even when pushed far away. Would you agree, Larry, that this is possible when an Orb the size of a basketball can have a thousand times the mass of one the size of a mountain, depending on the molecular density it chooses?

Here and there, I noticed Orbs taking particular delight in showing off the splendid, near-infinite variety of colors they can arrange on their glossy surfaces. Little did I suspect they were also communicating among themselves this way. When in close proximity, Orbs often remain stationary and replicate each other's appearance. This is no mere mimicry, for each Orb, in turn, creates modifications and enhancements that defy mere chance. After such an exchange, it was common to see them wander off in a specific direction (they have an entire planet over which to roam) or cooperate in some concerted activity. Body language, tone of voice, pitch, and timbre give nuanced meaning to human discourse. Orbs manipulate colors, shapes, patterns, and vibrations. Collectively, these qualities facilitate an exponentially greater sophistication of expression.

So exceptionally diverse and creative are the Orbs' means of communication that, as with all else they do, they derive sheer pleasure from the pastime. I witnessed groups of Orbs resonating back and forth, their vibrations propagating elegant wave patterns, which, depending on the phase of the wave, interacted in complex ways with the matter surrounding them. Similarly, they can modulate vibrational frequencies to be felt on touch (as we did) or heard (as did Angie). These were forms of communication and excitation I could fathom. There likely were many others I could not understand.

Venturing further, I encountered an extensive network of Orbs—well over a thousand—in sizes ranging from as small as a grapefruit to those whose bulk would not fit inside a coliseum. The larger Orbs were fewer in number; all appeared to be moving aimlessly. Closer observation revealed that a form of organized segregation was taking place. Orbs of similar size matched up, then arranged into long sequences like giant strings of multicolored pearls. As stunning as it was, this structure did not remain static, for it floated weightlessly in the OceanOrb, spinning and twisting while altering and harmonizing colors upon receiving some invisible unifying command.

I dove to depths where sunlight never penetrated, yet uninterrupted darkness rarely prevailed. Here, brightly illuminated Orbs sallied back and forth in zigzag patterns; others approached from out of the gloom like giant beacons, spreading a soft light wherever they went. They drifted aimlessly by, only to fade silently into the darkness. Orbs did not linger in this region for long, preferring or requiring sunlight. For this reason, I watched with heightened interest as several shifted their luminance to blue and drifted toward a faint glow from further below. I followed, plummeting into a realm well beyond the deepest of Earth's oceans.

There, I came upon a most startling sight. Hundreds of Orbs amassed into a vast, slowly rotating, tightly compacted sphere. From this fiercely glowing conglomeration, solitary Orbs repeatedly propelled themselves outward and back, their completed course of travel describing acute ellipses, their brilliant light reaching into the abyss to confound the distant blackness. This pastime, in itself quite intriguing, was made more so when it dawned on me that the spectacle radiated the same shade of blue as the planet's sun!

It was then, Bruce, that I saw them—growing upward from the jagged terrain below. Silent sentinels bathed in pale blue light—more of your spires. I can tell you nothing about them, as they were obscured in partial darkness. I hope this meager accounting will be of some assistance in your effort to solve their mystery.

Until this point, my entire being had been consumed by the fascinating behavior of individual Orbs, with scant attention devoted to that of the OceanOrb. Rising toward the surface, I tried shifting my perspective.

Beyond our present understanding of the structure of matter, there is an interface where the elemental becomes sublime. It is here (a word I hesitate to use, for it connotes *place*) that every Orb can instantly communicate with any ten or ten million fellow creatures. I know almost nothing of what was conveyed within this dominion. Not because anything was deliberately shielded from me—that would have required subterfuge—but it was of a nature I could not yet fully comprehend.

I was, however, able to sense, as we have all recently seen, that every Orb in existence celebrates the arrival of a new member born out of the OceanOrb. When one is born, another somewhere on the planet voluntarily disbands and is reassimilated. This act, too, is celebrated. The harmonious process explains how the entity can be so vast yet intimately connected, unimaginably old, and yet constantly renewed and replenished.

How it can exist as one, yet comprise a multitude.

Still, my understanding of the OceanOrb seemed to lack emotion, even though I was, in some mysterious way, permeating that which I wanted to comprehend. Funny-strange, the similar difficulty in understanding an entity to which I was even more intimately connected, namely, myself.

I considered all that had transpired on this expedition. I thought of my crewmates and what was learned from each of you.

Then I remembered Paul's words. I centered my being on what was, and will always be, simple.

As brilliantly simple as Angie, for whom the Orb has a great affinity.

I battled against my parochial, preconceived notions. Partly winning the fight, I accepted that you can never fully understand the universal ocean flowing within and without us. In doing so, I began to perceive the world from the OceanOrb's original, revelatory perspective—as joyous exaltation.

And there it was, before me all the time!

I saw the broad and glorious sky as the timeless sun rose and fell, lightness and darkness, one star and a million!

I felt the touch of the atmosphere's warm embrace imbued with feathery tracings of wind, wild and calm.

I heard the hush of ascending moisture changing to blustery squalls of descending rain.

And then, in my greatest triumph, I divined your presence, Kelly, as you sought my island of solitude, searching only for me, my love.

And I desired to return home.

To you.

To an abused Earth that has always been and will forever be the first and last sanctuary we have.

I centered my will on the invisible path before me and found myself back inside the Orb with Angie beside me.

Before I opened my eyes (I could just as easily say before I closed my eyes), one last image flashed in and out of view, an image not easily rectified with all the rest. The glint from the faceted sides of a slowly rotating cube. Of all the wonders I saw, this is the only one I cannot faithfully attest to.

Diverting my attention was another, more tangible wonder: Kelly peering down into the Orb and then stepping forward to hold me while it moved away.

You have been most patient with me…

Visionaries

"CONGRATULATIONS AND WELL DONE," said Paul, voicing the predominant opinion of my crewmates.

"Back on Earth, there'll be doubters," Diana cautioned, expressing the subordinate sentiment. With help from Thompson and Paul, she had interrogated me like a world-class prosecuting attorney, but I was only a little worse for wear.

"What do *you* believe?" I responded, realizing that if my encounter with the entity lacked credibility with my crewmates, I'd have zero chance of convincing the billions on Earth.

"What I believe won't matter. A shitload of scientists, no, *everyone* will be asking, 'Did you make contact with the Orb or merely with yourself?' By your own account, you fell asleep. You must admit that most of what followed has more than a passing semblance to a dream, a string of illusory images concocted by someone with a hyperactive imagination."

(Symmetry, I thought to myself, if I again found myself scrutinized and found lacking by the scientific community.)

"She's right," Thompson said. "Even those inclined to believe you may choose to focus on the unusually intimate nature of your contact. They will conclude that you could not evaluate exactly where your identity ended and the Orbs' began. You will be accused of being unable to distinguish between the two."

"Another example of the observer affecting the observed?" I said, once again finding something Thompson said worth paraphrasing.

"Take one more step," replied Thompson. "The observer, to some degree, becomes the observed."

"If so, isn't that the best evidence of contact? Of course, I was altered by the Orb. How could I not be, when every projection of our selves alters us in some way? If I plunge my arm into a pool of cold water, my arm becomes cold, and a host of physiological changes occur. It is still my arm when, in turn, it slightly warms the water. Well, I plunged my mind into the Orb. We took *something* from each other. Joy, I found— easily identified in Angie, and then found in me."

"Was that sharing enough to undo the damage Melhaus inflicted with his behavior?" Diana asked.

"That was never necessary. The entity perceived threats from the laser and *Ixodes* , but not the underlying motivation. To the Orb, emotions other than pure joy cannot be separated out because they lose meaning. Don't you see the irony? I, inside the Orb, imparted causative emotions like hubris, anger, guilt, and pride to our actions, not Larry individually or us collectively. How best to explain? To the Orb, everything is connected and unjudged, which is difficult for us to accept. Threats are perceived when something holds itself completely apart from, or is the antithesis to, that connectivity."

"A connectivity of which you became a small part," Diana commented.

"Small, yes, but far from trivial. I never felt completely…"

"What?" Diana said, cajoling. "Alone?"

"Yes. Alone."

"Because of your connection to the Orb?" Thompson asked.

"In part," I said, my voice wavering. "But not all."

"If not all, what then?" Paul prompted, even though he didn't need to ask. Having just heard my verbal report, he had a pretty damned good idea of my response.

"Kelly was with me. I felt her. I felt Angie. Behind them, each of you. Behind each of you, everyone and everything."

Looking around the table, I saw everybody smiling. All except Melhaus, fast asleep in the blue warmth of the late-day sun. I smiled back and said, "Perhaps I did find out more about myself than about the Orb."

"As I said before," Paul remarked, "congratulations."

We were to leave the planet mid-morning the next day. Diana was assisting Paul, who was dismantling his science station and securing it on board *Desio*. As for Thompson (and Diana, as well), the task of stowing equipment had been made easier thanks to the efforts of Melhaus and his laser. A few instruments had survived for the geologist to use, and he intended on doing so until, in his words, "the very last rays of light make work possible, and possibly beyond that."

We were sympathetic. Working in adverse conditions, the first expedition had come away with what they believed to be a representative sampling of the planet's geology. They had not, however, sampled the spires. From the start, these unusual structures presented an intellectual challenge that captivated and confounded Thompson.

Various tools were at his disposal, including a diamond coring bit, which he used to bore small holes into the spires. The extracted samples were then sliced into 'thin sections,' and examined under a petrologic microscope *and* a scanning microscope capable of resolutions to a fraction of a nanometer. At first, nothing in the visual analyses of these thin sections or their subsequent spectral and chemical analyses had shed any light on how the spires formed.

Now, suppressing excitement, the expert geologist appeared at my doorway and said, "Stop trying to emulate Hemingway. I need you to look at some microscope images."

"I thought your microscopes were toast."

"Crispy. Diana's scanner escaped destruction."

The first thing I noticed and commented on when entering Thompson's cabin was that the San bow, minus two arrows, had been remounted on the bulkhead. "They had better make that standard issue for deep space missions," I said.

The second thing I noticed was that he cleared his workstation of everything except the scanning scope, associated hardware, and a monitor where four colorful images, each occupying a quadrant, were displayed.

"Pretty pictures," I commented.

"Sit," Thompson ordered. "Try, if at all possible, not to act dumber about this than you are."

"I like a challenge."

"Study the surfaces of the thin sections displayed on the monitor. What do you see?"

"There is a noticeable difference in smoothness."

"Be specific."

The images were unambiguous. So much so that it was difficult to take Thompson's need for my opinion seriously. "The top two images are smoother than the bottom two. Of the top two, the one on the left is slightly smoother than that on the right. Does my answer please master?" I said.

"You're sure of your response?"

"Absolutely. Is this some kind of object lesson, like the juice container? What gives?"

"'What gives' is, once again, our assumptions have been turned on their head."

That was something Thompson would not joke about. "How so?" I asked.

"In due time. Get Diana. Don't tell her what this is about."

"Since I obviously don't know, that'll be easy."

I located her in the lab, helping Paul stow away his equipment. "You've been summoned to the king's chamber," I pronounced.

Both of us?" Paul asked.

"No. Just Diana."

"What the hell did I do now?" she asked.

"Remarkably, nothing," I replied. "Thompson appears excited about something."

Diana gave Paul a quizzical look. "Thompson? Excited? Hmm…"

On entering Thompson's cabin, I noticed the order of the images had been changed. Diana, concluding that the display was the purpose of her presence, approached the monitor.

"Pretty pictures," she said.

I looked at Thompson and shrugged. "I told her nothing."

"What's the resolution?" she asked, her face practically pressed against the screen.

"Point-six-five nanometers," Thompson replied. "The field of view is five hundred nanometers. The scans are of thin sections made from spire core samples. I want your opinion on the relative smoothness of the four scans shown."

Diana, reacting more or less as I had, stared at Thompson. "Is this some kind of trick?" Thompson shook his head. Seeing he was serious, she glanced back at the monitor. "Okay," she said, pointing. "Two have smoother surfaces and edges, one noticeably smoother than the other. Satisfied?"

"Very much so. This will need to be discussed. I'll transfer the images and others like them to your A.I.Ds.. Gather up Paul and Kelly. Melhaus, too. Not here. Too crowded. Meeting outside in five… no, fifteen minutes. I'll need more time." Thompson laughed. "Anyway, a bit longer to further consider what this all means."

The commander was never late for anything. Twenty minutes had elapsed, and we were still anxiously waiting for him to assume his place at the head of the worktable. In the interim, Kelly, Paul, and Melhaus had reviewed the images. The physicist, now alert, had joined us once again. I was glad to see that he was mending quite nicely. We began trading wild ideas about what was prompting Thompson's odd behavior when he appeared in *Desio's* open hatchway, pausing briefly to stare at the spires and then out to the returning Orbs.

Joining us, he said, "You've all seen the images?"

We nodded.

"Any disagreement?"

"Should there be?" Kelly asked.

"No. But what was obvious to my eyes was unacceptable to my mind. I could have been mistaken. I needed independent confirmation. Each of you provided that."

"You're welcome," Diana said. "Confirmation of what?"

"Today, I reexamined the first core hole drilled eight days ago into the spires. Although I had exhausted every means at my disposal, the mystery of their formation remained unsolved. Call what I did next either intuition or desperation, but give me credit to this extent: I realized that conventional thinking had to be transcended if a solution were to be found.

"Not knowing exactly why, perhaps I was subconsciously guided by something Kyle said, I removed a small chip from the interior rim of the first borehole. I then carefully prepared a thin section for analysis with the scanning microscope. When viewed under extreme magnification, I expected the sides of the borehole, represented by the chip I took from it, to appear jagged and irregular. What I saw defied belief. Not only had the jaggedness been smoothed out and all the voids filled in, but approximately forty nanometers of mineral, identical to the rest of the spire, had accreted onto the surface. Repeating my procedures, I scanned a chip from the interior of a borehole drilled four days after the first. I discovered the surface jaggedness to be nearly gone, and twenty nanometers of mineral accreted. I am rounding off here, omitting detailed methodology to get to the point. Dr. Melhaus, can you confirm my math and extrapolate the mineral accrual rate to more useful values?"

"Assuming the present rate continues, a growth of fifty meters in ten billion days. That's twenty-eight million Earth years."

"Help me out here," Diana said. "This mineral accrual occurs how?"

"Ah, that is the question, isn't it? Consider the other two images. One is from the surface of the first core, *not* the hole it came from, mind you, but the removed core; the other is a sample of a fragment that came from the spire's summit."

"You mean one of the fragments that nearly caved your head in?" Diana said as a gentle reminder.

"Right," Thompson said, frowning. "Neither sample shows mineral accrual. Only the spire itself is accruing material."

"Oh, I get it!" Diana declared. "You want us to believe the spire is repairing itself!"

"Why limit it?" Thompson said.

"You're saying the spires form themselves this way? That, like some giant stone tree, they grow?"

"That's exactly what I'm saying. The spires are, in some sense, alive. According to my calculations, some are as ancient as one hundred million years old. Ancient and alive."

"May I offer my opinion?" Melhaus said.

"Of course," Thompson replied.

"I would submit that if the growth rate is slower than the repair rate, the spires may be quite a bit older. As old as we're guessing the Orb to be."

"Good point. I hadn't considered that possibility. Unfortunately, we lack the time and the means to prove it."

"What the hell did I say that helped you with this?" I asked.

"Your description of the spires in the OceanOrb. You gave them living attributes. Said they appeared like sentinels growing off the bottom, or words to that effect."

"Yes. Yes, I did," I said, feigning my importance. "I had promised to solve the spires' riddle, so this discovery gets me off the hook."

"No, not quite," he replied. "Unless you make another offhand remark telling us how the spires originated here."

"Same way as the phytoplankton?" I volunteered.

"Can we back up a minute?" Kelly said. "You're asking us to accept a lot. I don't remember you answering Diana's question. What process is causing this growth?"

"Shall I coin a new term? *Molecular transmigration?*"

"Conjecture, Bruce?" Kelly responded. "That's insufficient to call something alive."

"I disagree. Reflect on the order of events that have challenged our idea of what constitutes life. Angie's first contact began relieving us of our hubris. Our horizons expanded with Paul's revelation concerning the OceanOrb and its link to the planet's weather. Lastly, Kyle's metaphysical journey has led us to question the nature of matter and the limitations of the mind. The spires are again forcing us to realize that life refuses to follow the rules we have laid down for it. We must expand the definition to encompass the entire planet as a living entity." Thompson swept a challenging gaze across us. "No, even that may be too confining. Should we act as visionaries and rewrite the definition? Will the next step in our evolutionary journey be to claim that life is inseparable from all of creation? Is that our simple answer, Paul?"

"I'm not prepared to go quite that far…"

Thompson laughed once again. "Neither am I. But I am prepared to go partway. If you can't follow me, you will find what I am about to do incomprehensible."

Turning to me, the commander asked, "Which compartment holds the collected rainwater?"

"Reserve Compartment 'B,'" I responded. "The smaller of the two."

"Good. Empty it."

"Say again? You lost me."

"Empty it. The main compartment is sufficient for our needs. We shall do our best to leave this planet as we found it. I will set a further example by leaving my collected samples."

"What?!" Diana shouted. "You want me to abandon all my specimens?!"

"I'm well aware of how much your work means to you. To all of you. Don't you think I wrestled with this decision? How long have you been able to keep specimens of phytoplankton alive?"

"Four hours."

"Figure it out. Keeping phytoplankton alive is impossible for the same reason that spire fragments do not regenerate. Everything on this planet is somehow an integral part of the whole. There is connectivity here. We should not assume any of this is ours for the taking."

"The last crew did," Diana said.

"In their ignorance. If it is any consolation, what they've taken from this planet is still available for study."

"What about the specimens I preserved or slide-mounted?"

"Since they are corrupted, I see no reason to leave those behind."

"You're going to be censured for this decision," Paul said.

"You bet."

"I, for one, will back you up."

"*We* will back you up, Diana added. "You saved our collective butts. It's time we returned the favor."

The day's unlikely events and the hard work of preparing the ship for departure left me little time for Angie. With the sun setting, I noticed she had discovered a new playmate. Who that person was gave me pause: Melhaus, propped against a boulder, gazing at the horizon, thinking of who knows what.

Angie sauntered over, dropped the stuffed duck, and stared up expectantly. She did this gamely, despite being rebuffed on numerous prior occasions. What followed next ranks in the top five surprises on Orb. Melhaus began tossing the duck! He did this gamely, wincing in pain with each throw but seemingly enjoying himself. Eventually, when the discomfort forced him to stop, I rescued him.

"She can be a little insistent sometimes," I said, scooping my pooch up. "Tell me if she bothers you."

"No bother. I was rather enjoying myself."

Out in the growing darkness, a few dozen softly glowing Orbs silently glided like ice skaters on a frozen pond.

Paul joined us. "Glad to see your spirits improving, Larry. Just to let you know, to comply with Bruce's directive, which Diana and I agree with, I have removed most of your samples from the lab. I petitioned Bruce to save one or two."

"So be it. There weren't many." The following words seemed difficult for Melhaus to get out, but he managed to say them anyway: "Thank you."

"Just keep getting well."

Paul had been Melhaus's biggest defender. Maybe now that was being noticed.

I felt like I hadn't been alone with Kelly for a hundred years. I was heading to my cabin to update my work when I bumped into her.

"I missed you," I said, picking up Angie and pressing the three of us together.

"I missed you both, too."

"Well, have I changed?" I asked, expecting "no" for an answer.

Kelly pressed her lips to the top of Angie's head, looked up at me with her dark eyes, and gave me a cagey smile. "A little."

"C'mon. What?"

"You seem a little happier."

"If so, you've only yourself to blame."

We spied Diana approaching. "Can I have some of this free love?" she said, spreading her arms wide and squeezing what was now the four of us, into one big embrace.

"You want to get everyone else in on this, too?" I asked.

"Speaking of, what's up with Larry?" Diana said, taking a step back. "Was I hallucinating, or did I see him playing with Angie? This is your handiwork, Kelly. It must be euphoria from the pain medication."

"Didn't you all see?" Kelly said, backing away from Angie and me. "No, you couldn't have; you two were in the ship talking to Bruce. Larry waded up to his waist in the OceanOrb. It was totally his idea. Interesting, no?"

"Interesting, yes," Diana responded. "*If* that's the reason. His turnaround has been rather sudden and remarkable."

"Hey, wait, I have an idea," I said. "We're tired and sweaty, and it will be our last opportunity. Tonight, let's all go for a communal swim. Right in front of *Desio*, under the brilliance of a starlit sky."

"Sounds wonderful," Kelly said.

"I'll run it by the commander," Diana volunteered, "but I'm sure he'll agree."

Diana and Kelly rushed off to finish their chores, and I headed to my cabin to review and quickly update my work.

Pending Additions/Notes:
On Earth, who will bother to read this?

Peering out of the box. Nice view.

To be inserted in narrative from recording: "Larry, one of the reasons I signed on to this expedition was to reinvent myself, even while doubting a person can. Well, if I have, you have. Twice."

Regarding loneliness: Paul, as usual, was right.

CSA wanted a different perspective on deep space missions; I guess they got what they wanted from me. And more.

Remove all details of sexual intimacy with Kelly?

Draw definitive conclusions? Be suspicious of absolutes.

Larry??

Will I regress when back on Earth? Fallback: Like it or not, we're stuck with each other.

We survived ourselves.

19 November 2232 21:38:22 Hrs
K. Lorenzo Recorder Download No. 728

Gilmore: Here comes Kyle now.

Thompson: Careful now, there's a drop-off.

Gilmore: On Earth, does Angie like playing in the water?

Lorenzo: Sometimes.

Unknown: *(Indecipherable)*

Lorenzo: Kelly, can you hold her? Be right back. I don't want to go in with my recorder.

Bertrand: It's waterproof.

Lorenzo: That's the problem.

Bertrand: Very funny. I see what you mean.

Takara: Larry, you can get that bandage wet if you want to.

Melhaus: *(Inaud)* forget about it.

Takara: Kyle, hurry back. Streaks of color are lighting up the water. It's beautiful!

Thompson: Doctor, you *(Inaud)*

(power off 21:39:53)

(lo battery)

Addendum

Date: 17 February 2235
Desio **Recovery Mission**
Deep Space Vessel *Marsden*
Acting Commander Carla Ramirez

I feel constrained to attach the following thoughts in an attempt to add a small measure of completion to the foregoing narrative, to which the author devoted so much of himself. I understand that this effort shall not bring closure to the matter I was sent here to investigate: the loss of *Desio* and her crew. After eight days on Orb and with Marsden's departure imminent, I shall ultimately be judged as having failed in that regard. In sum, I will not concede that the crew met with an untimely end, even though no trace of them has been found and no conclusive evidence exists as to the cause of their disappearance.

To many, the crew's fate was considered sealed when the *Desio* failed to enter Earth's orbit during the short window of time allotted. Their ability to survive a harsh, nine-month-long winter was considered impossible even if all life-support systems remained functional and Orb's vast ocean could somehow sustain human life.

There was speculation within the upper echelons of CSA that *Desio*'s fate was somehow linked to the adverse effects deep space missions have on human behavior. (How nearly true this was!) I can personally attest to what those effects are: during the outbound voyage, two members of my crew were administered psychotropics by the ship's doctor, and one was temporarily confined to quarters.

My crew had an additional reason to be restive. If *Desio's* problems weren't self-inflicted, we conceivably could be subject to the same tribulations that befell them. Keeping this in mind, I carried out the recovery mission with the utmost caution, which, pending my complete report, I will briefly describe.

The missing ship was quickly discovered by locking onto her locator beacon. When our hailing signals went unanswered, I positioned the *Marsden* in a geostationary orbit directly above the *Desio*. Utilizing teleoptics, I viewed both the ship and the small island on which she rested. She appeared to have arrived safely, mostly intact, although seeing that her turret laser had been dismantled and her submersible was in ruins gave us great cause for concern.

While still in orbit, and to avoid unnecessarily putting my crew in harm's way, I accessed and downloaded *Desio's* data banks. Commander Thompson's log and Mr. Lorenzo's narrative were most informative. It would be an understatement to say that I was astounded by their content.

Neither account foretold what befell the crew, though Mr. Lorenzo's (including the last automatic download from his personal recorder) best described what transpired immediately before all accounts abruptly ceased.

With increased foreboding, we left orbit and descended into the planet's atmosphere. *Marsden's* sensory array reconfirmed the absence of bio, chem, and radiation hazards. Satisfied with the results, we set down on the island at a prudent distance from *Desio*. Her hatchway was open. She appeared abandoned, though only the entryway exhibited minor damage from the elements. My science officer and I, wearing protective suits and carrying litescopes, navigated through the ship's dark interior, quickly surveying each compartment for the crew, startled at not finding their remains. We proceeded to conduct a more thorough inspection. Propulsion and life-support systems had gone offline but were in working order. Food and water were in sufficient quantity for the crew to have made the return voyage home. (Samples were tested for contaminants and proven safe.) The standard-issue packet of emergency-use L-capsules was still stored with Dr. Takara's ransacked medical supplies. I found Mr. Lorenzo's recorder lying on his workstation— probably just as he left it two and a half years ago. Other than missing a crew, nothing else was noteworthy.

Scouring the island offered no clues to a deepening mystery. *Desio's* flight recorder proved the ship had set down only once on the planet's surface, eliminating the possibility that some crew members were interred on another island where their remains might be found. The absence of remains prompted my issuing instructions, briefly questioned by my first-in-command, to have the forsaken ship checked out, repaired, and secured from further damage.

Having, I believed, collected all the facts available, I attempted to formulate logical assumptions: Mr. Lorenzo most likely returned to the ocean after depositing his recorder in his cabin. The device's log and his narrative indicate the time and date of whatever befell the crew. As evidenced by the excited tone in Dr. Takara's voice, colored streaks were lighting the ocean. On this only occasion, all crew members were in the ocean simultaneously. Finally, every member of the crew, not having departed the island by means of *Desio*, departed (willingly or not) via the ocean.

The question was how and why.

Theory: Dr. Melhaus, respected for his genius, took some calculated action, presently obscured by time and the elements, that adversely affected the entire crew. His improved demeanor (doubted perhaps only by Dr. Gilmore) suggests this was not the case. Furthermore, unless he was caught up in his own scheming, where was his body?

Theory: The Orb, intentionally or otherwise, was responsible for the crew's demise. By all accounts, the entity had the physical capacity to harm. If one is to believe mission logs verbatim, however, the entity was cognizant, dare I say, *protective* of anything identified as a life form. Nevertheless, our understanding of the Orb is so massively incomplete that nothing can be absolutely ruled out or in, including an accidental occurrence that killed the crew at the very moment they were all in the ocean. Due to this possibility, I ordered my crew to stay on land. Of note, the only indication of the Orb's presence after eight days was the faint colors seen when the water was swirled.

Not satisfied with my faltering attempts at an explanation, I sequestered myself in my cabin and meticulously went through it all again. I stared at the holographic images Mr.

Lorenzo took of the marooned *Ixodes*. Something about them troubled me. Leaving the *Marsden*, I made a second visit to the cove. The submersible was wedged between the rocks, in the exact position seen in images taken two and a half years ago. But there was one striking difference. The water now barely touched her!

I ran back to my ship, accessed and played back images that *Desio's* crew had taken two and a half years ago of the Orb and *Ixodes*, concentrating on the relative water level on rock slabs lining the shore and comparing it to my present observation. What I discovered was difficult to believe. The ocean level had dropped by almost a meter!

But that didn't make sense. There are no tides on Orb. The ice caps had not increased in size. Atmospheric saturation was essentially unchanged.

And yet, planetwide, a massive volume of ocean water (henceforth, I shall be reluctant to label it such) had vanished in less than three years!

I consulted with my science officers, urging them to find an explanation.

They were unable.

Then, I came to fully appreciate the melding of Mr. Lorenzo's creative imagination with Dr. Melhaus's brilliant science. If you have this same appreciation, you might reach a similar conclusion.

That delivered out of, and departed from, the planet was an enormous Orb.

This means the crew of *Desio* may still be alive.

Presently, there is insufficient evidence to support my contention, or any other for that matter. As Commander Thompson might say, each person, following their desire to create certainty, must choose what to believe.

Personally, I am inclined to end this report in a manner faithful to Mr. Lorenzo's narrative.

I propose that the crew is well and along for one hell of a joyride.

About the Author

Gary Tarulli holds a B.A. in Literature from the State University of New York at Oneonta. He is the author of the science fiction novel *The Symbionts of Murkor* and the social satire novella *TOO BIG*. He currently lives in Long Island, New York, with his understanding wife and a seventeen-pound pooch named Maggie.